REBEL

(Recoil Trilogy Book 3)

Joanne Macgregor

"In a time of deceit, telling the truth is a revolutionary act."
George Orwell

"It is the first responsibility of every citizen
to question authority." **Benjamin Franklin**

October 31

I never thought it would end like this, with him dead, a loved one dying, and me lying on my back, bleeding.

Yet, looking back, it seems inevitable.

The moment I joined the rebels, perhaps even the moment I left home to train as a sniper in the war against the plague, I stepped onto the path that ultimately brought me to this place, and this moment.

My hair whips in the downdraft of the helicopter that banks overhead and peels away. The sickening iron taste of blood fills my mouth.

I'm so sore, so tired, so tempted to slip into the beckoning darkness. But the desperate voice above me begs me to hold on.

Sirens grow louder, closer. I shudder from the scorching pain, feel my heart pump more blood out of me with each beat.

There's a loud bang, and another voice — harsh and hostile — yells impossible commands.

And I can't protect anyone, not the ones I love, not even myself.

Part One

Chapter 1

Stepping Out

October 4

The world outside is crazy.

Mutant rats infest the streets and parks, infecting people with the plague. Terrorist cells plan more attacks on our nation. The government continues to crack down on opposition to its repressive measures: monitoring protests, unearthing dissident activity, hunting rebels, detaining insurgents — all in the name of protecting the people.

For Quinn and me, the world is an especially dangerous place.

We stand together, holding hands. Neither of us moves. Both of us want to prolong this last moment of calm before the storm that waits outside Tallulah's Inner City Teen Shelter.

He squeezes my hand, and I look up at him, allowing myself to be distracted by his piratical good looks — the mahogany hair, the slate-gray eyes and olive skin, the slight cleft in his chin, and the silver hoop threaded through one eyebrow. A gentle smile curves his lips when he meets my gaze. I smile back and sigh.

It's time to rescue my brother, Robin.

I slip my sniper's rifle into my long duffel bag, sling a backpack over my shoulders, and open the door. Following Quinn, I step outside into the cool darkness of the evening.

That step feels huge, important, more like a momentous decision than a simple stride. I'm crossing a threshold from safety to danger, from the known to the uncertain. I'm moving from running away to running to, from escaping to confronting.

But Quinn holds my hand and tugs me forward, and I remind myself that with my hand in his, I can face anything.

As we set off down the sidewalk, I zip up my gray hoodie against the chill October wind that blows dried leaves against our legs and buffets trash against the run-down apartment blocks. Heavy clouds are gathering in the sky above, crowding out the stars.

The road ahead is dimly lit by the yellow glow of a streetlight, and deserted apart from two figures huddled beside a pile of bags in the shadow of a dilapidated old bus shelter a little way down the block. One of them is skinny, dressed entirely in black with chunky boots, and has her head shaven on one side — Evyan. I'm not surprised she's one of the rebels who has chosen to splinter off from the main group, because she's always had her eyes on the Quinn O'Riley prize. Wherever he goes, she'll follow.

The male figure next to her must be Mark, because wherever Evyan goes, Mark follows. But as we draw closer to the pair, I see that this man is older — mid to late forties — and has glasses and a straggly goatee beard. It's not Mark, it's Neil. That *is* a surprise.

If I'd had to pick a group to help me liberate my brother Robin from the clutches of PlayState and ASTA, it would have been trained fighters — big guys like Cameron and Bruce from my old sniper unit who knew how to handle themselves in a fight and shoot the pit out of a peach at forty paces. It would not have been a philosophizing pacifist and a girl who has always made it clear that she wished me, if not dead, then at least gone.

Even Quinn, whom I love and trust, wouldn't be anyone's first pick for a rescue mission team member. He's madly intelligent, yes — great at extracting meaningful information and patterns from raw data — but he's still more geek than guerilla.

"This is all of us," Quinn confirms.

"What do we do now? Maybe we could —" I begin.

But Evyan cuts me off. "Quinn, what do *you* think we should do?"

"Jinxy?" Quinn asks.

I shrug — I don't have any real plan. Until an hour ago, I'd been lying low at Tallulah's, licking my wounds and hiding out from the government and rebel forces, both of whom have seriously unpleasant plans for me.

"Okay then," Quinn continues, "I think the best bet would be to get to Neil's safe house, set ourselves up there, and plan our next step."

"Cool. Which way, Neil?" Evyan asks.

We follow Neil, heading up the street in a northerly direction. I wish we had a car and could move faster. Every minute that passes takes Robin closer to the moment he'll be moved from PlayState's headquarters to the detention center. What must it be like for my mom, stuck at home, unable to do anything to help either of her children? She'll be freaking out, terrified that she's about to lose another family member.

Feeling exposed and unsafe, I aim my flashlight into the shadows as we walk, alert for any movement or sound that might signal the approach of a curfew patrol or a plague-infected rat.

"Safe house?" I ask Quinn.

"Neil has a house in the north zone's outer sector."

"It's completely off the grid, and not registered in my name," Neil says. "So there's no way for the government to link it to me. No reason for them to search there."

"And do the rebels know about it?" I ask.

Government forces aren't the only ones searching for me.

Neil shakes his head. "They only know that I have one, but not where it is."

On the next corner is a long-abandoned convenience store. The security door of its entrance is still padlocked shut, but all the windows have been smashed and the shelves stripped bare. The wreck of an old van is parked outside, resting lopsidedly on the tireless rims of its wheels. This is exactly the sort of place where mutant rats might nest. And lurking inside the van could be an M&M — a plague-infected victim — or perhaps a government spook team set up to spy on the street.

Footsteps crunching loudly on the broken glass littering the sidewalk, Neil and Evyan march on, oblivious to any danger.

Chapter 2

Keeping an eye out

"Hold up there, guys," I say, taking my rifle out the bag.

Stepping around Evyan and Neil, I scan the gloomy interior of the store with my flashlight. Nothing. I take up position behind the van. Holding my rifle with the flashlight flush against its underside, I aim at the van's rusty doors, on which someone has spray-painted graffiti: *Only the rats are free.*

"Oh, for God's sake, is all this really necessary?" Evyan says.

I signal to Quinn. He opens one of the van doors and immediately steps back so that I can check the interior. Empty.

"Clear," I say.

"*Now* can we go?" Evyan sets off without waiting for an answer.

"We need to turn left here," Neil says.

"Wait!" I grab his arm before he can turn the corner. "Let me check it's safe first. Every time, okay? Every corner, every alley."

Evyan snorts and mutters something about me wanting to make myself feel useful. Keeping close to the storefront, I edge forward and crane my neck around the corner to search the street beyond. My eyes immediately lock onto a sudden movement about thirty yards ahead and to the right. It's only a scrawny stray dog, sniffing around an old entrance to the decommissioned subway system.

I hold my hand up in a stop sign to keep the others back. We need to be extremely careful. Dogs can also be infected with the plague — any mammals can, that's why the official policy is to destroy any and all stray animals. But I've always loved dogs, and I'm not about to shoot a healthy-looking specimen.

The dog walks over to a plumber's truck parked in the street, lifts its leg against a tire, and then trots off. The street is silent and still again. I turn back to the other three.

"Okay, it seems clear."

"If we're going to stop to check every street and shadow, we'll never get anywhere. We should just get moving," Evyan says.

Much as it pains me to admit it, even to myself, she has a point. It might not be safe or clever to move down a dark street without checking for potential dangers, but neither is spending too much time outdoors. The wind is picking up too, and there's the smell of rain in the air. Maybe it *would* be better to get to the safe house as quickly as we can.

"Fine," I snap. "Let's go."

I'm still saying the last word when I catch a glimpse of blue light, floating about ten feet above the ground, moving up the street.

"Get down!" I shove the others back toward the van. "It's a securodrone. Get underneath — now!"

We drop to the ground and slide under the old wreck, Quinn on one side of me and Evyan on the other. Neil manages to wedge himself under the lowest part of the chassis and starts trying to wrestle himself free of his backpack. I worry that his movements will shake the wreck, perhaps even bring it crashing down on us.

"Lie still!" I hiss.

But nobody needs the instruction this time — we can all see the flashing blue lights of the surveillance drone illuminating the asphalt and sidewalk. The beady eye of the camera under its pumpkin-sized body will be revolving as it hovers, taking in the images of the street and relaying them to an intel analysis unit somewhere. If we're detected, a strident alarm will sound, and a patrol unit will descend on us within minutes. We cannot afford to be discovered.

My muscles are tense, my mouth dry, and something sharp presses painfully into my right hip. I turn my head to look at Quinn, who lies on his back beside me. His fingers inch across to grasp mine, and we lie like that, hardly daring to breathe, as the lights pulse brighter, closer, glinting off the piercings in Evyan's ears and nose.

The drone must be level with the van now. Is it hovering beside us? If an intel agent, perhaps a cadet like the ones at ASTA, is monitoring its video feed in real time, they might direct it to descend and peer under the wreck. *I* would. But this one keeps moving, and soon the lights fade, then disappear.

We lie still for several more long minutes. Neil pants as if he's run a mile, Quinn wipes a hand across his forehead, and I ease a bottle of water out of my pocket to take a sip. Evyan studiously avoids meeting my gaze, as if she expects me to say, "I told you so."

No need, Evyan — I think we all understand the danger now.

"Think it's safe to move yet?" Quinn asks.

"I guess," I say, but I've no sooner eased out from under the van than I hear the sound of running feet.

I gather myself into a crouch and swing my rifle up at the

approaching figure, but it's just a kid — Carlos, the youngest kid housed at Tallulah's. He stops dead in his tracks, staring bug-eyed at the weapon.

"Kerry?" He calls me by the name I used in the shelter.

I lay the rifle down on the sidewalk beside me and beckon him closer. "What's up, Carlos?"

He edges forward slowly, wide eyes flicking from the rifle to me and back again. When he's right in front of me, he fishes around in his underwear and brings out an envelope.

"It's a message," he whispers. "From Miss Tallulah."

When I try to take the envelope, Carlos pulls it back. He holds out his other hand expectantly and smiles angelically at me. For Pete's sake, the kid is incorrigible.

"Does anyone have a cookie or some candy?" I ask the others.

Neil hands over a roll of ImmunyChews. I break the roll of candies in two and drop one half into Carlos's hand. He gives me the envelope, but his eyes are fixed on the rest of the candy.

"Just wait, okay?" I say, holding it up like a promised reward. "We may need to send a message back with you."

Carlos nods once, then pops two of the candies into his mouth and starts chewing, staring at each of us in turn.

I hold the envelope gingerly by one corner — not sure how hygienic the inside of Carlos's underwear might have been — and check both sides for a name, because I'm not sure if this was meant for me or Quinn. With an impatient curse, Evyan snatches it out of my grasp and hands it to Quinn, who tears it open and reads it quickly. His face tenses.

"What? What is it?" I ask.

"It's a message from Sofia."

Sofia Medina was one of Quinn's fellow cadets in the intel unit back at ASTA. She helped me establish that our sniping unit was really executing plague victims, and she fed fake information into the intel system so that I could get a message to Quinn about where his captured brother, Connor, was being detained. I discovered this evening that she also passed the information to Quinn that Robin's been captured and is being held at PlayState's headquarters, where they're grilling him about how he hacked into The Game.

"Sofia says they're moving Robin at dawn tomorrow," Quinn continues. "She doesn't know where to, but she does know it's so he can be questioned further and given a lie-detector test."

I meet Quinn's gaze. He looks worried, but my eyes, I know, must be wild with panic, because that's what I'm feeling right now — crazy, stomach-churning panic.

"Jinxy?" Quinn says.

"What's up with you?" Evyan demands.

I have to clear my throat before I can speak. "I know where they'll be taking him. To the place where they interrogated and tortured Connor."

To the place where they interrogated and tortured me.

Chapter 3

Outside the system

"Quinn, we need to get Robin tonight. Now! You said they'd tightened security at the detention center after your brother's escape — it'll be impossible to spring Robin once he's inside there."

"Yeah, but we don't have a plan," Quinn says. "We were going to discuss that tonight or tomorrow."

"We'll have to discuss it now. Let's get off the street though, before another drone or patrol comes by."

I ensconce Carlos in the driver's seat of the van and tell him we're playing a game where he drives us all the way to Mexico, then I clamber into the back with the others. In the far corner, a soiled respirator mask and a single sock lie beside an old romantic novel, its pages fanned open like it once landed in water, the paper nibbled at the edges by rodents or roaches. Did someone once shelter here? Where are they now?

"We need to get to PlayState as soon as possible," I say, sitting beside Quinn.

"Do we even know where PlayState is located?" Evyan asks.

"Yeah," I say. "It's virtually on the same grounds as ASTA. They're probably the same organization."

"Quinn said the security measures at ASTA were hectic. Is PlayState the same?" she asks.

I nod, thinking of the high perimeter fence topped with razor-wire and electrified strands, the motion-detecting lights and surveillance cameras, and the guards at the massive main gate.

"Soooo, how exactly are we going to get in?"

There's a long moment of silence as we look at each other and then at Quinn. But surprisingly, it's Neil who speaks first.

"What we need to do is to think like programmers," he says.

"I don't think computer code is going to help us with this, Neil." Quinn's reply is much more patient and polite than the retort which hovers on the tip of my tongue.

"No, but a logic flowchart will."

Neil snags a pencil and notepad from his backpack, turns to a fresh page and writes *Rescue Mission* at the top. He draws a diamond-shaped box, with an arrow marked *NO* coming out of the side and another labeled *YES* exiting from the lowest point.

"Can we scale the fence somehow and gain access that way?" Neil asks.

"Yes. And no," says Quinn. "I suppose it's possible to short the electric fence, but we'd be seen for sure, and then there'd be a major shoot-out."

Up front, Carlos growls like the souped-up engine of a muscle car, and squeals as we take an imaginary corner at speed. While Neil draws another decision diamond below the *YES* arrow, I take a moment to scan the street through the windshield. Still deserted.

"Do we have the manpower — excuse me, the human power — and the firepower to emerge victorious from such an encounter?" Neil asks.

"No," Quinn and I say together.

It's a stupid question. Neil knows as well as I do that we have exactly one weapon between us, and that I'm the only one who knows how to use it. No one else here could hit the broad side of a barn with a shotgun.

Neil draws a little skull with X'd out eyes at the bottom of the *YES* arrow — that's the end of that line of logic. He draws another diamond to the right of the *NO* arrow.

"Could we enter from above — yes or no?" he says, pushing up his glasses with a thumb.

"No," I say. "Unless you've got a helicopter at your safe house. And even then we'd be shot down."

Another *NO* arrow, another question box.

My foot jiggles. This is taking too long — we need to move faster.

"Can PlayState be accessed from below?" asks Neil.

"What, like via a tunnel? Not that I know of," Quinn says.

Neil traces over the *NO* arrow. "Then you've got to go through the door. Like the song says."

"Dude, what song?" Evyan's words are clipped with irritation.

Neil sings a ditty. "It's so high, you can't get over it. So low, you can't get under it. So wide, you can't get around it. You gotta go through the door!"

We all stare at him like he's nuts.

"Didn't any of you go to Sunday School?" he asks in a wounded tone.

Evyan rolls her eyes, Quinn looks baffled, and I snap, "Neil, if you've got an idea, please spit it out in plain English." And when he doesn't immediately reply, I add, "Now would be really good!"

I know I'm being rude, but we haven't got time to mess around. Carlos is also in a hurry — he shouts at imaginary M&Ms to get out of the way.

"The logical conclusion is that you have to enter through

the front gate," he says, as though this should be obvious to all of us.

"That's your grand plan? Ring the front door bell?" Evyan asks.

"They'd never let us in, Neil. Worse, they'd arrest the lot of us," I say.

"That would be true, if the people at the gate were you."

Evyan curses violently.

I say, "Who else *would* they be?"

"The more useful way of phrasing that question is: who would they let in?"

"Aah," says Quinn in a voice of dawning comprehension.

My irritation levels rise, because I'm still totally clueless.

"The only people they let into the compound are those who they're expecting," I say.

Neil draws another question-diamond.

"I swear to God, I am done with those little shapes," snaps Evyan. For the first time ever, she and I are entirely in sync. "I am ready to crumple up that piece of paper and shove it —"

"Is there a way we can make them *expect* an arrival tonight?" Neil asks.

"No," says Quinn, and his face has that earnest expression he always gets when he's thinking hard. "We can't. *We* can't."

And suddenly, I get it.

"We can't because we're outside the system," Quinn continues. "But someone on the inside could, someone like —"

"Sofia!" I finish for him.

"She could plant a message in the security system that someone is expected?" Neil checks.

"Yeah," I say.

"Easy," Quinn adds.

"Then the next logical question is: who would they

feasibly have to admit, in the middle of the night?" Neil asks. "Who would you need to be?"

"Some emergency service. Like a doctor, maybe! If someone was sick, they'd have to admit a doctor," I say, excited that there may be a way in after all.

"My sister's a doctor," Neil says, surprising me again. I've never thought about the lives of the rebels beyond their involvement in the resistance. "But she would *not* be keen to join a liberation mission, and besides, we live clear across town. If we had to wait for her to join us before we set off, we wouldn't make it in time."

"Okay, so who else might come to the gates?" Quinn says.

"Someone making a delivery?" Evyan suggests.

"Nah," I say. "Not at night. Besides, ASTA get their deliveries mainly by drones. PlayState would be the same."

"An official transport. A purification center disposal unit?" Quinn suggests, but then immediately shoots the idea down. "No, that won't work, they have special vans and trucks, and where would we get one of those?"

Truck. The word sparks something in my brain.

"How about," I say, "if they had a plumbing emergency?"

Three faces turn to look at me. Quinn is smiling, Neil nodding, Evyan has an eyebrow raised. Carlos is now beeping an imaginary horn, and fiddling with every button and dial remaining on the dashboard.

"Look over there." I point through the windshield. "It's a plumber's truck."

"You think the keys will be inside?" Neil asks.

"It's possible," I say.

There's a lot less theft these days, with people off the streets. Crime, like most everything else, has redirected itself online.

"We won't need the keys," says Evyan, and I'm shocked to see she's grinning widely. Have I ever seen her smiling before?

"Are you going to hot-wire it?" Neil asks.

"Hullo? 1990 called — it wants its technology back," Evyan says, digging around in her backpack. "You can't hot-wire cars built this century, dude."

I glance at the truck — it doesn't look new, but it's not that old.

"Then how?" I ask.

"Jammer and clone key programmer." Evyan holds up two small objects.

One looks like the sort of remote control device my mother had to open our garage's electric roller-door — in the days when Mom still drove and left the house. The other is a palm-sized gadget with an LCD screen and some cords dangling from it.

"What the heck are those?" I ask. "And why do you have them?"

Evyan merely says, "Stay out of sight until I signal you, then come running."

Chapter 4

Out past curfew

Evyan scrambles out of the van and heads off down the street toward the flatbed truck. I clamber up front and get Carlos to duck down behind the dashboard with me. There's a rumble of thunder from somewhere in the distance, but inside the van, all is quiet. I glance back at the other two. Neil is stroking his beard and smiling vaguely at his flowchart, while Quinn is writing the message to Sofia.

"Tell her to disable the cameras covering the entrance to the building and the lobby inside," I tell Quinn.

He nods and asks, "What's the name of the plumber — can you see?"

"Royal Flush Plumbing."

Evyan has just reached the truck. As she passes it, she swings her hip into the driver's door. A car alarm shatters the silence, but Evyan is already ducking behind the railings of the old subway entrance. A minute passes, then a short, dumpy man appears from the entrance of the apartment block, holds out his own remote key, and switches off the alarm.

Silence is restored. He walks around the truck, presumably checking it hasn't been broken into, and then walks back toward the apartment, relocking the truck with his remote.

Nothing happens for a couple of minutes, then Evyan emerges from her hiding spot, walks casually up to the truck, opens the driver's door and slips inside.

"She's in!" I tell the others.

"Here's the note for Sofia," Quinn says.

I pass the paper to Carlos, who stows it back in his underwear.

"Give it to Miss Tallulah straightaway, and tell her it's really urgent. Do you understand?" I hand over the rest of the candy.

Up ahead, the truck's lights are flashing.

"I think she's done it!" I say, amazed at the ease with which Evyan has committed grand theft auto.

We grab all the bags, exit the van and run up the street to the truck. Its engine is purring, and Evyan has killed the lights. She fiddles for a minute with the padlock securing the two metal flaps that cover the flatbed's back, and then the lock pops open with a soft click.

"How did you *do* that?" I ask as Quinn tosses our bags into the back.

"Let's go!" Evyan urges.

She gets behind the wheel again. Quinn climbs inside the cab of the truck and slides over to make room. I follow, but Neil says, "I'm not coming."

"No?" Quinn says.

"No. I don't want to have more to do with *that* than I have to."

He gestures to my rifle as he says it, but it's hard not to feel that what he really objects to is me. Whatever. I'm glad he's not coming with us — he'd be more of a liability than an asset, no two ways about that.

"I'll go ahead to the safe house and get things ready. Here, take this." Neil leans over me to hand Quinn a cellphone, and shows us he has another. They're those cheap disposable types with preloaded airtime that you can buy from *Smart Vendor* machines.

"Do you always carry a pair of burners around with you?" Evyan asks, sounding impressed.

"No," says Neil. "I always carry at least three. I've programmed my number on speed-dial number one. Text me when you're out and clear, and we'll decide on a meeting spot."

"Can't we just finalize that now?" Evyan asks.

Quinn and I both shake our heads. "In case we get caught, we should know as little as possible," Quinn explains.

"Speaking of which," I say to Evyan, "this is going to be dangerous. It's entirely possible that we'll get caught or … worse."

"I know that," she says, looking ahead at the road.

"You should go with Neil, it'll be safer."

"Do I look scared?"

"Fine, don't say I didn't warn you." I pull Carlos up onto my lap.

"Why's the kid coming with?" Evyan asks.

"We'll drop him off at Tallulah's on the way."

"He ran here — he can run back. Scram, kid."

Carlos makes to get out, but I put an arm around his waist and hold tight. "No, Evyan. It's dangerous out there. We'll give him a ride."

"It'll only take a minute or two to drop him off," says Quinn. "Bye, Neil, good luck."

"Just look out for rats and drones, okay?" I say.

Neil says something as he closes the door. I can't hear perfectly because Evyan's revving the engine, but it sounds like, "May the goddess be with you."

"The goddess?" I ask Quinn as we set off, shaking my head at the enigma that is Neil. How can someone be both so brilliantly logical and so unbelievably flaky at the same time?

Carlos leans forward to open the glove compartment, searches through its contents, finds a packet of gel-filled liquirats, and crams a fistful into his mouth. Quinn reaches around the boy. pulls all the papers out of the compartment, and examines them — ever the intel agent analyzing the information.

"Where did you learn to pick locks and steal cars?" I ask Evyan.

"I learned how to pick locks in juvie."

"What's juvie?"

"Juvenile detention — kiddy-prison. God, you are so vanilla!"

"And stealing cars?" Quinn says.

She gives him a grin and says, "Why d'you think I was sent to juvie in the first place?"

Fabulous. I'm on the run with a hot rebel, a sugar addict, and a convicted felon.

After we've dropped Carlos and his candy rats off at Tallulah's, we head south, in the direction of PlayState. As we drive through the mostly deserted streets, I snuggle up close to Quinn, reveling in the sensation of being near to him again.

"What have you got there?" I ask him.

"Registration and license" — he tosses two documents back into the glove compartment — "and something even better. It's an all-hours permit for Cletus Mayberry, plumber, and one assistant, to travel outside of curfew hours in the business of attending to plumbing emergencies."

"Good find!" says Evyan, fist-bumping Quinn.

It *is* good. If we're stopped by a curfew patrol, we have a free pass. But I've spotted a problem.

"Cletus is a male name, which means Quinn will have to be the plumber," I say.

"Your pipes are my pleasure, ma'am," Quinn drawls in a

broad Southern accent, giving me a sexy wink.

"And the permit only allows for one assistant."

"That'll be me," Evyan says quickly.

"Why you? Why not me?" I ask, peeved.

"Because you don't look old enough to be a plumber's apprentice," she replies. "What are you, fifteen or something?"

"I'll be seventeen next month!"

"Whatever, we still don't have a pass for a third person."

"Then what?"

In answer, Evyan pulls the truck into a dark side street and, keeping the motor running, engages the handbrake. "You'll have to ride in the back."

I wish I could think of a good argument against this plan, but I can't.

"Sorry," Quinn tells me softly as I climb into the flatbed. He looks more like a wild pirate than ever, silhouetted against the lightning-streaked sky with the wind in his hair.

I shove the bags and backpacks behind some stacked lengths of guttering and lie down uncomfortably on the corrugated truck bed floor. There's just time to wave goodbye to Quinn before Evyan slams the panels closed and I'm left in the darkness.

"Don't lock it," I hear Quinn say.

Yeah, don't lock it, I think. I'm already feeling trapped and claustrophobic. What if, when we get to our destination, Evyan can't pick the lock again? Or *says* she can't?

I hear two doors slam, and then the truck is rattling down the road, with me bouncing around in the back, and thunder reverberating all around us. I can only hope that Tallulah gets the message to Sofia okay, and that Sofia has enough time to plant an alert in ASTA and PlayState's system that the gate guards should expect the arrival of Royal Flush Plumbing.

The ride feels like it goes on forever, and is so bumpy that I reckon Evyan must deliberately be aiming for potholes and speed bumps. The only thing more uncomfortable than rolling around in the darkness, banging elbows and knees against the plumbing equipment, is when it starts raining, and cold water leaks through the gaps between the panels, splashing down onto me. And the only thing worse than *that* is when the truck starts slowing to a stop. Because that's when the banging of my heart begins — a rapid, percussive accompaniment to the strident blare of a police siren.

A

Chapter 5

Out of sight

Crap.

I shine my flashlight inside the confines of the enclosed flatbed, desperately searching for a way to hide in case the cops decide to check back here. Pipes, wrenches and shovels, a white toilet seat with attached lid, a toolbox — there's nothing large enough to conceal me. Then I register the long ladder hanging from hooks mounted on the low sides of the truck. I tilt it up, squeeze myself behind it with my rifle on my back, and drop it back down, just as the truck comes to a halt.

Evyan keeps the engine running and gives it a couple of loud revs. Is she deliberately keeping its noisy to cover any sounds I might make? I stab an arm through the spaces between the ladder rungs and drag the toilet seat up against the side of the ladder. It's a start, but my legs must still be visible.

"Good evening, ma'am, sir." That must be the cop's voice. "Please turn off the engine."

The truck goes silent, but now I can hear the radio loudly playing a rap song. I pull a coil of yellow PVC piping up to the ladder to hide my legs, and open the lid of the toilet seat so that double the length of the ladder is covered. But this leaves my face visible through the oval center of the seat.

Outside, the cop says something, then repeats himself more loudly. "I said, kindly lower the volume."

The music is turned down and I hear Evyan say, "Is there a problem, officer?" I've never heard her sound so respectful.

"You're out past curfew. Papers, please."

I'm too scared to pull a shovel or the fire extinguisher closer — for sure they'd make a noise that the cop would hear, even over the sound of the rain. All I can reach that is light enough for me to lift, rather than drag over, is a plunger and a silicone glue gun. Working as quietly as I can, I lift them and arrange them against the toilet seat gap.

"Cletus Mayberry?"

"That's me, sir," Quinn replies.

"And you are?"

"I'm … Eve, his assistant."

"Your pass seems to be in order. Mind me asking why you aren't driving, sir?"

"I never did think there was much point in keeping a dog and barking yourself." Quinn is speaking in the accent again.

"Where are you folks headed?"

"We've been called out on a plumbing emergency to PlayState, on the south side."

"You have any proof you're expected there?"

Why is this cop so suspicious? Why isn't he in a rush to get back into his dry cruiser?

"No, sir. But you're welcome to call them and check," Evyan says.

She sounds supremely confident, but it's a dangerous bluff. What if he does check?

"I think they're mighty keen for us to get there quick as we can, officer," Quinn says. "Seems there's sewage spread from one end of their ladies' room to the other."

"It's going to be a crappy job," the officer quips, and

Quinn and Evyan laugh sycophantically. "Tell you what — I'll escort you there. That way you can help those folks with their emergency even quicker."

And he'll get to check out the cover story by seeing whether we're admitted to the ASTA grounds.

"Thank you, officer, that's much appreciated," Quinn says. Evyan doesn't reply. She's probably using all her energy to prevent herself from cursing or rolling her eyes. "May we be on our way then?" Quinn asks.

"Sure," says the cop. I sigh, but my relief is short-lived, because the cop continues, "In just a minute. First I need to check the back of the truck."

"Of course, sir." Quinn must be feeling as panicky as I am, but there's no trace of it in his voice. "Let me help you lift those panels."

I kill my flashlight, take a deep breath, and pull my knees up as high as I can in the cramped space, cursing silently when my movement bumps the ladder, sending the plunger toppling over. It makes only a small noise, but it rolls out of arm's reach, and now my white face is clearly framed by the rim of the toilet seat. Any second now, the cop will see me.

One of the panels lifts up, allowing the yellow glow from a nearby streetlight into half of the interior. Rain blows in. I cover my face with my hands — but they're white, too.

"The other side, sir."

Frantically, I tug the sleeves of my hoodie down over my hands and clutch the inside of the cuffs, covering my face with the dark-gray fabric just as the other panel creaks open.

"As you can see, officer, we're fully equipped for any plumbing emergency," I hear Quinn say.

I stay frozen in place, breathing as slowly and shallowly as I can, but my heart thuds so loudly in my chest, I'm sure it must reach the cop's ears. I can feel sweat prickling under my arms, and my rifle presses painfully into my back. What's taking so long? Is the cop planning to climb inside and check the contents? I nearly squeak in fright when the panels bang shut again.

I stay where I am, even when the engine starts up and we begin moving again, the siren sound of our unwelcome escort coming from up ahead. After about fifteen minutes, we slow to a stop, and I hear the exchange between Quinn and a guard. We've arrived at PlayState. Sofia must have come through for us, because we're immediately allowed in.

When the plumber's truck comes to a halt, I ease myself out from behind the ladder but wait until Quinn gives me the all-clear before I climb out. We're in the parking lot in front of the PlayState headquarters, and the only vehicle there is one of the reinforced people carriers that organizations use to transport essential staff to and from work under armed guard. From the back of the truck I grab a coil of wire and a heavy wrench — I figure they may come in useful — and offer them to the other two. If there's going to be any shooting, I'll need my hands free. Quinn takes the coil of wire, and Evyan eagerly grabs the wrench.

"You okay?" Quinn asks.

"Yeah."

I'm relieved that the rain has eased up — I'm already uncomfortably damp and have no desire to drip my way into PlayState.

I've been here once before, when I won The Game and was invited to play a simulated sniper session inside the massive gaming arena around the back. I've never been inside the headquarters itself.

Fitting the suppressor attachment onto the end of my rifle, I look over at the building. It's four stories high, with sealed windows and a multi-person decon unit set into the glass-fronted bottom level. The fish-eye camera mounted above the entry doesn't have the usual red power light glowing. Thank you, Sofia.

We climb the stairs up to the entrance and peer through the glass front but don't see anyone inside the brightly lit interior. I point to the lock on our side of the decon unit.

"Can you pick that?" I ask Evyan.

"Sure. This type of low-grade lock will be easy." She snags a small kit out of an inner pocket, removes a couple of metal picks. "Done," she announces a minute later.

The first time I met Sarge, our cadet sniper unit's tough-as-nails commander, was during that "real-life" simulation in the arena. He told us that there's a weak spot on every target — the sniper just needs to find it and hit it. It looks to me like PlayState's weak spot is that they rely too heavily on their tight perimeter security and are laxer about defenses inside the grounds.

Trusting that the building's alarm won't be armed while people are still inside, I push the door of the decon unit.

Chapter 6

Outside the door

The door of the decon unit swings open under my hand. I pause, holding my breath, but there's no beeping or screeching of an alarm.

We all go into the unit at the same time — it's roomy, big enough to take ten people at once — and cover our eyes with our hands to protect them from the ultraviolet light bath and disinfectant mist. When the decon unit beeps to signal completion and the inner door pops open, I step out, scanning the lobby of the building for potential dangers.

A surveillance camera is mounted on the wall near the elevators. It, too, looks dead. The metal detector directly in our path *is* switched on, but I'm able to ease out sideways and avoid passing through it. I step forward, cradling my rifle in my arms.

The only living things in the lobby are the small trees in massive planters lining the walls, and the long vines of ivy trailing down from above. Looking up, I see that above us is a triple volume of open space crisscrossed by suspended walkways. I tilt my head and listen intently, but hear only the faint hum of the air-conditioning.

When I signal, Evyan enters, then Quinn, who closes the

door softly behind us. Unsure where to go, I study the information board on the wall behind the reception desk. The first two floors seem reserved for offices, while the third houses the *Operations Room*, and the fourth the *Data Center (Networking Room and Server Floor)* and the office of *Roberta Roth (CEO)*. This is proof, if I needed it, that PlayState and ASTA are one and the same, because Roth is also CEO of ASTA.

"Sofia said Robin's being questioned in the programming division," Quinn whispers.

I point to the board that lists the *Programming Suites* on the second floor. Evyan walks over to the bank of elevators, and I only just reach her in time to bat her hand away from pressing the button. Placing my finger on my lips in a shushing gesture, I lift my eyes to the lights above the elevator door. She pulls a face but follows me over to the emergency stairwell. I pull open the door and hesitate, wondering if they're expecting me to take the lead. I'm beginning to understand why the military is organized in ranks, with clear leaders for every mission. I gesture to Quinn to go first, but he shakes his head and mouths, "No, you."

I'm only marginally less clueless than they are, but I go first, moving as quietly as possible up the stairs, hugging the outside wall so as to be less visible to anyone above who might look down. The stairwell smells of smoke — I hope no one comes to have a cigarette in the next few minutes.

The stairs end on the second landing. I open the door a crack and peep out. All clear. It occurs to me that I ought to set up some signals with the others so we can communicate silently.

"This means stop," I whisper, holding up a hand. "This means follow me, wait, crouch down. And this means on the count of three, one, two, three." I unfold my fingers in time to the counts.

"Who died and made you queen?" Evyan hisses.

I'd like to give her a different kind of hand signal, but I step aside and murmur, "You want to take the lead on this, be my guest."

"I want Quinn to lead."

Quinn shakes his head. "I know my limits."

"So with your permission, Evyan, may I go now?"

I ease through the opening of the door and, once I'm sure it's clear, signal the other two to follow me into the big open-plan area filled with desks and chairs. Framed posters of stills from The Game decorate the walls — repbots and Alien Axis Army soldiers and their leader Jahkil — and the usual *If you see something, say something* notice is stuck above the coffee machine in the corner. The main lights are off, but several of the desktop computer monitors glow faintly in the dark.

At the far end of the office space is the suspended walkway that leads over and above the lobby, to the other half of this floor. The bridge has a Plexiglas dome, giving the effect of a glass tunnel. If Robin is here, he must be on that opposite side, because I can tell at a glance that this half of the floor is empty.

No sooner have I thought this than a sudden noise makes us jump. I give the signal to duck down, and we each crouch behind a desk.

"It's the printer," Quinn whispers, pointing to a huge machine now spewing papers into its print tray.

Wait, I signal. What if someone comes to collect the print job they sent?

After a few minutes, I figure no one's coming. Signaling to the other two to stay put, I creep over the carpeted floor to the walkway, crouch behind one of the giant plant pots trailing ivy vines below, and lift my rifle to peer through the scope to the other side. It, too, is dimly lit. From what I can see through the enclosing tunnel, it consists of several smaller offices, some with their doors open and others closed.

My eyes are drawn immediately to a strip of light shining out from beneath a shut door. I move my scope across and see a pair of shined black boots, then move my gaze up the legs.

My heart gives such a kick of shock that the scope dips, and I have to take a deep breath before I can steady it again.

It's Sarge. He's standing outside the door, smoking a cigarette. And he's armed.

I slink back to Quinn and Evyan. First, I tell them the good news. "I think I've found the office where Robin must be — it's on the other side."

"How do you know which one it is? Can you see him?" asks Evyan.

"It's the only one with a light on, and it's guarded." I look at Quinn when I give them the bad news. "Sarge is standing outside, and he's carrying a submachine gun." I gesture with hands about fifteen inches apart, so they have some idea of the sort of tactical-style weapon I'm talking about.

Quinn purses his lips in a silent whistle, while Evyan asks, "Who's Sarge?"

"He's the worst possible person who could be standing outside that door right now. I have no idea how we'll get past him."

"You could shoot him," Evyan suggests at once.

"No I couldn't," I whisper back furiously.

I may have shot infected animals and terminally ill plague victims, but I've never shot a healthy person.

"And anyway, they'll hear the sound of the shot," I point out.

"But your gun's got a silencer on," Evyan protests.

"It's called a suppressor — because it only suppresses the sound. It doesn't eliminate it completely."

"Well, that's a fat lot of good. Can you sneak up and hit him on the head with this?" Evyan holds up the heavy wrench.

I shake my head. "There's no way to sneak up on Sarge." Besides, a blow to the brain from that heavy chunk of steel would surely kill him.

"What would happen if you just walked up and appealed to his better nature?" Quinn asks.

I love Quinn a lot, so I don't tell him not to be stupid. But I do cock my head and shoot him a disbelieving glance when I reply, "If I walked up holding a weapon, he'd shoot first and ask questions later." Scratch that — if Sarge shot me, there would *be* no later. "And if I went unarmed, he'd take me hostage, and then he'd have the Robin and Jinx twin-set."

"Maybe we could distract him somehow?" Quinn says.

I can see he's desperate for things not to get violent. He's probably fighting off flashbacks of the time he shot a guard.

"In the movies, they always distract the guard by throwing a stone. I'll give it a shot," says Evyan.

"And then what?" I ask.

"We'll wing it," she says with a shrug. "We can rush him and pin him down when his back is turned."

I don't think it'll work, but what do I know? I don't stop her.

Evyan moves in a low crouch over to the walkway and positions herself behind an enormous planter. She sets the wrench down and picks up something — a pebble or a piece of bark — from the base of the plant, takes aim and flings it through the walkway tube, aiming it as far away from Sarge as she can get it.

From where we're hunkered down, I can't hear the sound it makes. But Sarge obviously can. His head snaps up to check the direction where the sound came from, but he doesn't do anything as stupid as going over to investigate. Instead, he pinches out the glowing tip of his cigarette and tosses it aside, lifts his weapon and scans the entire office.

We've only succeeded in making him more alert.

I signal to Evyan to retreat. She steals back along the wall and hides behind a desk.

Having apparently assured himself that nothing is amiss on his half of the floor, Sarge takes a few steps toward the walkway. The red light of his weapon's electronic sight moves from side to side as he checks the area.

Quinn curses. I move around to the side of the desk closest to Evyan, where the shadow is deepest.

"Shoot him!" Evyan says urgently.

Without my consciously willing them to do so, my arms lift the rifle, nestle the butt against my shoulder.

Sarge reaches the walkway. He's going to come across. He's going to find us.

I rest the stock against my cheek, align my eye with the scope.

"Shoot him! Before he shoots us!" Evyan hisses.

My sniper's gut instinct is to shoot him in the chest. A kill shot would be easy at this distance, in this still air, and it would instantly incapacitate him — preventing any possibility of his raising an alarm.

I'm immediately shocked and ashamed by the impulse. This is *Sarge.* He's a real person to me, not just some nameless "tango". He's somebody's son — he may even be someone's husband. He might have kids. I know firsthand what it does to a family to lose a husband and father, and I won't put anyone else through that pain and grief.

But there's a dark, angry part of me that *wants* to take him down.

This is the man who christened me Blue, who plucked me out of the stifling boredom of home and pushed me to the limits of my endurance, who helped me find a depth of inner strength that I'd never suspected I had. This is the man I grew to respect and trust. This is the man who drank coffee while in a nearby room, I was tortured. This is the man who didn't tell me that I was actually killing, not tranquilizing, my targets.

He's halfway across the walkway now, and my finger curls around the cool trigger of my weapon.

"You could just wound him," Quinn says quickly.

The sniper inside me that Sarge selected and trained, the girl he called his ice-maiden angel of death, shakes her head at Quinn's suggestion. She reminds me of what Sarge told me just two months ago — if you don't end a threat to life permanently, it'll come back and bite you on the ass. Put an enemy shooter down, and you eliminate the danger. Merely injure him, and he'll be back to kill you or one of yours.

Sarge takes another step. He's squinting in our direction. In another second he'll spot us.

I take aim. Center the crosshairs on his chest.

As he steps off the walkway onto our side, Quinn says, "Jinxy, please."

His voice is a low plea. It tugs at my heart, nudges my conscience, and shifts my position ever so slightly a split second before I squeeze the trigger.

Chapter 7

Monsters out there

The rifle thuds. Sarge drops his weapon and clutches his right forearm. By the time he looks back up, Quinn and I are charging straight at him.

I snatch up Sarge's weapon as Quinn tackles him with a hard shoulder to the gut. The breath leaves Sarge in a grunt, and he doubles over, winded. He gasps a couple of times, then straightens up and gapes at me.

"Blue? That you?"

I point my rifle at his head. "Don't even think about yelling," I warn him. My voice sounds cold and icy calm, but inside, I'm full of doubts and fears.

"Princess, you just turned a corner you can't go back round," he wheezes.

"You took my brother. I never did buy that 'squad before blood' crap."

"How does the door open, the one you were guarding?" Quinn asks.

"There's a secret knock," Sarge says, his voice heavy with sarcasm.

His wound is bleeding through the fingers gripped tightly over it, and it must be hurting like a mother, but apart from his white face, I see no sign that he's in pain.

I peer at the office across the way through the scope on my rifle. "It looks like a biometric scanner, so we'll have to take him along. Move," I say, jabbing my rifle in Sarge's ribs.

"You are in a whole world of trouble, my girl," Sarge says.

"She's not your girl," snarls Quinn. "Now shut up and do what she says."

"Walk slowly. And don't try anything stupid," I order.

"Or what? You'll shoot me again?" he replies, his face twisted in a scornful grimace. "Go ahead —I've got another arm and a couple of legs. But you and I both know, princess, that under your big talk you're still just a bleeding-heart softie. You won't kill me."

"Maybe not, but *I* will," says Evyan, snatching the submachine gun out of my left hand and pressing it against Sarge's temple. "Now I'm no super-sniper, but at this range, I don't think I'll need to be. Move!"

He glances at Evyan and apparently sees something in her face to convince him that she, unlike me, means business, because he turns and starts walking. At any moment that door could open. We need to move quickly, and we need to keep Sarge quiet.

"I'll get a gag," Quinn says.

He darts to the coffee corner and is soon binding a dishcloth around Sarge's mouth. We march our prisoner over the walkway, across the open central area on the other side, and push him to his knees in front of the scanner beside the closed door.

"You okay to stay and guard him?" I ask Evyan, speaking as softly as possible.

"Oh, yeah," she says with an evil grin.

"We'll need to move quickly once the door is open. Any ideas what we should do when we get inside?" I ask Quinn.

Sarge rolls his eyes and shakes his head. I swear he's

laughing at us, at my pathetic attempts to lead.

"I'll do Sarge's finger. You go in first with your gun. But after that…?" Quinn gives me a helpless shrug.

I know what he means. He's a data guy, and we've got no data. Without knowing who and what and how many are behind that door, how can we plan?

I aim my rifle at the door. Evyan presses her weapon against Sarge's back while Quinn seizes his injured right arm, stretches it up and presses the index finger on the scanner pad. Sarge hisses in pain, but otherwise nothing happens. Quinn repeats the process with the middle finger and thumb, but the scanner's display light glows red, and the door stays locked. Quinn stops, thinks for a moment, then hauls Sarge to his feet and gets him to position his eye over the scanner. A green light flashes, and the door opens with a soft pop.

I charge into the room, yelling, "Nobody move! Nobody move!"

In a single glance, I take in the whole room. Seven people, three of whom I know well, are seated around a long table. Automatically, my eyes scan for possible sources of danger.

Leya!

Leya, who pretended to be a sniper cadet at ASTA, who pretended to be my friend while she spied on us for Roth, is sitting on a stool in the corner of the room. Her mouth is open in shock, but her hand is already reaching for the sidearm holstered at her waist.

"Freeze!" I yell, aiming my rifle at her.

She holds her hands still, about a foot away from her body.

"Behind your head," I say, and she reluctantly crosses her arms behind her head.

Quinn steps up to Leya and removes her firearm. He returns to my side and holds it out to me.

"Point it at *them*, Quinn?"

"Oh, right."

He aims it at Leya and then at the group around the table. Of course, I know he would never shoot unarmed people, but *they* don't know that.

"Just what the hell are you doing, Jinx?" Leya yells.

"At least I'm not betraying my unit by spying on them."

"No, you're just betraying your country," she retorts.

"You," I instruct the high-value target seated at the table. "Go stand next to Leya."

Looking completely unruffled by this turn of events, Roberta Roth walks over to stand beside her agent.

Only then do I allow my gaze to travel to my twin brother, with his blond hair and blue eyes so like my own. He's seated at the center of the table, surrounded by what must be the computer security experts who are investigating how he hacked their systems. Nearby, in her blue ASTA jumpsuit with its silver intel unit pin, Sofia sits wide-eyed and absolutely still.

"Robin! You okay?" He looks to be unharmed.

"Well, hi, Jinxy," he says, smiling bemusedly. "What brings you to this neck of the woods?"

I only just stop myself from running around to give him a hug.

"Are you going to screw this up, too?" Leya's face twists in anger. "Do you realize that every time you impede us, you help them — the terrorists?"

"Robin, come over here, quick. And you too," I say to Sofia. "You can be our hostage."

I'm not sure exactly where Sofia's allegiances lie. She may want out of ASTA, but that doesn't mean she wants to join the rebel movement, so I'd rather leave Roth with the impression that Sofia isn't coming willingly.

"You don't want *me* as your hostage?" says Roth, tossing back her sleek black hair, with its iridescent purple underside.

I shake my head. "I'd be too tempted to murder you, and I don't want another death on my conscience."

At the words, "another death," Robin cuts me a sharp glance. He doesn't yet know that his sister has killed several plague victims, one of whom was a good friend.

"C'mon!" I tell Sofia.

"O-Okay," she stammers convincingly, wiping a hand over the filigreed henna tattoo surrounding her eyes. "Just d-don't shoot."

"You are making a serious mistake here, Miss James," says Roth. "Once again, you are acting like a very silly little girl."

"I thought you said I wasn't just a girl, that I was a combatant in the war against terror," I say, throwing her own words back at her.

"It seems we failed utterly to install a correct mindset in you," Roth continues. "You were supposed to be on our side fighting the terrorists, not on their side opposing us."

"I'm not on their side," I say, gesturing to Robin and Sofia to stand behind me, and to Quinn to hold Sofia's hands behind her back as though she truly is our prisoner.

"War is coming, and we need to be ready for the fight. You should be supporting your country in any way you can," Roth says.

"It isn't that simple," says Quinn.

"You are such fools! You'd be a joke if you weren't doing so much damage to our country," Leya says.

"Have you ever thought about how what *you're* doing is damaging this country? Betraying everything our Constitution stands for?" Quinn snaps.

Oh, Quinn, are you really still trying to convert them with logic and integrity?

I gesture to the tech-heads to move to the side of the room where Leya and Roth stand, and when I see that one of the older men is trembling and has tears in his eyes, a pang of guilt stabs at me.

"Just do as I say and you won't come to any harm," I tell them all.

"*No harm*," Leya mocks. "People like you make me sick. Newsflash — there isn't any way to win this war without causing harm! You can't fight killers by being nice and kind and understanding. You can't keep your hands clean."

"So we're supposed to fight dirty? We're supposed to become as bad as them?" Quinn says.

"That would take some doing! I don't know how you can even compare us. We have a hacker who's compromised national security, and we're just questioning him about —"

"Yeah, you are now," I say. "But in a few hours you planned to do more than just *question*, didn't you?" The thought of Robin in that room with the chair and the drain sends a shiver through me.

"Only if he didn't tell us what we need to know."

"How can you justify torturing and interrogating a kid who hacked a computer game? What gives you the right?" Quinn asks.

I see Roth and Leya exchange a glance. They're good questions. In the mad rush to get here and free Robin, I haven't stopped to think why they consider hacking a game to be an issue of national security.

"You're just corrupt," says Quinn. "You're abusing your power to protect your profits, same as always."

Roth shoots him a filthy look. Leya looks like she's not above adding a physical charge to her verbal attack.

"Robin, can you tie them up with this?" I motion to the coil of wire looped over Quinn's shoulder.

"With pleasure."

While I keep my weapon trained on the group in the corner, Robin gets them to stand in a tight, outwards-facing circle with their hands behind their backs.

"We have to fight fire with fire." Leya continues her tirade as Robin binds her hands behind her back, and then loops the cord around the programmer standing next to her in the same way. "Don't you get it? There are monsters out there preying on us, committing evil deeds. Everyone lives in fear because the monsters prey on innocents, like wolves on sheep. And they'll keep doing that until someone stops them. That's what we're doing here — we're finding ways to stop them, smart ways. We're training people who will be ready to take the fight directly to the terrorists."

Roth starts to say something — to Leya, I think — but there's a banging at the door. I sling my rifle over my shoulder and across my back and take Leya's handgun from Quinn. It's a Ruger 9mm. Slim, compact and accurate, it's a better weapon for these close quarters. I ease off the safety and hold it ready while Quinn opens the door a crack. I'm ready for an attack, but it's just Evyan.

"What's taking so long in there?" she says. Her eyes are fierce, and there's a sheen of sweat on her face. "Hurry up already!"

Chapter 8

Out of the frying pan

"We're almost done. Just keep that weapon on Sarge," I tell Evyan, because I know he's a trained soldier who must be searching for some way to turn this situation around. "And don't stand so close to him, back up."

"You're a coward," Leya yells. Trying to bait me into a time-wasting discussion? "You don't want blood on your hands, but bad things happen when good people do nothing!"

"Are you still talking?" I ask.

Robin, who has finished tying up Roth and her team, now yanks the long cord out of a landline telephone and starts winding that around the group for good measure. We're almost ready to go, but Leya is not yet finished having her say.

"You of all people should be supporting us — after what they did to your father. You should be out there avenging his death, not in here resisting our efforts. You're a traitor to his memory!"

"Shut up about my father. You have no right to talk about him, or to tell me how I should feel, or live my life," I snap.

My throat is suddenly tight, and my old doubts are crowding my mind. I *do* want to fight those responsible for my father's death. If the terrorist who injected him with rat-fever serum was standing in front of me right now, I'd shoot him myself.

Or would I?

What would my father want me to do? What would make him proud of his daughter?

"Maybe not. But I have a right to talk about my life. See this?" Leya turns and tilts her head so that the tattoo on the outer corner of her left eye is facing me. "Ever wonder what it means?"

I'm curious, in spite of myself, in spite of the urgency of the situation.

"Cactus Rock," she spits.

"Cactus Rock?" Quinn says the words like they mean something to him.

They sound familiar to me, too, though I can't quite think from where.

"Yeah, Cactus Rock High. Remember that attack?"

I nod slowly. I do remember. It was right at the start of the wave of attacks. A group of terrorists posing as parents came to a basketball game at a high school in Reno, Nevada. They sealed the doors to the gym and injected dozens of kids, parents and teachers with the serum before the tactical response team arrived. The kids were taken to the hospital and examined, tested for poisons, kept overnight for observation, but no one knew about rat flu yet, and the victims weren't quarantined. They were discharged the next morning. By the time they started showing symptoms, it was too late. They'd already infected others who were out in the city — virtual viral bombs, waiting to explode.

"*I* remember. I was there," says Leya, her voice hoarse with emotion. "I was in the restroom washing my hands when the screaming started. I tried to get back to my team, my friends, but they'd jammed the gym doors shut, and I was stuck outside, close enough to hear the screams and the shouting and the begging. But not able to do a damn thing about it."

Tears are streaming down her cheeks now.

"Leya …"

"And I was there at the hospital when my friends were dying — bleeding and screeching and falling apart. I saw it all. I saw half my class suffer and die. And there was nothing I could do about it." She lifts a shoulder to wipe her cheek and glares back at me with blazing eyes. "I vowed never to be that helpless again. I promised to get revenge, and I will. I am. So don't you talk to me about 'fighting dirty'. Because I've seen *dirty*, and I don't think we'll beat them by playing nice."

For a few moments we're all still, silenced by the horror of her account.

Then Robin says softly, "I'm done here."

For a moment I think he's talking about the war, then I realize he's finished tying up everyone, and has also thought to collect all their phones, which he bundles into a turquoise scarf he takes from one of the programmers.

"Time to go," I say, nodding at Quinn to open the door.

He gestures to Robin and Sofia to leave first, then follows, leaving the door open. I can't see Sarge from where I'm standing, but I can see Evyan. She still has the submachine gun pointed down at him.

"Bring him in here," I say to her and Quinn.

I back up from the doorway and raise my weapon, not wanting to be within grabbing distance of Sarge when he enters. While I wait, I try to think of something to say to Leya. I know she won't want my pity or attempts at consolation.

In a way, we're similar, she and I. We both lost people we cared about to the plague, we both hold the terrorists responsible, and we both want to do something to help in the war. But Leya's a real fighter — more of a soldier than I'll ever be. She's fighting the monsters who've attacked our nation directly, while I'm trying to prevent us from becoming monsters ourselves.

Quinn says that killing people who are killing people, to show that killing people is wrong, is a crazy strategy. And I agree, I do. But I'm still not sure I've chosen the right side. Hell, after my time with the rebels, I'm not sure there *is* a right side. I want Leya to know that I'm not her enemy.

"Leya, I'm —"

My head snaps to the side at the shot that comes from outside the office.

I'm out the door in the same instant, taking in many things at once — Evyan, uselessly pulling on the trigger of her weapon; Sarge in a half-crouch amidst a litter of cellphones, holding a handgun awkwardly in his blood-slippery left hand; Robin collapsing, clutching his shoulder, where a bloom of vicious red is spreading. Quinn is stepping toward Sarge with his hands outstretched. Sarge is unsteadily raising his weapon.

Instinct takes over. It's instinct which calculates that Sarge's shot will hit Quinn square in the chest. It's instinct that lifts my arm and aims, selecting the one sure and immediately incapacitating shot. It's instinct that pulls the trigger. It's not me who sends a 9mm round into the dead center of Sarge's forehead. It's instinct.

It's me who rushes over to Robin. It's me who calls his name, heedless of the scuffles and yells behind me. The world narrows to this moment, to my brother, to the blood streaming out of his shoulder and his wrist.

"Robin!" I cry over and over. "Robin, please!"

His eyes open and he stares at me blankly. He's alive. Someone pulls the weapon out of my hand, and a moment later the deafening bang of another shot jolts me from my panic.

I glance over my shoulder in time to see Quinn sending a second shot into the scanner lock mechanism. The door is sealed and won't easily open now.

"Help!" I cry.

Sofia rushes over, grabbing the turquoise scarf from where Robin dropped it. She wraps it tightly around his wrist.

"We need to get him to a doctor, quick!" she says.

I try to get one shoulder under the arm on Robin's uninjured side, but Quinn sets me aside gently.

"Here, you take this," he says, handing me Leya's handgun. I tuck it into the waistband of my jeans, behind my back. "I'll get Robin."

He lifts my brother over his shoulder in a fireman's lift. Sofia removes her jacket, wads it up into a ball, and wedges it between Robin's shoulder and Quinn's back. "You'll need to go ahead with the weapons," Quinn says, grabbing Robin's bleeding wrist and squeezing tight.

The weapons! I scramble over to the door, where Sarge was when I … Where Sarge was.

He isn't there anymore. Quinn and Sofia and Evyan must have dragged him inside the office already.

No, not him. His body.

Evyan is outside the door, holding Sarge's weapons.

"What happened?" I demand, taking the submachine gun from her and running to get in front of Quinn, who has already started striding back to the walkway with a groaning Robin slung over his shoulder. "Where did he — where did Sarge get the sidearm from? Why didn't you shoot him?"

Sofia runs past us across the walkway. "I'll get the elevator."

"That gun you left me with wouldn't fire, I tried and tried, but nothing happened," Evyan complains from the rear.

I glance down at the sub, see at once that the safety is still engaged. Sarge would've noticed that, would've known it would give him precious seconds in an attack. Why didn't I think to take it off? Or show Evyan how it worked?

We cross the office on the other side of the walkway and slip into the elevator Sofia is holding open for us.

"And then," says Evyan as the doors close and we move down, "as he got up, he reached across to his other leg, and suddenly he was shooting! And Robin had his hands up like this" — she holds her hands up against her shoulders — "and the shot went through his wrist and into his shoulder."

Oh God. Sarge must have had the sidearm hidden in a leg holster under his pants. Why didn't I check? I know better. I should've checked. Of course he would have had a backup weapon. I was an idiot not to have patted him down. I'm supposed to be a professional shooter, but I made an elementary mistake. And now my brother might die because of it.

"Robin?" I touch the back of his head, smoothing his silky blond hair.

He groans an unintelligible answer as the doors of the elevator slide open and I step out.

And come face to face with two people who know exactly who I am.

"Blue?" says the big guy with buzz-cut hair, at the same time as I say, "Bruce?"

Chapter 9

Bleeding out

"What did you do to your hair, Blue?" Bruce asks.

But the other guy, the geeky-looking one with glasses, isn't studying my appearance. His gaze travels from the weapon I'm holding, to the one Evyan is now pointing at them.

"Whoa," Cameron says, holding his hands in front of him.

He has a bunch of papers in one hand and nothing in the other. As usual, Bruce has his Leatherman multi-tool clipped on his belt, but apart from that, neither of them appears to be armed. And they're both dressed in civilian clothes, not the black jumpsuits which are the standard uniforms of the ASTA sniper cadet unit, where they were my teammates.

"Back up," I tell them, stepping forward so the others can get out of the elevator.

"What the hell's going on, Blue?" Bruce asks, taking in the weapons, the rest of our group, and Robin lying limply over Quinn's shoulder.

"They snatched my brother and we came to get him, but Sarge shot him. We need to get him to a doctor, so don't even think of trying to stop us."

I keep walking forward as I talk, forcing Bruce and Cameron to back up. I can hear Quinn panting behind me, struggling under the weight of Robin.

"Sarge shot your brother?" says Bruce, sounding stunned.

"Yeah, and she shot him back, so just get out of our way before she shoots you, too," says Evyan, waving her weapon at them.

"You shot Sarge?" Bruce asks me, his eyes round with shock.

"What, is there an echo in here?" says Evyan.

"I killed him." The whispered confession is out my mouth before I can stop it.

"Holy shit!" Bruce shoots a glance at Cameron.

"*Why?*" Cameron asks.

"He had his weapon up and was about to kill Quinn. What was I supposed to do?"

"Couldn't you just have wounded him?" Bruce says.

"I already did. It didn't stop him. There was a shot to drop him, and I took it."

"Jinx, we need to go!" Quinn gasps from behind me. "I can't carry him much longer."

"He's still bleeding," says Sofia.

I take a few more steps forward. Bruce and Cameron take two steps back. They're both still looking at me with shocked faces.

"I had no choice, okay? There was no time," I say, and my voice sounds like a plea.

Cameron and Bruce exchange a long look, as if they're having some silent conversation.

"Things are going to get really bad, now," says Cameron. "Even worse than before."

"Oh, yeah. Much worse," Bruce agrees.

"It's now or never," says Cameron.

"You think so, bro?"

Cameron nods.

Bruce clears his throat. "Right, we're coming with you. Here, let me help you with that."

He eases Robin off Quinn's shoulder and slings him over his own as though he weighed no more than a sack of potatoes, spins around and heads for the door, with Cameron beside him.

"Wait, what?" Now it's my turn to be amazed.

"We were leaving already," Cameron says.

"What is going on here?" Evyan demands. "Whose side are these guys on?"

"We've been chucked out of ASTA," Bruce says. "Well, technically I've been discharged and Cameron quit."

"That's true," Sofia confirms. "Everyone was talking about it today."

"Then what are you doing here?" I ask Bruce, as I follow him to the doors.

Through the glass front I can see the rain has started up again, harder than before.

"Discharge papers," says Cameron, holding the door open for Bruce and Robin to pass through. I follow them.

"We were due to get a transport home in the morning, but Sarge said he'd be off base then," says Bruce.

Yeah, he'd have been at the interrogation center, supervising Robin's torture.

"So he told us to bring our discharge papers over here tonight so he could sign them. Hell, Blue, you really shot him? Sarge is dead?"

"He shot my brother and was going to kill Quinn," I repeat. "He only missed *killing* Robin because he was shooting with his left hand. It was self-defense!"

"Justified," says Cameron. "But …"

"Yeah, '*but*'," says Bruce, shaking his head.

We're all out of the building now. Quinn and Evyan

stride ahead to the plumber's truck. I pull up my hood against the pelting rain and run past them to the back of the truck. I open the panels on the flatbed and tell Bruce, "Lay him down, gently."

"Can't say I think much of your wheels, Jinx," Bruce says, eyeing the truck dubiously. But he lifts Robin over the side panels and, muscles bulging, deposits him carefully on the corrugated base.

"Neil said his sister's a doctor, we'll go directly there. Evyan can call him on the way to alert him, and to get the address," Quinn says.

Sofia climbs into the back of the truck, jamming herself between Robin and the side, pressing the ball of fabric hard against his wound. Evyan hands me Sarge's sidearm then gets behind the wheel and starts the engine.

"Why were you thrown out? Why do you want to come with us?" Sofia asks Bruce and Cameron, when they hop into the back of the truck.

"They can explain on the way. We need to hurry!" I urge, swinging off my rifle and climbing inside after them.

"Hang on. Just one sec," says Quinn, from where he stands in the pouring rain at the foot of the flatbed. "Jinxy, do you trust these guys?"

I glance quickly at Bruce and Cameron, but there isn't time to think it through logically. I go with my gut, like I should've when we were upstairs, instead of allowing Quinn to persuade me into merely wounding Sarge.

"Yeah, I do."

"With our lives?" Quinn presses.

"You heard her, dude," Bruce says.

"I think so. Yes."

In truth, I'm not sure who I can trust. I just know we have to get Robin to a doctor. Now.

I squeeze myself in between Bruce and Robin. We're all

soaking wet and jammed in the back like five sardines lying side-by-side in a can, with me in the middle. If we get stopped again, there'll be no way to hide us, we'll have to fight. As Quinn closes the panels, shutting us in the darkness, I hand the submachine gun to Bruce, and Sarge's sidearm to Cameron. I hang onto Leya's Ruger and place my rifle on the floor of the truck, with the bags.

With a lurch that jerks a moan of pain out of Robin, the truck moves forward out of the lot in front of PlayState and down the drive to the main entrance. A minute later, it stops — we must be at the gate. We strain our ears above the rain drumming on the metal flaps above us to hear what's happening outside. Bruce, Cameron and I engage our weapons and tilt them up in readiness, but the guard must just wave us through, because a moment later we're off again.

"Safeties back on," I say.

Bruce sniffs. "It stinks in here, man. You think this Royal Flush dude washes his equipment before he chucks it back here?"

I retrieve my small flashlight from my pocket and turn it on. Robin's eyes are closed, but his face is screwed into a tight grimace of pain, so he's not unconscious. I can see Sofia has his uninjured wrist under her fingers, taking his pulse.

"How's he doing?" I ask her.

She moves her head in a gesture which could mean anything, and says, "This is soaked through. Does anyone have something else we could use to staunch the wound?"

Oh God, how much blood has he lost?

Our bags are back behind our head, but they won't be easy to get into. I twist around and manage to wriggle out of my hoodie and hand it to Sofia, who folds it tight and presses it against Robin's shoulder. I turn onto my side, facing Robin, so I can check on him.

"Many's the night I've dreamed about having you lying

next to me in the dark, squirming up against me," says Bruce. "But I never thought it would be in the back of a stinking plumber's van."

I shine the flashlight directly at him. "My brother is bleeding out beside me, Bruce — do you think you could just control yourself for once?" I snap.

"Sorry," he says, sounding chastened and holding his hands up in apology.

The beam of the flashlight glints off something metallic at his wrist. "Your ID bracelets!"

Bruce gets such a fright that he sits up, banging his head on the metal panel above.

Cameron curses softly.

"Get them off!"

"Chill, Blue," Bruce says, retrieving the multi-tool from his belt.

"Don't tell me to chill," I say. "They could be following you even now."

Was this intentional? Did I make another mistake in trusting my two ex-cadets?

Bruce fiddles with the attachments until he finds the wire-cutting extension. He cuts through first his own and then Cameron's bracelets and is about to feed them through the crack between the side of the truck and the roof panel when Cameron lays a hand on his arm to stop him. Cameron takes the bands and wraps them through and around a short piece of PVC piping, then he inches back and hammers a fist loudly on the partition between the truck's back and the cab. We brake suddenly, and even before we've come to a complete stop, Cameron opens a panel and leaps out of the truck. Bruce and I sit up to watch as he runs into the rainy darkness. A minute later he's back and we're moving again.

"What did you do with them?" I ask him.

"Storm-water drain," he replies.

"Good idea."

With this deluge, the plastic pipe and its wrapping will float down the drains and into the Chattahoochee river, and with any luck will be halfway to Florida by the time they locate and retrieve it. It's a great decoy.

I turn onto my side so I can keep an eye on Robin. When I shiver at the cool metal pressing into my side and the wind whistling through the gaps into the truck, Bruce snuggles up behind me. I tense, but he doesn't take advantage of the situation to grope or make any more off-color quips, so I don't push away his warmth.

"So Sarge is dead? You really killed him? Man, I can't get my head around that," Bruce says. "I dunno what I feel, even. Sad or angry or just stunned."

I ignore Bruce's comments about Sarge, even though they pretty much mirror my own, and instead ask, "So, can you two explain why you're in here with us?"

Bruce does most of the talking, with Cameron tossing in the odd laconic phrase.

Turns out ASTA has changed radically since I went AWOL. Security is up, freedoms are down, and all R&R weekends home have been cancelled. Two new cadets joined the sniper unit to replace Leya and me. Bruce and Cameron suspect one of them, a guy from Memphis, of being the new mole in the unit.

"He's a little guy — shorter even than you, Blue."

"I'm not short."

"I reckon they thought he'd look like a teenager."

"He's older," says Cameron.

"He's twenty-five," says Sofia. Being in the intel unit, she would've had access to his file.

"That figures," grunts Bruce. "I think he's a marine or something, man, he's too good."

From which I conclude that he outperforms Bruce on the

shooting range.

The other new cadet is a girl, and she's eighteen, according to Sofia.

"She could also be the new rat for Roth," says Bruce.

"Can't shoot," adds Cameron.

"Can't shoot for shit," agrees Bruce. "Got tits out to here, though." His hand comes over the side of me and protrudes a good half-foot in front of my own chest. "Maybe that's why she can't shoot — her puppies get in the way," he adds thoughtfully.

"So you quit because you think there are more moles?"

"Not just that, man. I told you — the whole place has changed. They search our rooms, they stopped Dasha selling cash cards, cut off our internet access. Plus, what they did to you when you were detained — I'm still pissed off at that."

The truck bounces and rattles, and a cry of pain escapes Robin's gritted teeth. I want Evyan to drive fast, so we can get Robin help sooner, but I also don't want him to suffer even more pain. It's killing me to see my brother like this.

I wipe a cool hand over his sweaty face. "Hang in there, Robin. We're going to get you help soon," I tell him.

"Tests," says Cameron.

"What tests?" I wonder if Cameron's intentionally trying to keep me distracted from my fears.

"Oh, I forgot about that!" says Bruce. "They've been taking all the cadets, unit by unit, to this medical center and running a bunch of tests on us. We had fitness tests and weird stuff, too — brain scans and testing us on virtual reality sims while we had wires stuck on our heads."

"FMRIs and EEGs," Sofia says.

"Did they do it on y'all, too?" Bruce asks her.

"Not yet. We're only due to go the week after next. But I know about it because three of the other intels are working on analyzing the data."

"Jeez, man. They control everything we do, and now they want inside our heads too."

"But I never figured you'd quit, Bruce," I say.

"Yeah, and I never figured you'd kill Sarge, Blue," he retorts. "Besides, I haven't told you the worst of it."

Chapter 10

Outraged

"There's more?" I ask Bruce.

I want all the details. Concentrating on this story keeps me from sliding into full-on panic over Robin.

"Two days ago, Sarge and Roth called me in. Sarge said nothing." Bruce pauses, and I know he's still trying to grasp the fact of Sarge's death, just as I am.

"And Roth?" I prompt.

"She was all smiley-like. Which makes her look pretty scary, let me tell you," Bruce says. "Tells me she needs a new set of eyeballs on the unit now that Leya has been redeployed to other duties."

"She asked you to be a mole?" That would *not* have gone down well with Bruce.

"Yeah! Can you believe it? She genuinely thought I'd be pleased to be her new pet rat! And Sarge just sat there, not objecting or anything. So I told Roth — I thought that's what the new cadets were for, but she just laughed and told me not to be paranoid. I didn't know what to think. Either she didn't trust the others and wanted me to spy on them, or she didn't trust me and was testing me, and would compare my reports to the ones from the others."

"So you refused?"

"Of course I did. I told her nothing would make me spy on my squad. And she was all, 'Nothing? Really?'" Bruce simpers in imitation of Roth. "'Then we have no use for you in the program, cadet. Either you follow orders, or you can pack your bags and leave.' Just like that."

"Huh." Just like Zonia was with me, when I refused to shoot President Hawke for the rebels.

"So I told her where she could shove her orders, and she told me I was dismissed."

"Then me," says Cameron.

"Yeah, we figured Cameron would be next, so he saved her the trouble and quit. And now with you icing Sarge and snatching your brother, I reckon they wouldn't even have let us leave tomorrow."

"Lockdown," says Cameron.

"Yeah, they'd seal the whole place and we'd be stuck tight as spam in a can. But I'm not too bummed about leaving, to be honest. I was getting cabin fever — we were hardly even going out on missions anymore."

Ah, *missions*. "Guys, there's something you need to know."

"Why you went?" Cameron asks.

Perceptive, watchful Cameron knew there was something really wrong those last days I was at ASTA. He'd told me that whatever I was planning to do, I wouldn't be able to do it alone. And that when the time came, he'd want in on my plans.

"Are we about to hear the real reason you went AWOL? Because they've told us a stack of crap about you, Blue," Bruce says.

"About me?"

"They said you'd run off to join the terrorists and are behind a bunch of attacks at government sites, and are planning to assassinate the president."

"Never. Not Jinx," says Cameron, his voice confident with conviction.

I'm touched by his faith in me, but I squirm a little. The story about the planned assassination, at least, is not completely groundless.

"Yeah, Cameron and Mitch and I didn't believe that, no way."

"And Tae-Hyun?" I ask, wondering what the remaining member of our unit thinks of me now.

"He never said. Mind you, he spends most of his time drooling over the new girl's assets, and showing her how to hold her weapon. I bet he wishes he was showing her how to hold *his* —"

"*Bruce.*"

The truck corners sharply, turning Robin onto his injured shoulder. He whimpers and passes out. I bat away the plunger that rolls up against my head and ease him onto his back again. Sofia and I exchange fearful glances, but neither of us knows what more we can do.

"Yeah … so we reckoned if they would tell us such BS about you, they'd lie about anything, and we couldn't trust a thing they said." Bruce pauses for a moment, then lays a hand on my upper arm and asks softly, "You haven't joined the terrs, have you, Blue?"

"No!"

Behind me, Bruce gives a deep sigh of relief. Then he asks, "So why *did* you run away?"

"I found out something — something bad — and Sofia checked it for me. Guys, we've been shooting M&Ms. Maybe even terr suspects."

Cameron sucks in a quick, shocked breath of comprehension and mutters, "Not acceptable."

But Bruce says, "Yeah, and?"

"Killing them, Bruce, not darting them. Those M&M

rounds were filled with poison, not tranquilizer. Some of the darts for suspects too, for all I know."

Bruce lets loose with a stream of curses and complaints. He's not so much appalled at the realization that he's been killing plague victims and perhaps suspected terrorists — Bruce has always believed that both those groups should be "neutralized" — but he is outraged that he's been doing so without his knowledge, that ASTA have been lying to him about more and for far longer than he ever suspected.

"I feel like a fool, man. I should've guessed."

"Yeah, you and me both. Anyway, I couldn't stay after that, after I knew what we were really doing."

"You never did like shooting live things," says Bruce. "But now you've taken out Sarge. I still can't process that, man. Sarge!"

"So now I'm with the rebels. Sort of. And you two need to decide if you're in with us, or if you want us to drop you off somewhere."

Lightning cracks nearby, loud as a .50 caliber rifle fired beside my ear. The rain pounds down heavily on the panels above. Sofia has found a grease-stained towel — perhaps what Cletus usually wipes his hands on — and we hold it above Robin, doing our best to shelter him from the drops of icy rain splashing down on us.

"First I want to know exactly what y'all are up to. What's your agenda?" Bruce asks.

"We're *not* out to aid the terrorists, whatever they may have told you at ASTA. We just don't think that the government is going about fighting this war in the right way. They're too focused on making profits and staying in power. They want to keep the civilian population scared and obedient. Did you know that rat fever isn't spread by airborne contact, or by food or touching surfaces?"

"No?" Cameron asks.

"No. It's more like AIDS — transmitted by blood and bodily fluids. Plus bites, of course."

"Is there *anything* they've told us that's true?" Bruce says, sounding irate.

I don't reply, and in the silence that follows, I hear Robin's breath coming in shallow pants. I pray it's just from the pain, and not that shock is setting in from the blood loss. How much longer will this journey take?

Bruce is speaking again, asking me something.

"What?" I say.

"What do y'all plan to do?" Bruce asks.

"Uncover the truth, if we can, and let the country know."

"I'm in," says Cameron. "Told you I was on your side."

"Yeah, I'm in, too," says Bruce. "Just so long as you understand my fight is still with the terrs and the plague. A rabid comes anywhere near me, I'll shoot it. If we find a terrorist, I'll shoot him, and shoot anyone who tries to stop me from shooting him. And if I discover you rebels are doing anything to assist the terrorists —"

"Let me guess, You'll shoot us, too."

"That's about the sum of it. And," Bruce adds, "just as long as that leprechaun doesn't piss me off too badly. Are you still with him?"

"Yes."

"Like, *with him* with him?"

"Yes!"

"Just checking," Bruce says, sounding disappointed.

At that moment, to my huge relief, the truck stops. There's a knock on the panels. "It's just me, don't shoot," Quinn says, before flinging them open. "Neil and his sister are here, they met us halfway."

"Everybody out, we're ditching the truck," Evyan orders.

We're parked in a dark, deserted side street. Bruce and Cameron lift Robin, carry him through the sheeting rain over to a black SUV, and lay him on the plastic sheeting covering the back seat. The rest of us grab all the bags and weapons and load them up in a blue panel van parked behind the SUV.

"You're his sister?" says a plump woman with short, graying hair and a kind face. She's sheltering under a large umbrella and carrying a black bag which I hope is filled with medical supplies.

"Yes, I'm Jinx. You must be Doctor …" I realize I don't know Neil's surname. The rebels only ever used first names.

"Call me Beth," she says. "You come with us."

She climbs into the back of the SUV and crouches down beside Robin. I clamber into the seat behind them and, not waiting for an invitation, Sofia follows, still clutching my bloodstained hoodie. Neil is already behind the wheel, and the engine is running.

"Are you okay? Do you want me to come with you?" Quinn asks from where he stands at the door of the SUV.

"No. You keep the others under control," I tell him, wiping a hand across my wet face. "Don't let Bruce shoot anyone."

"Love you," he says, sliding the door of the SUV closed before running back to join the others at the van.

Cameron is already inside the back, but Evyan and Bruce are standing in the downpour beside the van. They appear to be arguing over who gets to drive.

I neither know nor care who wins. Beth is handing me an IV bag to hold up above Robin, and a second after she slips the needle into a vein in the crook of his elbow, I yell, "Go, Neil, just go!"

Part Two

Chapter 11

Hiding out

October 9

I'm hiding out up in a giant hickory tree, trying not to move a muscle.

A woodpecker clings to the trunk of a nearby tree, cocking its head from side to side as if to see beneath the bark where a juicy borer beetle or some termites might lurk, blissfully unaware of their imminent death. It's a handsome bird with a scarlet head and striking black-and-white plumage.

That red head reminds me of Zonia and Connor and their band of red-bereted rebels plotting assassination and other bloodthirsty missions in the woods.

The bird hammers away at the tree trunk with its short, sharp beak. The bursts of hard drumming are surprisingly loud, like the rapid fire of an automatic weapon.

I don't want to think about weapons. Or Zonia and her rebels. I just want to sit here and watch the pretty bird attack the tree, and think of nothing.

My father once told me that woodpeckers slam into wood with such force that their eyeballs would fall out if they didn't have an extra set of eyelids. He said they also have an especially thick skull which prevents brain damage by absorbing the shock of impact to their foreheads.

Sarge had no protection against the impact that slammed into his forehead. A sudden flash of memory turns my gaze inwards and backward, blinding me to the beauty of the bird and the trees. Again I hear the explosion and feel the recoil in my hand. Again I see that wound — jelly-red in the center and scorched black around the edges — and Sarge slumping to the ground, lifeless as a crumpled heap of old clothes.

I bang the heel of my hand against my own forehead, forcing myself back into the present. Startled by my movement, the woodpecker takes flight with an aggrieved *qweah*! It flies toward the thicker wood of trees at the far end of the property, black-and-white wings flashing through the air like a checkered flag at the end of a motor race.

We're not at the end of our race — I'm not even sure we've started — and already there are casualties.

I stare back at the curved lines and flat roof of Neil's adobe house, which is unlike anything I've seen before or could have imagined. The mud-brown exterior looks like it would fit better in a desert than this wooded corner of the south.

The whole house is off the grid. Two of the outer walls are made from plastic water bottles packed in concrete, studded with solar jars that collect sun in the daytime and glow softly at night. Electricity comes from the solar panels on the roof, water is pumped from a private well into faucets fitted with purifying filters, and used water passes into a hi-tech recycling unit, from where it goes to irrigate the fruit, vegetables and berries growing in greenhouse tunnels out back. While Neil would never allow animal flesh to pass his lips, he does keep a couple of goats for the milk and cheese in a small, fenced-off section. A few chickens mosey about in the long grass, so we always have fresh eggs, and he keeps a flock of geese too, but not for food.

"Geese are the best watchdogs. I let them wander loose at night and they'll make an almighty racket if there's an intruder. Attack him, too," Neil had told me.

Inside the house it's all open spaces, with exposed ceiling beams, wooden furniture and rounded cement benches. Brightly patterned Mexican rugs lie scattered across the polished concrete floor, Navajo woven baskets and Cherokee pottery nestle beside the massive stone fireplace in the living area, and Aztec figurines and Inuit carvings crowd every surface. Dream-catchers dangle over the front and back doors, and one expanse of roughly plastered wall is covered with a mural of bold raven, wolf, bison and sun motifs.

It's all a bit overwhelming — especially the fiercely grimacing mask, complete with real-looking hair, that glares down at me from the landing when I climb the stairs to the second floor. It gives me the creeps.

Neil says the house is guarded by ancient spirits, but he's hedged his bets with a high-tech security system which includes steel reinforced doors, surveillance cameras at the gate, infrared sensor beams which crisscross the front yard and driveway, and an electrified fence to rival ASTA's — all of which are managed by a control panel located near the front door. Neil doesn't trust the government further than he can spit it, and he's paranoid about being invaded.

The yard behind the house is a tangled wilderness of weeds, long grass and trees which grow more densely toward the back of the property, eventually merging into the woods beyond. A suspended plank walkway connects the balcony outside Neil's upstairs bedroom to the nearest tree, which in turn bridges out to a bunch of other trees. A couple of the trees have rope ladders hanging from their boughs, but the web of interconnecting walkways, branches and trunks eventually ends in an enormous loblolly pine situated well into the woods. Beth says that last tree hangs over the property line. On two of the trees in the yard, there are wooden platforms, and in another is the tree house in which I'm now sitting.

I asked Neil why he'd constructed this maze in the boughs, and he replied that sometimes he just likes to get away and sit in the trees to think. So, I've found, do I.

Which is why, on this sunny morning in October, with the leaves just beginning to take on the orange-and-gold richness of fall, I'm sitting up here alone. Thinking.

Thinking about Sarge — what he said, what he did, how he died. Thinking about how Robin very nearly lost his arm and could have lost his life. Thinking about the bad decisions I made and the trouble I got us into. Because that whole disastrous mission is on me.

We had no plan, no intel, and I made stupid mistakes. I was trying so hard not to let anyone get hurt that I risked us all. Guilt eats at me like the termites devouring the branches in the woodpecker's tree. It's my fault that Robin was shot, that even now he's still weak as a kitten and confined to bed. And I'm obviously to blame for Sarge's death. I also feel bad that Bruce and Cameron are here with this group of disorganized misfits instead of safe at home. They've had to order new clothes and toiletries online, because all their stuff got left behind at ASTA.

I insisted on paying – giving them the last of my cash cards — but Bruce waved them aside, saying, "Neil's footing the bill, and trust me, Blue, he won't miss a couple of C-notes. Guy's loaded."

We've been here four days, and we've accomplished nothing further — nobody seems to know what to do or where to begin. Evyan is impatient to get going, as long as she can follow Quinn. Quinn wants to follow the data and find out more about what's really going on. Cameron told me that he'll follow me. He ought to know better.

Bruce just wants to follow the sights on the end of his weapon. He's itching to shoot something — his first choice would be a mutant rat or a terrorist, but I reckon if we're cooped up here for much longer, he'll settle for taking a potshot at Evyan, because those two get on like a pair of cats in a sack.

Neil doesn't seem to want to follow anyone. He spends his days down in the basement, where he has a full-on network room filled with monitors, a huge 3D printer, and a bunch of servers and powerful computers connected via the forest of satellite dishes mounted on the roof to networks beyond. Back when I was with the rebels based in the state park, Nicky told me Neil was some kind of computer genius. It turns out that he was the founder of an IT start-up company back in the early nineties. He built it up from nothing, made a fortune when he sold up, and now lives as a recluse — when he's not hanging out with the rebels in the forest trying to undermine the government he loathes — playing with his bits and bytes in the temperature-controlled basement of this odd house.

I don't know who I want to follow. I only know that I'm not fit to be in charge of anything or anyone. I'm clearly incompetent as a leader, and I have absolutely no desire to be in charge again. I don't want the responsibility of leading the others into danger, or of hurting, possibly even killing, another person.

Sofia and I have been alternating shifts at Robin's bedside. When she's with him, or when Beth is busy with him, like she is now, then I head for the trees — to think or nap or cry. To be alone.

If only the others would let me be.

Evyan was in the backyard earlier, visiting the goats. As she passed by my tree, she threw stones up at me.

"Will you stop feeling sorry for yourself already!" she yelled. "You're pitiful."

Bruce tried to tempt me down with his idea of an irresistible offer.

"C'mon, Blue, let's go shoot some rats in the woods. I'm bored," he whined. "I'm as bored as a shlong at an abstinence party. I'm so bored that I'm even considering hitting on the Goth girl."

Cameron comes past every now and then, looks up at me for long moments, sighs and then disappears back inside.

The only one I allow up is Quinn. He sits with me, reassuring me that I'm not to blame. At night, he stands silently beside me as we gaze up at the night sky, squeezing my hand when we see a shooting star. Sometimes he just holds me close, running his fingers through my short hair. He seems as fascinated with the cherry-red ends as he was with the blue streaks I had back when my hair was still long and blond.

"Hey."

Quinn's deep voice breaks into my navel-gazing, and I look up to see him crossing the walkway to my tree. He carries a travel mug filled with coffee and a chocolate muffin. I think he's afraid I'll get weak from hunger and fall out of the tree, because he's always bringing me snacks.

"Hey yourself," I say.

"Good news," Quinn says. "Doc Beth has finished her examination of Robin, and she's given him the all-clear."

I close my eyes in relief for a moment.

"She says he'll only need to stay in bed for another day, and won't be able to use his arm for several weeks, but there's no sign of infection. And she says there's no reason why, in time, he shouldn't regain moderate functioning in that arm, and even some in the hand."

Some function. Not most. Not all. I know, from Beth's previous reports, that the bullet ripped through his wrist and shoulder, tearing ligaments, tendons and muscle, shattering bone, destroying nerves. That it caused permanent damage.

The spasm of guilt I feel must cross my face, because Quinn says, "Jinx — it's *good* news! He's going to be fine. In fact, he's asked for all of us to have a meeting with him, says he's got something big to tell us."

"What?"

"His exact words were that we should all gather around his bedside this afternoon for a 'spectacular show and tell'. He seemed pretty amped about it."

I have no idea what it could be. I only hope it's something good. I don't think I could handle more bad news.

Chapter 12

Making out

"So what time is Robin giving us this big news?" I ask Quinn.

"When he wakes up. Beth insisted he have a nap and gave him something to make sure he did."

"Want to go for a walk?" I ask.

"Some alone time for you and me? Yes, please. That house may be a wonder of the modern world, but there's no privacy."

Quinn's not kidding. Everything is open plan — the only rooms that actually have doors are the toilets. Even the bathrooms are only partially sheltered behind waist-high adobe partitions. There's no place where you can be alone, nowhere you can talk without being overheard.

Quinn pulls me to my feet and walks ahead of me across the plank bridge to the next tree, tugging me along behind him. When we reach the first platform, he pulls me close and hugs me tight. For a moment, I relax, breathing in the fresh scent of him, relishing the sensation of being surrounded by arms stronger than my own. I wish he could scoop me up and carry me off, like a real pirate. I wish we could sail off into the sunset on a schooner and drink tankards of rum, or whatever it was pirates and their wenches quaffed. I wish we could be on the opposite end of the world from this plague — with no responsibilities, no worries, no shame.

"I feel like we've hardly seen each other," Quinn says, tilting my chin up to drop a soft kiss on my lips. "I miss you."

"I'm here now."

"No, you're not. Not here, not really. You're back there." He jerks his head. "With Sarge."

He knows me so well.

"Look, I know what you must be feeling. I killed a man who was about to shoot my brother, remember? If anyone knows what you're going through, it's me. And I say you're being too hard on yourself."

I give him a quick smile, but I guess it doesn't fool him, because when I cross the next bridge, he follows me, saying, "It wasn't your fault, Jinxy. He was aiming at me — he probably would have killed me. And he may have shot you or any of the others. We all would have been arrested and sitting in that damned torture chamber right now! You did what you had to do."

My eyebrows lift in disbelief. "Never thought I'd see the day when you were justifying my shooting and killing someone."

"I don't think violence is the answer, but that doesn't mean I think we should just lie back and let ourselves to be taken out without a fight," Quinn says. "And anyway, Sarge was a soldier. He knew the risks of what he was doing."

"I know. It's just … I knew him, you know? I even once respected him."

A fiery-orange oak leaf twirls down from the branches above us. Quinn plucks it from the air and hands it to me with a little bow, as if presenting me with a bouquet of flowers.

"It's beautiful." I trace the sharply scalloped edges and dark veins with a fingertip, wondering how one leaf can change so dramatically, can hold so many colors — red and green and gold and brown — and still know what it is.

"*You're* beautiful, *mo chuisle*."

"Is that Irish? What does it mean?"

"My beloved. Literally, pulse of my heart."

"I prefer that to 'wench'. Tell me some more," I say as we walk around to the wide platform built onto the far side of the oak's trunk.

"I don't know many — you're my *chéadsearc*, my first love."

"That's a nice one, too." It shouldn't matter, but it pleases me mightily that he's never loved another girl.

We lie down, side-by-side on the rough planks, holding hands.

"More!" I demand.

"*Is tusa mo spéirbhean, mo stóirín.*"

"Your spear van? Your storeen?" I struggle to get my clumsy tongue around the lilting music of his words.

"You are my sky woman — a beauty to match the sky. And my little treasure."

Sky woman. I like that one a lot. I love being Quinn's treasure and his heartbeat. I wish I had beautiful endearments for him, but I'm a sharpshooter, not a poet.

"You are my love," I say simply.

"That'll do," he says, and I can hear the smile in his voice.

We lie quietly for long minutes, staring up at the leaves quivering in the soft breeze, listening to the sound of the geese honking and the goats bleating below us.

"I spy, with my little eye, something beginning with an E," I say.

"An eyrie?"

"What's an eyrie?"

"Kind of like what we're in now," he says.

"No, not an eyrie."

"An ear?"

"No. Give up?"

"An egg? An eagle? An elm?"

"No, no, and still wrong. Give up?"

"Sure. You win."

"An elephant."

"You're seeing elephants now? Faith, maybe I should get Doc Beth to take a look at you, too."

"Over there." I point at a large white cloud, high up in the patch of blue sky visible between the treetops. "See, there's its trunk and ears, and its legs and tail. Do you see it?"

"I do indeed. Right, my turn. I spy with my eye, something beginning with a C."

"A cloud?" I guess.

He gives me the look that deserves.

"A cabbage?" I wave at the small round cloud beyond the elephant. "Or one of those crabbeeny things you made me eat at —" I cut myself off. I don't want to think about ASTA. But what comes out of my mouth next is even worse. "A Connor?"

"No, Jinxy," Quinn says, capturing my hand and bringing it down to hold against his chest. "I am not lying here beside my love on a fine, sunny day, imagining I see my brother's face in the clouds."

But he must be missing Connor, and his mother and father and little Kerry. Got to be. I'm missing my mother.

"Have you heard anything from him?" I ask.

"Not a peep. I think he's excommunicated me from the O'Riley church."

"Nah, I reckon he'd take you back in a heartbeat."

Just so long as Quinn ditched me, the girl who got him detained, the girl who came between the brothers and broke up the family. I should get myself a T-shirt made: *Here comes trouble.*

He traces a finger over the henna yin-yang tattoo on the back of my right hand. It's faded a little now.

"Are you worried about your mom?" he asks.

Using one of Neil's burner phones, we got a message to her that Robin and I are okay, but we haven't dared more contact.

"Yeah, I am. After my father died, she got real depressed. Now, without Robin or me to keep an eye on her and take care of her, I worry that she'll sink under again."

I'm getting uncomfortable lying on my back on the hard wooden surface. The Ruger 9mm tucked into my waistband is digging into the small of my back. I keep it with me all the time now. I know there's a real risk we'll be tracked and found, plus there have got to be mutant rats out in these woods. Just because the government's out to get us, doesn't mean the rats aren't too.

I roll onto my side and feast my eyes on Quinn — his dark golden skin, the slight cleft in his chin, the stubble that darkens his jaw. When I run a hand through his thick hair, his eyes open, and I see they're a deep slate-gray today — the color they are when he's relaxed and happy.

"It's getting long," I say, giving his locks a tug.

"And your roots are starting to show." Now he is the one playing with my hair. "Are you going to go back to blond?"

"Would you prefer that? They say gentlemen do," I tease.

"Ah, now, my father advised me never to make the mistake of telling a lass you prefer her this way to that. 'You canna win by answering those sorts of questions, lad. Just tell her she looks beautiful every which way,'" he says, in a broad Irish accent. "He's a wise man, me father. Also, me mother is a fierce woman!"

We spend a few delicious moments kissing in the golden light under the shifting, sighing leaves. Reality intrudes in the form of a sharp rapping nearby. The woodpecker is back.

"Perhaps I should go redhead, like that character," I muse. "Or I could go black and white, like a skunk. I could back-shave it, and maybe just leave a horizontal ring, like a monk. Though, easiest of all, I guess, would be to shave the lot off."

I sneak a sidelong look, expecting him to fall into the trap of protesting against me going bald — I know he loves my hair — but instead he takes a deep breath and holds up a silencing finger for a minute. He is clearly thinking hard. Then he clears his throat and begins.

"That Jinxy James, that Jinxy James, I sure do love that Jinxy James. I would like her as a skunk, I would like her as a monk. I would like her bald as coot, 'cos she is sexy and she's cute!"

"Green Eggs and Ham, O'Riley — really?"

"It's love poetry," he says, all mock-offended.

"So would you like her here or there?" I ask him, playing along. "Would you *still* like her with no hair?"

"I would like her here and there. Faith, I would take her anywhere," he replies, wiggling his eyebrows suggestively.

"Would you like her in a box?"

"Sure I'd like her in a box … um …" He pauses, searching for a rhyme, then grins and says, "Have you seen her? Girl's a fox!"

I laugh. And it feels good. It's been a while.

"Would you like her in a house?" I challenge.

"I would *love* her in a house, if she'd take off her stupid blouse." At this point, he pulls off my long-sleeved T-shirt in one swift movement, leaving me gasping. Before I can protest, he continues, "'Cos mostly I would love her bare, so I could touch her here" — he cups one lace-covered breast — "and there" — and then the other.

His touch ignites a fuse in my core.

"I could love her everywhere." His hand moves lower. His eyes are heavy-lidded.

I want to see more of him, too. Feel more. I grab the

bottom edge of his T-shirt, slowly roll it up and pull it off, murmuring, "Would you? Could you? In a car?"

I trail my hands along his shoulders, down over the planes of his chest and the muscles of his flat abdomen. When I lightly trace the line of dark hair that leads down, he sucks in a breath. He leans forward, and along the curve of one breast, he kisses a soft line and whispers, "Girl, I will love you near and far. All of you. Always. Everywhere."

"That doesn't rhyme," I say, breathless with my own pulsing need.

Quinn doesn't reply. His mouth has other things to do than form words.

Chapter 13

Smuggled out

When we all file through the open archway into Robin's room, my eyes go immediately to his right arm. The shoulder and wrist are bandaged, and the whole arm is immobilized in a complicated-looking sling. I examine his face. It's pale, with dark shadows below his eyes, but he looks … cheerful.

"Quinn said you had news for us?" I ask him.

"Take a seat, y'all, it's a good story."

I sit on the bed by his feet, since Sofia already has the chair beside him, and Quinn stands behind me, his hands resting on my shoulders. Evyan slouches in one corner, while Bruce and Cameron sit up against a wall, and Neil perches cross-legged on one of the low adobe partitions. Everyone looks expectantly at Robin.

"So, you know I hacked into ASTA's database and then into The Game?" Robin says.

"I *told* you to stop doing that," I say, irked.

"I was very careful. But what I was seeing in there was just too interesting to stop."

"What did you see?" asks Neil.

"Some really weird stuff. Like double-layer coding, stacked architectures — the thing is structured like the double helix of a DNA molecule."

"What do you think it is?" Quinn looks intrigued.

They seem set to sidetrack this into a technical discussion, but I want to know what happened when Robin was captured.

"How did they catch you?" I ask.

"I think I triggered an alert when I went into the bottom layer of that code. I wasn't sure they'd detected my intrusion, but when I got your message I decided to destroy the evidence, just in case they came knocking. Good thing I did."

"I thought experts could still recover stuff from computers even when you've deleted and wiped them clean," Evyan says, sniffing. She caught a cold after our adventures in the rain and has been in a foul mood ever since.

"They can," Neil confirms. "Did they take your PC when they detained you?"

"Yup," says Robin, looking pleased with himself. "But all they'll find on that is my schoolwork, gaming history, my movie collection, and non-incriminating emails."

"I don't understand," I say.

"Because I wasn't using *my* laptop for the hacking."

"Good!" I say. That was clever of him. Then a thought hits me. "Wait — do you mean you were using *mine*?"

He grins guiltily.

"What the hell, Robin!"

"You weren't using it, and it was more powerful than mine."

"No, it isn't. Mom bought us identical models for our sixteenth birthday."

"Yeah, well, I pimped your drive." At my look of incomprehension, he explains, "I added some upgrades. It was a thing of beauty."

Another thought intrudes. "Why are you talking about my laptop in the past tense?"

"When I got your warning, I grabbed it and ran to the basement, and … well, I chucked it in the biohazard incinerator."

"Grand techno meltdown. Linux to lava. Very cool!" Bruce nods approvingly at the thought of the carnage.

"You destroyed my laptop?" I ask, equal parts outraged and relieved.

"Yeah, sorry about that, Jinxy," Robin says, looking anything but. "Anyway, I was back on my machine, playing games when the goons arrived."

"Mom?" I say, even though I'm scared to ask.

"You won't believe it, but she was great, like *fierce* — yelling at them to leave me be, demanding to see warrants for the search and my arrest —"

"They had warrants?" Quinn asks.

"Nope. They said under Emergency Regulation number whatever they didn't need them. They asked her a few questions and confiscated her PC along with mine, but she very obviously knew nothing about anything."

"Do you think she'll be okay?"

Robin knows what I'm asking. He nods. "Last I saw her, she was threatening to sue them for false arrest and to complain to her senator. And declaring she was going to lay a charge of theft with the police for the PCs. She didn't look like she was set to go curl up in a corner and cry."

I guess if there's anything that would make Mom come out fighting, it would be a threat to her kids.

"And when they got you to PlayState and questioned you?" Quinn asks.

"They were fishing in the dark. Without that laptop, they knew next to nothing," Sofia says.

She tells us how when Roth wanted an intel representative in on the questioning, she volunteered so she could feed information on where Robin was being held to

Quinn.

"Of course, they still knew I'd hacked their systems," Robin says. "They must have traced the IP address somehow, even though I'd used a subnet mask and proxies."

Yeah, or maybe they just knew because Zonia left a tip on the SEE-SAY line, as she threatened she would if I refused to assassinate President Hawke.

"But without your machine, Jinxy, they didn't know exactly what I'd done, where I'd penetrated, what I'd seen. They didn't know, for example, that I'd installed a back door to access The Game programs in the future."

Neil gives a whistle of appreciation, and behind me, Quinn murmurs a soft, "Huh," sounding seriously impressed.

"And while they were questioning me at ASTA, no one asked about that, so I'm pretty sure they haven't found out."

"They would have, once they got you to the interrogation center," I say.

"And they didn't know that I downloaded huge chunks of code and APIs, protocols, mods, libraries and specs onto a microchip that I smuggled out of home and ... that I still have with me!" he declares, sounding mighty proud of himself.

Neil and Quinn look amazed. Sofia is frowning, the filigree pattern of the tattoo surrounding her eyes crinkling in concerned lines. But Evyan, who appears to have no more trust or liking for my twin than she does for me, is visibly skeptical.

"No way. They would have searched you," she says in a pissy tone.

"They did search me. Very thoroughly. But" — Robin's grin is maximally mischievous — "only on the outside."

"Eww!" I exclaim. "You don't mean that you hid it up your —"

"No! A.) No. B.) Do you think I've gone five days without ... going? And C.) Just no! Gross," he says, looking offended.

"We're going to need the doctor to extract it though."

"I'll get her," Sofia volunteers, and Robin calls after her, "Tell her to bring a light and tweezers."

"Dude, you didn't stick it in your flesh-flute?" Bruce says, wincing. "That's gotta be some kind of uncomfortable."

Robin rolls his eyes to the heavens. "Get your minds out of the gutter, people."

When Beth comes in, he tilts his head to one side and taps his ear.

"Your *ear*?" I demand. "You hid a microchip in your ear?"

The doc tuts with disapproval as she shines a light into Robin's ear. "You could have done some serious damage. And didn't it irritate you?"

"It only made a noise when I moved my head quickly."

"I see it." Beth inserts the ends of a set of tweezers and extracts something which she drops into the palm of Robin's waiting hand. "Here you go."

We all crowd close to see the tiny chip, even Evyan. It's miniscule — less than half the size of a cell phone sim card.

"Careful!" Neil says when Evyan sneezes. "That's a fifth-generation nanochip. It can hold terabytes of info." He sounds awed and looks eager to begin exploring the contents immediately. "May I?"

"As long as I can play, too." Robin moves as if to get up.

"You're on bed rest, you're not going anywhere," Beth says firmly.

"If Mohammed won't go to the mountain … I'll bring everything we need up here," Neil says as he scurries out of the door.

"And I'll be your right hand, if you like," Sofia says, directing a shy look at Robin from her liquid brown eyes.

"I do like," Robin replies, and Sofia blushes.

Ah, so that's how it is. Things have clearly been

developing between the patient and his pretty nurse while I've been hiding out up in the trees.

"So that's my story," Robin says. "That's all, folks."

Sofia, Neil and Quinn are clearly excited to analyze the information on the chip. The more action-oriented members of our group look less impressed by Robin's story.

"I'd like to terabyte your bits," Bruce says to Evyan as they make to leave the room.

"Roses are red, violets are blue. I've got five fingers, the third one's for you," she replies, suiting the action to the word.

"Guys, can I have a few minutes alone with my brother?" I ask Sofia and Quinn.

But when we're alone, I struggle to find the words to say what I need to say.

"Thanks for the blood, by the way," Robin says. "Beth told me I've got of pint of you sloshing around inside of me."

"It was the least I could do after I let you get shot," I mutter. "Look, Robin, I've got two things to tell you."

"I've also got something to tell you."

"Me first." I want to get this over with. "First, I'm sorry. I'm so, so sorry." I lightly brush his arm.

"Jinxy, you didn't do this to me. It's not your fault."

"It is. I screwed up. I should have checked Sarge, I should've been the one to guard him. You could have lost your arm. You could have died!"

He waves away my words with the hand on his uninjured arm and says, "And the second thing?"

I look down. There's a loose thread in the quilted patchwork bedspread. I tug at it, unraveling a few stitches.

"Jinxy?"

"Did Sofia tell you what we found out, about the sniper unit?"

He shakes his head, frowning in puzzlement.

I tell him about the poison-filled ammunition, the killing.

"Oh, Jinxy." He pulls me into a careful, one-armed hug. "That's why you ran away?"

"Yeah." I gulp, swallowing tears.

"We'll figure this all out. We'll find out what they're up to and tell the world," he promises.

"That's the plan. So" — I sit back, wiping my eyes with the back of my hand — "what did you want to tell me?"

"It's about Dad."

"*Dad*?" That's the last thing I was expecting.

"After you told me about the bank attack and how he died, I went looking. I wanted to see for myself."

"Oh, Robin, why?" I'd wanted to spare him that. "And where? *How?*"

"All of that footage is still available, if you know where to look. There are sites, on the dark web, where you can see anything — photos of murder scenes and dead bodies, videos of autopsies and executions and … well, there's some seriously sick stuff cached out there, including footage of those early plague attacks and deaths."

"You saw? Dad?"

Robin swallows hard. "Yeah, I saw."

We sit for a long, quiet moment, both of us reliving those awful last hours of Dad's life.

"But what I wanted to tell you — something good in all that horror — was that there were interviews with the survivors, those bank staff who were safe behind the security window, remember?"

I do. "I remember the one — a young woman with a birthmark here." I trace a strawberry shape on my forehead. "She had a poster. An ad for the bank, I think."

"Yeah, those were for Dad," Robin says.

"They were? Why would Dad have wanted a giant bank advertisement?"

"Dunno. She said in the interview I saw that he'd asked

her for some advertising materials — promotional pamphlets and posters and stuff like that. That's why she left the bank floor and went to the back, to get it for him. It saved her life."

He looks pleased to tell me this good news. To let me know that although Dad may have died, a life was saved because of him. But I'm not pleased, because the words "advertising materials" have jogged a memory. My scalp tightens. My stomach clenches. Somewhere the tally of deaths against my name increases by one.

"They were for me," I say, and my voice is flat, toneless, dead.

"Huh?"

"We had that assignment for English — to analyze examples of advertising, remember? You did pop-up ads on websites, I think. And I was going to do financial services. I asked Dad to collect some examples for me from the bank … They were for me," I tell Robin, who's staring at me, openmouthed. "He was there, in that bank on that day when the terrorists struck, because of me."

Chapter 14

Workout

I rush out of the room before Robin can say anything more. I want to get away, to be alone, but the treetops are not an option, because what I really don't want to do right now, is to think.

Upstairs, in the room I share with Sofia and Evyan, I change into my sweats and running shoes. My plan is to exercise all thought and emotion out of myself, to run until I feel nothing but exhaustion, until I remember nothing except how to take my next breath.

On my way back downstairs, I cross paths with Quinn, Sofia and Neil. They're laden with computers, monitors, keyboards, external drives and a rat's nest of differently colored cables. Clearly, Robin's bedroom is going to be transformed into the new tech central. Neil, whose face is shining with excitement, doesn't spare me a glance as he passes, but Quinn takes one look at my face and knows something is badly wrong.

"Jinxy, what's the matter?" he asks.

"Nothing. I don't want to talk about it."

Really, what is there to say?

I can see Quinn would like to push the issue, but he's

tethered by a fat braid of red and black cables to a machine Sofia is carrying, so he has to follow her. I disappear to the south side of the house, where there is a solarium — complete with glass walls and roof. In amongst the virtual forest of potted plants are exercise mats, weights, a cross-trainer, and a treadmill with a virtual reality setup.

I'm surprised, when I fit the VR goggles and headphones on and power up the system, to see the PlayState logo in the corner of the screen. I didn't know they made these kind of things as well. The program urges me to choose "one of twenty different immersive environments to enhance your running experience". I'm tempted by *Sahara Sands* and *Brazilian Rainforest,* but settle for the more mundane *Cityscapes* option. The belt under my feet starts moving, and I'm running along a busy city street. And to me, it's just as exotic as any jungle or desert.

These scenes are at once utterly strange and completely familiar. They're strange because we've always lived in the suburbs, never in the center of a city. And for the last four years, we've lived mostly inside our own house. But they're also familiar because I've watched thousands of shows and movies on T.V. with urban settings from before the plague. Now, skirting the sidewalk tables and chairs of a Parisian-style coffee shop where hipsters sit with small espressos and large croissants, I realize I've come to view those televised locations as something like fantasy settings — Hogwarts, maybe, or the hobbit village in Lord of the Rings. But this is real, or at least, it's a highly realistic version of what life was like until just a few years ago.

Was the VR footage filmed on a real street somewhere where there is no plague, like Sydney or Cape Town? Or was it filmed on a set created in a warehouse like the one for gaming simulations at PlayState? That bicycle messenger, weaving between the yellow lines of honking cabs, and that loving couple cooing over a baby in a stroller, are they real people or actors? Or perhaps just lifelike computer-generated images?

I run past an Asian grocer who waves a friendly greeting at me and then returns to stacking exotic fruits and vegetables in great balanced pyramids of purple, ochre and cerise, as if food can be left out in the open, displayed like edible art, with no worries of contamination or attracting rats.

In real life, the streets of our city are mostly empty. Whatever can be, is done virtually or remotely. But when I cross a street in this cityscape, the flow of vehicles is so dense that the traffic light's stern red hand must hold them in check.

I run into a park, pushing myself harder and faster now. I can feel that I've lost condition — there was no way to exercise at Tallulah's. While Robin, Neil, Sofia and Quinn work to make sense of what they've found, I'm going to work to get properly fit again. And if it leaves me too tired afterwards to do anything but sleep, so much the better.

The green spaces of this virtual park still belong to people — college kids playing a game of touch football, a dog-walker being dragged along by three eager beagles, a potbellied father grilling hot dogs for a party of hungry kids, a stooped grandmother sitting on a bench beside a pond, throwing breadcrumbs to a raucous flock of ducks.

Is it possible to miss something you've never had? To be fiercely homesick for somewhere you've never lived?

I want this back, even though I've never had it before. I miss it, even though it's never been mine. In a different world, I would have chosen to have lived someplace like this. I could have planned, after high school, to go to college in New York or Boston or London; to meet people face to face, and go to museums with them — to be in the same room as a Van Gogh or a Michelangelo, inspecting the thick smears of paint and the soft curves in the hard marble up close, rather than merely viewing them on a small screen.

I feel a pang of grief for what I've lost, what we've all lost and are still missing out on — neighborhoods pulsing with life and energy and noise, communities of people who know and trust each other, the freedom and beauty of open spaces. Our lives now are shrunken, narrow little things, sterile and inadequate imitations of what once was and what might have been.

I'm sweating and breathing heavily when the simulation ends at the entrance to a busy street market, but I'm not so tired that I can't still think of my father and Robin and all the rest of it. I grab a pair of ten-pound dumbbells and find Bruce and Cameron in the living room with Evyan. Cameron is reading a book. Bruce is cleaning my rifle while nagging Evyan to teach him how to pick locks.

"Come on, E, what else have you got to do? The brainiacs obviously don't think you've got the smarts to help them."

"Did I miss the part where they asked for *your* help?" she snaps back.

"Hey, I know I'm more brawn than brain. Here, look at this." Bruce clenches the muscles in his chest, making them bulge against the fabric of his tight T-shirt. "Impressive, right? *Right?*" He smiles down at his pecs as first the left and then the right one jumps. When Evyan doesn't respond, he makes them jiggle faster.

She ignores him and continues to file her nails.

"What? If you don't like that, I can make them move together — check it out!"

"Hey, Bruce?" I interrupt his display. "I could use a little of that. Not of your chest, —" I hasten to add when he gives me a look of delighted hope. "But your strength. I mean, I want to work out — abdominals and upper body strength — and I wondered if you and Cameron would help, maybe train with me?"

"Sure, Blue, any time!" Bruce leaps up enthusiastically.

Cameron nods and tosses the book aside.

In the backyard, under the curious gaze of the goats and the geese, the boys put me through my paces — crunches and sit-ups for my abdominals, planks for my core and back, plus pushups, bicep curls and shoulder presses to work my feeble arms.

"We need a cross bar for pull-ups," Bruce says, evaluating the railing on the balcony outside Neil's bedroom for its potential to serve as exercise equipment.

"There," Cameron says, pointing to a horizontal log ladder which connects two trees.

"Perfect!"

I groan. Pull-ups and monkey-bar swings were the two exercises which always defeated me in boot camp training back at ASTA. I jump up a couple of times under the ladder, but I can't reach the bars.

"Can you lift me up?" I ask Bruce.

"Blue, any time you want me to wrap my hands around you, just say the word."

"Bruce!" Hands on hips, I glower at him. "You and me — it's not going to happen, you know that. Heck, I don't even think you really want it. So do me a favor and cut it out already, okay? *Okay?*"

He grins sheepishly, shrugs and nods.

"Cool. Now can my *buddy*, Bruce, give me a hand?"

He pinches his lips together — no doubt some comment about hands and giving me was on the tip of his tongue — then comes behind me, places his hands on my hips and effortlessly lifts me up to the cross bars.

"Ready?" he asks as I struggle to get a tight grip on the rough wood.

"As I'll ever be," I mutter.

When he lets go of supporting my weight, I fall straight down, which causes the boys no end of amusement. I hear the echo of Sarge's voice in my head, "They're called pull-ups, princess, not fall-downs." An image of him — of his face in that last second before I fired, of his forehead in the split-second afterwards — flashes across my mind.

Bruce gives me another boost, and this time I hang on tighter, managing two chin-ups before dropping to the ground. Even the goats seem to be laughing at my efforts.

"Monkey bars," I gasp.

"Hehe, this should be good," Bruce says, lifting me up again.

Three bars. That's all I manage — three bars, *including* the one I start out on — before I drop back down. But I'm spent, my arm muscles are shaking, and I just can't do more. Worse, the exercise appears to have done more to summon the memories of Sarge than to banish them from my mind. Right now he's reminding me, "Pain is … what is pain, my little piglet? Pain is *good!*"

"Tomorrow morning?" I ask Bruce and Cameron from where I lie, flat on my back in the dirt, glaring up at the monkey-bar bridge.

My new goal is to be able to cross that whole ladder in one go, and I won't quit until I can do it.

As I get to my feet, dusting the butt of my sweats, I glance over at the house. Quinn is standing there, watching us. I smile and give him a wave. It's a small wave, but it's all my exhausted arm is capable of. He returns the greeting, but not the smile.

"Your leprechaun doesn't look happy to see you hanging out with us, Blue," Bruce says.

I'd like to elbow him in the ribs, but I don't have the energy.

"You need to take a teaspoon of cement and harden the hell up, princess," says Sarge.

Chapter 15

Outbreak

October 10

I spend most of the next day working out — alternating running on the treadmill and P.T. sessions with Bruce and Cameron — and taking my turn at kitchen duty. Beth has drawn up a roster of chores, from which only Neil and Robin are excused because they're so busy decoding. And because of Robin's arm, I guess.

That night all of us except Robin and Sofia gather in the big living area to eat our supper. The food here is a lot better than in the rebel camp, partly because of the fresh fruit and vegetables growing out back, but also because Neil is not only paranoid about being spied on and invaded by the government, he's also obsessed about being cut off from the supply chain of living essentials. He has a massive pantry stocked to the ceiling with canned fruit and pickles, sacks of rice and beans, every kind of canned and freeze-dried vegetarian food, packages of organic baking mixes, and long-life milk. Beth, who isn't a vegetarian, does order in frozen meat and fish, but only in small quantities.

"I didn't suddenly want to increase my orders, in case the

deviation from our established pattern flags a warning somewhere," she explained the first day here, when her weekly grocery order arrived via driverless vehicle delivery. "Neil says they monitor everything."

Tonight's meal, which Quinn and I made under Beth's supervision, is vegetarian chili topped with grated cheese and slices of creamy avocado. I polish off two bowls full — all the exercise has left me with a huge appetite — and then sit around watching television news with the others.

The world seems much the same as the last time I looked. Our government has sent an envoy to Beijing to formally protest the recent nuclear testing in the South China Sea; drought is devastating Sudan; in the House of Congress, one of the Southern Sector's senators has introduced a bill proposing to lower the voting age to sixteen years; and the Middle East is still as violent as it's ever been.

My eyes are drooping as I snuggle up to Quinn on a giant beanbag, and I'm wondering if I dare go out for a run on the actual streets tomorrow morning when three sharp pips sound from the T.V.

It's a public service announcement by Alex Hawke, President of the Southern Sector. Though his thick wavy hair, just greying at the temples, is as perfectly styled as ever, tonight his strong, square face isn't smiling in its usual reassuring way.

"Since when do they have the power to interrupt programming?" Quinn asks.

"They've been doing it for a while now," Beth explains. "This will be playing across all channels right now."

"All channels?"

"Even the cartoons get interrupted, and all radio stations, too. And the channels will need to rebroadcast it at three-hourly intervals for the next twenty-four hours. Newspapers will have to print the transcript in all editions tomorrow."

"So much for freedom of the press," Quinn says.

Bruce shushes him. "Let's hear what he has to say, man. It could be important."

"— because war is coming," Hawke is saying. "This evening, we have received reports of a heinous new attack in Orlando, Florida."

"My father lives in Orlando," Evyan says.

"Terrorists have released thousands of mutant rats, presumed to be infected with Mononegavirales Zoonotic Viral Hemorrhagic Fever, into the grounds of a onetime vacation and entertainment resort."

As he speaks, new images appear on the screen — footage from the security cameras at Disney World? The heaving mass of disgusting giant rats floods through the deserted, cobbled avenues where once there were parades, climbing dead trees and green plastic shrubbery. They stream across empty fountains and drained canals, pour over bridges and course into fairytale castles. They scramble over figures of tiny children in national costumes and scuttle into a hall with life-sized models of all the presidents, climbing into Lincoln's lap and weaving through George Washington's powdered white curls.

Mermaids, mice, princesses and pirates, carousels, spaceships and pumpkin carriages, all writhe with the twitching, scrabbling swarm of rodents. They mount a bronze statue of two chipmunks, and climb lampposts and rollercoaster rails as if seeking a view of the territory they've conquered.

I nearly gag when the footage switches to images of the vermin pouring through food courts, clambering over soda fountains, squeezing into old ice-cream trucks and pretzel carts.

The close-ups show that many of the rats have bulging tumors and oozing sores on their bodies. Their black eyes glitter with the threat of death and decay.

"Ah man, look at that! I need to be out there, eliminating the vermin," Bruce says, banging a fist on the arm of his chair.

A dozen of the rodents claw their way to the top of a giant model of a roaring T-Rex and stand erect on two legs on the dinosaur's head. It's like a new epoch has dawned, and it belongs to the rats.

Evyan sneezes and asks, "But why release the rats there? It's been closed for years, there's no one for them to bite."

"Symbolic," Cameron says.

"Huh?"

"It's a symbol of western capitalism. And of our vulnerability too, I guess, because it was supposed to be the happiest place on earth for children and families," Quinn explains.

"Plus, the rats won't stay contained for long," I add.

Sure enough, there's a shot of rats pushing through the bars of the ticket gates, squeezing under fences, and squashing through the grids of drain covers.

"The real question is why they're allowing this footage to be shown," Quinn says, frowning. "They usually suppress footage of attacks, or at least censor it."

"While there have been no confirmed reports of infections linked to this attack as yet," Hawke's voice-over continues, "there is no doubt that the threat level to our citizenry has further increased, not only in Orlando but all across this great nation. According to our intelligence reports, more such cowardly attacks are imminent, and it is only prudent that we implement more stringent security measures without delay."

"Ah, here we go. Less freedom and more crackdowns," says Quinn.

"You don't think this is real?" Bruce challenges.

"Oh, I'm sure the attack is real enough. But they're only

letting us see it so we'll accept what's coming next."

What's coming next is that Orlando and its surrounding areas have gone into lockdown until further notice, and the nationwide state of emergency has been extended "indefinitely".

"That means the media censorship continues," says Sofia.

But the changes are more sweeping than restrictions on the media. New regulations mandate that anyone out on the streets, at any time and in any state, needs to carry their social security card with them as proof of identity.

"I can't believe this," says Neil. "It's totalitarianism."

It is now compulsory for non-US citizens to be listed on the Alien Persons Register and to wear their alien ID cards at all times for rapid identification. The screen shows a smiling dark-skinned couple modeling examples of the laminated photo identification cards — photographs of their own faces set on a blank flag against a neon orange square. She wears hers on a lanyard around her neck; his is pinned to his shirt.

"Jaysus, it's like the Nazis with the Jews," says Quinn, sounding appalled.

Nighttime travel permits, Hawke announces, will henceforth be subject to even more stringent qualifying criteria, and the nationwide curfew has been moved up to eight pm. Anyone can be stopped and searched at any time, as can any private dwelling or business premises, with fewer requirements for suspected cause.

Basically, if I understand it correctly, anyplace can be entered and searched, and anyone can be taken in for questioning for no reason other than that the cops, the military, or Hawke's own guard don't like the look of you.

"Your government and fellow citizens expect your full support in abiding by these new measures. We cannot protect you from the dangers that threaten us all without your cooperation. Help us to help you," Hawke says, and never has his toothy smile seemed so smarmy to me. "And remember, if you see something, say something."

The PSA ends with the familiar SEE-SAY jingle, while a message scrolls along the bottom of our screen, advising responsible citizens to tune in to the official information channel for more news on the attack and an updated list of America's most wanted.

Cameron snags the remote and switches over to the channel. The screen flashes photographs and identikit sketches of alleged terrorists and suspected dissidents.

It's not long before my own face appears on the screen. It's the photo of me that was on my ASTA ID, looking all fresh-faced and eager, but Roth and Leya must have told them about my changed appearance, because they've photoshopped short brown hair with red tips onto the image. They call me an extremely dangerous killer and kidnapper, and I am, they insist, responsible for a series of attacks on government sites and military installations. They actually show a map with red dots pulsing over Chicago, Atlanta and San Diego.

"You sure do get around," Quinn says, ruffling my hair.

Residents of the Southern Sector are urged to be on the lookout for me, and as an incentive, there's a $250,000 reward offered for information leading to my arrest.

So much for going for a run on the streets tomorrow.

I am presumed, the announcer continues, to be associating with other known rebel insurgents and plotting the downfall of the government. Quinn's face appears, as does Connor's and Zonia's, but there are no images of Neil. Evyan curses when she's listed. If it wasn't for the name beneath the photograph, I'd never have recognized her. The girl on the screen looks no older than fourteen.

"Where did they get that picture?" I ask.

"My juvie records. They must have fingerprinted that damn wrench." She blows her nose and stares glumly at the screen.

"Look, Mom, I'm on T.V.!" says Bruce, not sounding too thrilled about it, when his and Cameron's photos appear.

He snatches the remote and kills the T.V., and for a while we all sit in a silence broken only by the sound of Bruce cracking his knuckles, absorbing the news and its implications.

I'm trapped. Again. Confined in a house that is smaller than the forest camp that was smaller than the ASTA compound. Every move I make seems to take me further away from the freedom I so crave.

We're all trapped in this house, in this life, not so much by the SEE-SAY alerts and securodrones, but by the government's crazy rules and regulations. We'll never be truly free until the plague is conquered, and I don't think we'll conquer the plague until we're free to think and move and speak and challenge. And to do that, I'll most certainly need to leave this house.

Neil says he's got to get back to deciphering code, and Evyan says she's turning in early, but I need to make a plan to dye my hair. Again. Plus I need a new hoodie — I had to toss the one we used to staunch Robin's shoulder wound.

"Beth, if I place an order for drone delivery nearby, will you fetch it for me?"

She nods.

"Anyone else want to add anything to my order?"

"Me, but I need to check some details with Robin first," Bruce says, sounding grim. "I'll place my own order."

He gets up from the couch and heads down the hall.

"Don't forget our training session in the morning," I call after him.

"I'll be there, Blue," he calls back.

Beside me, Quinn gives a soft sigh.

Chapter 16

Cop out

October 11

The next morning, still stiff and sore from the previous day's exercise, I put myself through the same rigorous training schedule, and when Bruce hoists me up to the monkey bars, I manage to get across four bars before dropping to the ground.

My annoyance and disappointment must show on my face, because Cameron says gently, "Takes time."

"I want to do this three times a day, every day," I tell them. "You boys up for that?"

"Sure, but haven't you got anything else to do?" Bruce says. "Don't you have a conspiracy to uncover or a rebellion to lead or something?"

"No, I have nothing better to do. I can't help the geniuses break that code. And as for leading a rebellion? Don't make me laugh. I have no idea where to start, even," I say, shivering. The fall air is cool once I stop exercising. "Besides, every time I do something, someone gets hurt."

Bruce snorts. "That's a chicken-shit cop-out. Hell, Blue, there's no guarantee that if you do *nothing* people still won't get hurt. Today, a rat or a cat that we haven't shot will

108

probably bite somebody in this very city, and they'll die."

"I don't want the responsibility for making any more decisions that go FUBAR, okay?" I collect the dumbbells and start toward the house.

"Not making a decision *is* a decision," Cameron says from behind me.

"Yeah, thank you, Yoda," I snap back, irritated. But it's food for thought.

I remember Leya saying something similar — that bad things happen when good people do nothing. Right now, I just don't want the bad things to be my fault.

Back in the house, Beth is handing out parcels. I don't know what Bruce ordered, but his package is way bigger than mine.

I go upstairs and dye my hair. Jinxy James, dangerous dissident and armed rebel, is now a platinum blonde. I examine myself in the mirror. I look younger again, a little more like myself, except for a new hardness around the eyes and mouth. At least I look nothing like the girl in the most-wanted image. Quinn, meanwhile, is growing a beard to help change the look of his face. He volunteered to go blond, too, but my revolted reaction was enough to squash that idea.

After a midday training session with Bruce and Cameron in which I forbid them to give me any more unwanted advice or character critiques, I go check on the eggheads.

"There's good news and bad news," Robin says.

"Let me have the bad news first," I say.

"It looks like they detected my intrusion into The Game, because that back door that I set up? It's been shut down. And RATs are out of the question, too."

"Rats?" I have a sudden image of us sending rodents to go destroy The Game with their sharp teeth.

"Random Access Tools."

"Robin, please speak a language I can understand."

"Bottom line is: no more remote access to The Game."

"Great. That's just awesome. And the good news?"

"We're making progress!" Robin says, his face shining with excitement. "We're working on the substrata of code that was added more recently, and finding out some crazy stuff. Sofia and Quinn are helping me make sense of all the acronyms and recurring patterns."

"Anything I'd understand?"

"Not yet," Robin says.

"Anything I can do to help?"

Robin merely laughs at that, but Quinn says, "How about I take you through what we're doing while we get some lunch?"

In the kitchen, I make sandwiches with bread fresh from Neil's bread-maker while Quinn tries to explain some of what he, Neil, Sofia and Robin are attempting to do. I understand only a fraction of it — it's filled with obscure terms like sniffing and fuzzing, rootkits and stringboxes — and don't like the feeling of being completely useless.

"I thought a sandbox was something kids used to play in." Back when kids still used to play outside.

Quinn tries to simplify it for me, and he looks so keen for me to get it that I nod and say, "Right," "okay," and "sure," every so often.

I'm loading the dishes into the washer when a series of soft thuds completely distracts me.

"What's that?" I ask, immediately on the alert.

Quinn shrugs. "It's coming from outside."

Peering out of the window, I see Bruce and Cameron in the backyard, shooting at makeshift paper targets pinned to trees.

"What are you doing?" I ask them when I get outside. And when I catch a glimpse of the unfamiliar attachments mounted on the end of both Bruce's submachine gun and

Cameron's handgun — the Sig Sauer P220 Scorpion that was Sarge's — I add, "And what are those?"

"New suppressors," Bruce says.

They don't look like any suppressors I've ever seen, let alone used.

"Cool, aren't they?" Bruce grins.

Cameron takes a bead on the target, which is about fifteen meters away, and fires off three shots, hitting the dead center in a tight cluster. The report of his pistol is surprisingly soft.

"Next-generation sound-suppressing technology. Muffles up to ninety percent of the sound," Bruce explains.

"Where did you get them?" I'm equal parts amazed and worried.

"Off the dark web. Robin told me you can get anything you like there, and he was right."

I need to have a talk with my brother.

"I could've ordered a fully equipped tank if I had the money," Bruce continues, "but I just got these beauties and some more ammo for all of us. Here, have a go."

I take his weapon and fire off several shots in quick succession. My aim is off, but that's probably due to the fact that I haven't done target practice for ages, rather than due to the new equipment. The sound-suppression is fantastic — no report echoes among the trees.

"Did you get one for me?" I ask, eager to find out what my rifle will sound like.

"Of course. I always take care of you, Blue, you know that," Bruce says.

Unfortunately, he says it just as Quinn arrives at my side. The hostility in the glare Quinn gives Bruce is almost tangible.

"I need to go help Robin. Join us?" Quinn says, putting an arm around my waist and giving me a little squeeze.

"I would if there was anything at all I could contribute.

But I'm worse than useless at that stuff," I apologize.

"Right. See you later?"

"Definitely."

I give him a quick kiss on the lips and wait until he's disappeared indoors before following to retrieve my rifle from the closet in the girls' room upstairs. Back in the yard, I insist that we practice deeper in the woods.

"If Neil sees us, he'll give us hell for shooting his trees," I say, pulling down the targets.

Cameron's knowing look tells me he, at least, knows that I'm actually trying to hide my shooting from Quinn, not Neil. It's silly, I know. And Quinn probably guesses that the boys and I aren't disappearing into the woods for a picnic, but I don't like to shoot under his disapproving stare.

I feel like piggy-in-the-middle of our band of rebels. I sincerely hope that Quinn's more intellectual and peace-loving approach will win out, because in my heart I don't like violence either. But I've seen enough of both our enemies to know that some insurance is probably a good idea.

I spend that afternoon and the next few days shooting and exercising. It doesn't take me long to get my shooter's eye back in, and I rapidly grow very fond of Leya's Ruger 9mm semi-automatic. It's lightweight and compact, so it suits my smaller hands. I like the light, crisp trigger, and it's as accurate as any sidearm could be. I'm never without it now.

My physical fitness comes harder, but despite my aching arms, I can cross seven monkey bars by the end of the second day. And a full five days after I started my training schedule, I finally make it. I'm proudly swinging to the last bar on the ladder bridge when Quinn tells me that they've figured out at least one part of the monkey-puzzle of code that Robin downloaded.

"And you'll never believe what it is," he says.

Chapter 17

Figuring it out

October 14

"We've got them! We've caught them with their hand in the cookie jar — just wait until the world finds out about this," Robin announces.

With the exception of Neil, who is busy in the basement, we're all crowded together in the living area, even Robin (who has been given permission by Beth to get out of bed) and Sofia, who sits beside him on a wide sofa, a laptop perched on her knees. Quinn's face is bright with excitement at their discovery. Robin grins like an alligator who's just snapped its jaws around a juicy turtle.

"Finds out about what?" I ask.

"Okay, so there were three parts of the code architecture we downloaded that puzzled us," Robin says. "One part is seriously encrypted, and we haven't made much headway with that yet. We cracked the most recent addition, and Neil's now working on the third part, which looks very similar to the one we figured out. He says he's *this* close to cracking it." Robin holds his thumb and forefinger a millimeter apart.

"But the part you guys already figured out?" I ask.

"It's advertising!" Robin says.

"Huh? What is?" Evyan is clearly as confused as I am.

"The Game – it's riddled with advertising. They must be making megabucks in revenue."

"I've been playing The Game for years and I don't remember any in-game advertising," Evyan says, looking at Robin skeptically.

"It's subliminal," Quinn says.

"Sub-what now?" says Bruce.

"Subliminal. 'Sub' — meaning *below*. And 'liminal' — relating to the threshold of sensory perception."

"Yeah, still going to need a translation, Paddy," Bruce says.

"Fine, I'll see if I can make it simple enough for even your mother's son to grasp," Quinn replies acidly, and launches into a detailed explanation.

If I understand correctly, subliminal messages are stimuli that a person isn't aware they've been exposed to, like an image flashed so briefly that you don't know you've seen it, or sounds transmitted below or above a person's normal range of hearing.

Normally, an image flashed for mere milliseconds wouldn't have much effect on the person seeing it, if they only saw it once or twice. But kids play The Game for hours at a stretch, and often every day, meaning that they're exposed to a message thousands of times in a gaming session, *every* gaming session, day after day, which will influence what they think, believe and do.

"And you won't know you've been influenced, because it's happening at a subconscious level," Quinn says. "You might be focused on one task, say playing a computer game, but subconsciously you're still absorbing other details like colors, patterns, music."

Bruce still looks unconvinced, but I think I get it.

"You know how when you're setting up a shot," I tell him, "and you're all focused on the target, but at some level your brain is busy registering the wind speed, temperature and elevation? And you factor that all in, even if you've only got seconds to take the shot. You can be aware of things that you're not consciously focused on."

"So what's in The Game?" Cameron asks.

"Yeah, what exactly have they been pumping into our brains?" Bruce demands.

"Loads," says Robin. "There are messages laced into the music, and logos hidden in the graphics of scenery and objects, but mostly they've been flashing very simple images of products or company logos. Advertisements."

"They've been messing with our heads, man!" Bruce says, rubbing a hand over his buzz-cut hair and looking majorly pissed. "My little cousin is only six — she plays the cartoon edition. You think this crap is in that version, too?"

"Oh yeah, no doubt with ads for kiddie products. Come see, I've isolated some screenshots," Robin says.

We gather behind the sofa while Sofia clicks through a series of images on the laptop. I may not have been an intel cadet, but even I immediately spot a pattern.

"Most of the ads in The Game are *for* The Game?" I say, pointing at one of the screenshots with the PlayState logo and the text: *Play The Game.*

"Yup. They've been getting players to grow totally addicted to The Game," Robin says.

"And they show the ads at highpoints — like when the player has just scored bonus points, or won a round, or taken down a repbot," Quinn says. "So they're piggybacking the message on that emotional high."

"It's classical conditioning, that's what it is," Beth says, clearly disgusted. "That's basically how we learn — by linking something with a pleasurable sensation. So if you're feeling great when you see an advertisement for a product, then your brain connects that product to the feel-good sensation, and you're more likely to buy it."

"It's mind-control. Bottom line, it's brainwashing." Quinn shakes his head and gives a bitter bark of laughter. "When I think of the ASTA slogan now — *Inform, Protect, Improve* — it's like an inside joke. They inform on potential cadets, protect their interests, improve their profits."

Quinn must be feeling mighty vindicated right now. He's always said that ASTA was up to something more, something sinister, and now he's helped discover and prove what it is.

"And get this — it's illegal!" he says.

He paces up and down while he explains that subliminal messages are powerful and dangerous because they sidestep our critical thinking. We don't know what messages we're taking in, so we can't consciously decide whether we believe them or not. We're being manipulated into thinking and feeling certain things, without our knowledge, permission or control.

"So ASTA and PlayState are showing adverts for all these products, and getting paid by the companies that manufacture them? This is all about *money*?" I ask, pointing at a screenshot for Hygeiney-Rides, and the next one for ImmunyChews.

"Always follow the money trail," Evyan mutters.

"It's more than that," Sofia says, tapping the screen in front of her. "When Quinn and I researched the list of advertised products to look for patterns and commonalities, we found —"

At that moment Neil rushes into the room, his face more animated than I've ever seen it.

"I've cracked it!" he declares.

Chapter 18

Outsmart

"That other section of code? It's also subliminal messages," Neil says.

"More advertising?" Quinn asks.

"Yeah, but with a very different product."

"Spill it, man." Bruce looks like he has no more patience for all the suspense.

Come to that, neither do I.

"They're subliminal ads for the United Nationalist Party in general, and President Alex Hawke in particular!"

There's an explosion of outrage at Neil's announcement. Sofia and Robin's mouths fall open in shock. Bruce leaps to his feet and bellows a string of curses. Evyan demands to know what the hell is going on. Cameron shakes his head — more, apparently, in disappointment than surprise at this latest example of devious activities by the government. My mind is racing ahead to why Hawke would want to put political messages into a computer game.

"Do you mean they've been manipulating voters to support their party?" Beth asks.

"Yes! It's more proof of the government's perfidy," says Neil, looking delighted.

"God knows where else they've been planting these messages — on T.V.? Radio? The internet?" says Quinn. His lips have thinned, and his eyes have paled to silver — a sure sign that he's livid. "But it's worse than that. The Game is played by kids, not adults who vote."

"Yeah, so what's that about?" I ask.

"He's growing a whole new generation of supporters brainwashed to vote for him one day," Quinn says.

"Last night, on the news, there was an item," I say, struggling to remember exactly what was said before the rat attack put all thoughts of it out of my mind. "Something about a bill to lower the voting age to sixteen."

"It's a coup," says Cameron.

"Faith, you're right! It's a virtual coup d'état," Quinn says. His hair is sticking up in all directions because he keeps running furious fingers through it. "Hawke is seizing future control of the government without anyone even being aware of it. Hell, kids may already be pressuring their parents to vote UNP."

"It wouldn't surprise me," says Neil. "Apart from the blatant 'Vote Hawke' messages, there are loads which present him as lovable and fatherly — photos of him holding kittens and puppies, and playing baseball and soccer with little kids. Plus, there are messages: 'Trust Hawke', "Hawke is good', 'Hawke is honest'" — Evyan makes a gagging noise at this and then explodes in a fit of coughing — "and 'Hawke knows best'."

I think about how I was always very fond of President Hawke, how I told my mother I figured him for a strong, honorable, trustworthy guy. Had that merely been the result of brainwashing? Mom had never liked him. She'd said he was too smooth, a typical slick politician. Tallulah hadn't cared for him either — she'd called him a smarmy son of a bitch and marveled at the fact that all the kids in the shelter seemed to like him so much. She'd been on to something.

The reason kids favored him was because they were all playing The Game, being regularly exposed to his sick mind-games. The reason that adults like Tallulah, my mom, Neil and his sister didn't was that they never played it. It was simple when you analyzed it.

Once I was in ASTA and then with the rebels, no longer playing The Game myself, my feelings for Hawke had waned. But they'd still been strong enough to make me refuse point blank to assassinate him when Zonia and Connor insisted I do so. Or was that just me? Would I have refused to shoot any president, any person, in cold blood like that?

"Connor was right," Quinn mutters furiously beside me. "Hawke *is* evil and corrupt. The reason he's so powerful is that he cheats and manipulates and controls. We've got to get a message to Connor and Zonia and all the other rebels across the country. For all we know, they could be doing this in the other sectors, too. We've got to expose this to the nation. To the whole world!"

"Hang on a sec," Robin interrupts. "Neil, are you certain this code, about Hawke and the UNP, was inserted first, before the product advertising?"

"From what I've been able to determine, it looks like it was there from the inception."

"You think he got The Game built just as a vehicle for this?" Quinn asks.

"Wouldn't surprise me," Robin says.

This brings on a fresh round of cursing from Bruce. If Hawke was here in this room right now, I reckon Bruce's hands would be wrapped around his throat and squeezing tight.

"What I'd like to know," says Sofia, "is whether Hawke even knows about the other advertising, or whether he still thinks he's the only one benefitting from the secret strategy."

"That's a very good question," Quinn says.

"You mean Hawke commissioned PlayState to create this game, and when it seemed to be working well and no one had picked up on the ulterior agenda, they simply added more advertising to make even more profit?" Robin says.

"And don't forget the recruiting," I remind them all. "The Game identifies kids with talent for shooting and coding and intel and stuff, and then hands their names to ASTA, who recruit and train them —"

"— and ultimately sell them back to the government as ready-trained soldiers, spies and other specialists to fight the war," Quinn finishes my thought.

"And they'd be eager and willing to do it, because they've been brainwashed into believing Hawke is such a great guy."

"It's brilliant!" Neil says.

"Neil, it's despicable!" his sister chides him.

Neil shrugs. "I only meant that as a business model, it's pure genius. They've been engineering a generation of super-consumers and political supporters."

I remember, back at ASTA, Quinn told me he thought the government was socially engineering our society. At the time I'd thought that was far-fetched to the point of paranoia, but it turns out my pirate was more right than even he knew.

"I seriously do not like this, dude. I've been playing that game for years. And they've been pushing me around all that time, telling me what to buy and who to like?" Bruce says, cracking his knuckles.

"What about the advertising?" Evyan asks Sofia. "Before Neil told us about Hawke, you said you'd found out more about the products being advertised."

"Oh, right. Can you bring the spreadsheet up?" Robin asks Sofia.

She taps a few keys, and then we're all squinting down at a series of columns, populated with clusters of names.

Robin points to the left-hand column. "These are the advertised products. And in this column next to them are the companies that manufacture them."

"Sofia and I did some digging on the companies," Quinn says. "And we discovered that most of them were owned by holding companies, who in turn were nested inside other holding companies."

Robin traces his finger horizontally across the screen, and I see that there are fewer and fewer names in the columns to the right.

"It's like a pyramid which narrows as you get to the top," Robin says. "Ultimately, all the producers of these products and services trail back to just a handful of organizations: PlayState, which obviously manufactures The Game; Tasty Plate which manufactures snack foods, candy, sodas — the kinds of food kids go for; SpaLyte — they produce hand sanitizers, UV lights, hot-boxes and decon units; and Style Tapa, which makes kids' and teen fashions, as well as disposable protection suits, latex gloves, shoe-covering booties, respirators, that sort of thing."

"Those names," I say, frowning down at the spreadsheet. "PlayState, SpaLyte, Tasty Plate, Style Tapa — they're all kinda the same."

"Jinxy gets a gold star!" Robin says, beaming proudly at me.

"They're anagrams of each other — not exact in every case, but close enough," says Sofia.

"So … They're all the same company?" I ask.

Quinn nods. "As far as we can trace the connections, they're all ultimately held by an outfit called A Play Test. Who also own ASTA plus an outfit called Stapla who do medical research and manufacture pharmaceuticals, though those two aren't advertising on The Game — not their target market, I guess. Most of the companies at the bottom of the pyramid were businesses that were in trouble or near bankruptcy three years ago. They were snapped up over the last few years, at bargain-basement prices, by these holding companies in the middle."

"Huh," says Bruce. "So this Play Test crowd buy up businesses that make goods for kids, and then advertise them in The Game and make huge profits when their sales go up?"

"That's the scam," Quinn confirms.

"They must be making a mint off manipulating young minds," says Neil.

"It's obscene," says Beth, frowning at her brother, who still seems more impressed by the technological sophistication of the program than outraged at the moral offensiveness of it.

"Hang on," I say, because one of the names Quinn rattled off seems familiar to me. "Did you say 'Stapla'?"

Quinn nods. "Yeah, why?"

I bend over to peer at Sofia's spreadsheet. Seeing it typed and on a computer screen like that brings the memory back. In my mind's eye, I see again the computer screen describing my medical treatment and showing the record of my interrogation and "interventions," back when I was detained after I helped Quinn escape. At the top of the screen was the name Stapla *Inc.*, I'm sure of it.

"That's where Connor and I were taken for interrogation. 'Medical research' must be the new name for torture," I say.

I can almost taste the bitterness on my tongue. It tastes like fresh blood and acrid sweat and helpless tears. It tastes like the pain of that room. I rub a hand across my face, as if I could wipe underneath my skin and bone, as if I could erase the flashbacks from my mind.

"Test place, too," Cameron says.

"What?" asks Evyan, who's had less practice decoding Cameron's cryptic utterances than Bruce and I have.

"Yeah, man, you're right," Bruce says to Cameron.

"That's the place they took us, where we had the brain scans and fitness tests done. I told you about it, Blue, remember?"

"That was at Stapla?" I ask.

It's hard to get my head around there being both torture rooms and cadet examination facilities under that one roof.

"That's where all the units eventually go to be tested," Sofia says. "So they must be doing at least some medical research."

"Maybe they consider human rights violations to *be* medical research," Beth says. "Sad to say, it wouldn't be the first time doctors had experimented on prisoners and patients."

Neil returns to his chair and begins sketching circles and arrows on a piece of paper. Another flowchart?

"But how would interrogations help with advertising and profit margins?" Quinn asks. It sounds like he's thinking aloud more than expecting an answer from any of us.

"They probably just get paid to do it," I say. "When Roth had me there, she said they'd been authorized by the Southern Sector government to question 'subversives'."

"They're sub-contracting the dirty stuff," Quinn concludes.

"Maximum deniability if anything ever gets out," Evyan says, nodding.

"So Play Test owns PlayState, who recruit kids for ASTA's cadet program, who then train and get examined at Stapla, along with alleged rebel dissidents," Quinn says.

"And suspected terrorists," I remind him.

"And the good, obedient specialists volunteer for the Southern Sector's military, civil surveillance and control programs, who in turn advertise on PlayState. It's a great big self-sustaining and hugely profitable cycle," says Quinn, sketching a circle in the air.

"And all roads lead to Rome!" Neil says, holding up his

diagram. It shows an outer ring of rectangles with names written inside — ASTA, PlayState, Southern Sector Government, A Play Test — all with arrows connecting them to a circle in the center, which is labeled Stapla.

"Then that's where we begin, yeah?" says Quinn, looking around at everyone.

My stomach clenches. I would go anywhere, do anything, rather than return to the place where I was held and hurt, where I was yanked out of myself, permanently changed, and only partly returned — a damaged, weak and fearful version of my past self.

When Quinn's gaze finally comes to rest on me, I swallow hard and speak in a voice which sounds anything but certain.

"Okay, yeah. That's where we begin. Let's do it. Sure."

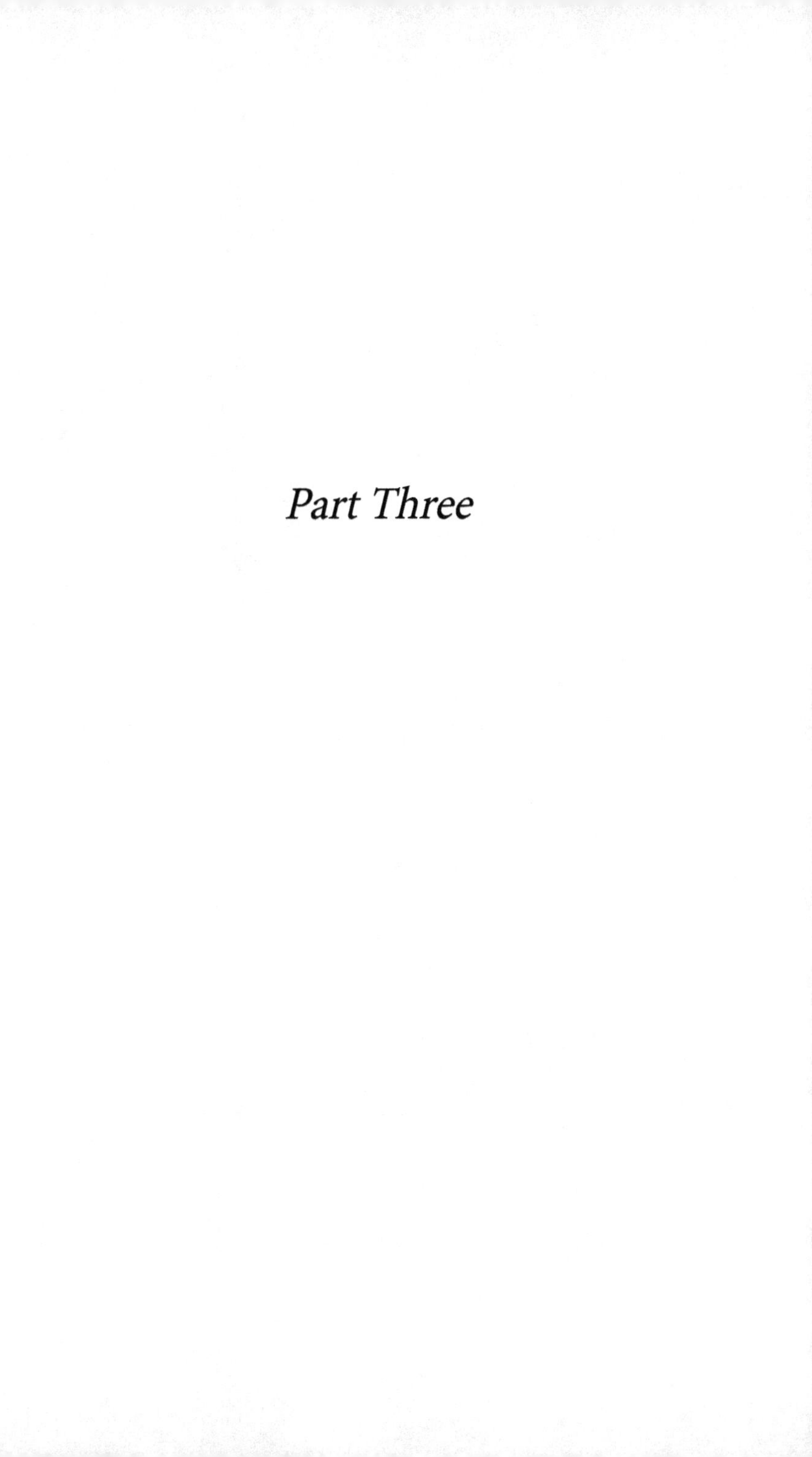

Part Three

Chapter 19

Flat-out no

October 17

"So who's calling this mission? Who's our team leader?" Bruce asks, looking from Quinn to me to Sofia.

"Not you, if that's what you're angling for," Evyan says over her shoulder.

She's our driver again, this time behind the wheel of Neil's black SUV, which is similar enough to one of ASTA's transports, we hope, not to raise immediate suspicions. Large magnetic decals adorn the sides and back of the vehicle, proclaiming it to belong to "Trojan Supplies" — "Because we're going in like the wooden horse carrying the Greeks into Troy," Neil had explained when we gave him funny looks.

Cameron, who turns out to have a gift for drawing, designed the logo of a horsehead, and Neil printed it off on the massive 3D printer in his basement, along with the large decals bearing the ASTA logo that we've also brought along.

Quinn, Evyan, Sofia, Neil, Cameron, Bruce and I are all on this mission. Robin stayed back at Neil's place. He wanted to come, but no way did I want him exposed to danger again. When he argued that he'd make a better fake intel candidate than I would, I went for a low blow.

"Even if your arm didn't make you a liability, I think we've established that you're no good when it comes to action," I'd said, giving him a hard stare and ignoring the hurt expression my words brought to his face.

Beth also stayed behind. She reluctantly supplied us with what we needed, but drew the line at actually joining the mission.

"I'm too old for shenanigans like that. But I'll be ready in case any of you gets injured," she said ominously. She also advised us to pack and take bug-out bags stuffed with the essentials we'd need if we had to make a sudden run for it, and had added, "Neil, you should probably pack a bug-out vehicle, and park it out back, too."

Sofia's unit is scheduled to come to Stapla for their testing at 9.30 am today. I'm keeping my fingers crossed, because our whole plan hinges on that not having changed. Hoping to avoid a repeat of the chaos of our rescue raid at ASTA, we've spent the last three days doing everything we can to prepare for this mission and to anticipate every potential problem.

Quinn, Sofia and I are all wearing the royal-blue jumpsuits we ordered off the internet. Neil scanned the silver intel unit pin and embroidered ASTA badge from the jumpsuit Sofia was wearing when we took her "hostage" and printed one of each for the three of us. They're made of plastic and glued to our jumpsuits, but I think we look enough like ASTA intel cadets to pass casual inspection. Which is a good thing, because we plan to intercept the intel unit and replace their members with our own.

Without Quinn and Sofia, the ASTA intel unit of graduated specialists will be two short. That leaves four members — two male and two female. Sofia will take the place of Dasha, the heavily tattooed girl who used to sell bootleg cash cards to her fellow cadets at the training compound. I'll pretend to be Natalie — a girl who also has blond hair, though she's a couple of years older than me — and Quinn will substitute for a guy called Alejandro. But we don't have anyone to take the place of the other male in the unit, Tyrone, because Neil is clearly too old to be an ASTA cadet, and Bruce and Cameron were examined at the center just a few weeks ago, so we can't take the risk that they or their brainwaves will be recognized. We're all hoping like mad that there's no one at Stapla who will recognize either Sofia, with the distinctive henna-colored tattoo around her eyes, or Quinn.

All of us have basic, form-fitted, particle-excluding gauze masks hanging around our necks that we'll wear to help disguise our appearance, and Bruce, Cameron and Quinn are also wearing beanies. Sofia added a pair of large-framed spectacles with clear lenses and applied a bunch of temporary tattoos on her arms and neck. Quinn shaved off his stubble, but left a horrible, thin moustache to match Alejandro's. I'm wearing heavy eye makeup, scarlet lipstick and a pair of dark-brown disposable contact lenses, ordered off the net. The lenses are uncomfortable, and I've developed a habit of blinking hard.

We pumped Bruce and Cameron for all the details of what happened when they were examined here, and can only hope we don't trip up somewhere. Until now, though, we'd planned everything together and hadn't thought about who would be heading the team.

"I vote for Quinn as leader," Evyan says, steering the SUV around a sharp bend without reducing speed. She drives like a maniac.

"Of course you do," I mumble.

"And what's that supposed to mean?" she asks, scowling back at me in the rearview mirror.

"Nothing, nothing," I say. Now is not the time for us to have a spat. "I vote for Quinn, too."

"Well, I don't," says Bruce, looking mulish.

"Shocker," says Evyan. "Let me guess, you vote for yourself or the girl with the gun."

"Annie Oakley," Neil chuckles.

I swear, I don't understand half of what he says.

"We're armed and on a mission," Bruce says.

"We won't be going in armed," Quinn points out.

We've already agreed on this. Carrying arms, we wouldn't get past the front door. We stashed all our weapons, including Quinn's double-bladed knife, under the seats.

"We should have a leader who knows how to shoot and is prepared to do so," Bruce insists. "Someone who knows at least some basic battle tactics. How about it, Blue?"

"I vote Jinxy, too," says Quinn. He gives me a glance with a side eye at Bruce, and I know what he's saying. Bruce is too gung-ho to be allowed to take the lead. He'll shoot before thinking it through, without properly evaluating the consequences. "I trust Jinxy."

Evyan makes an annoyed sound, but when Sofia, Neil and Cameron also give me their vote of confidence, she snaps, "Fine. Whatever."

There's only one problem — I'm not fit to lead. This ragtag group of rebels might not have realized that, but I certainly have.

"No," I say. "I won't do it."

Evyan gives such a satisfied smile that I'm tempted to take back my words, but I don't. My flat-out refusal sparks off another debate and round of voting. In the end, everyone agrees — Bruce only very reluctantly — that Quinn should lead the mission.

At 9.10 am precisely, we turn in to the side road that leads to Stapla and pull over to let Neil out. He takes one walkie-talkie handset, hands the other to Evyan, reminds us not to forget him on the way out, and then disappears behind a large bush.

We take off again down the narrow road, passing no traffic. We took back streets to get here, and they were mostly deserted too. I guess the government's new measures are taking effect.

I've been down this stretch of road twice, but both times I was blindfolded. Now I can see that it's mostly bordered by thick underbrush, with small bushy trees, long grass and unpruned hedges. Quinn, who remembers it from the raid to spring Connor two months ago, swears there's a part of the road which will be ideal for our plan.

Sure enough, after a minute's slow drive, we hit a section — about twelve yards long — where a high brick wall towers on one side of the road, and tall palisade fencing entwined with wild creepers borders the other. Evyan drives into the middle of this section and parks diagonally across both lanes, before killing the engine. While it looks innocent enough — like the SUV has merely stalled in the middle of a three-point turn — the gaps on either side are too narrow to allow a car to pass by. We've effectively blocked the road.

I wind a scarf around my neck, using one end to cover the ASTA badges, and sling a small purse across my shoulder. Hidden inside is the extra piece of equipment I'll soon need.

"Right, does everybody have what they need? Clear on what we —" The crackle of the walkie-talkie interrupts Quinn's final check.

"Car! It's a car, headed your way! A yellow car," Neil's voice warns. "Actually, it's more orange than yellow. Tangerine, you could say."

Bruce rolls his eyes, and Quinn begins, "I suppose we should —" but I yell, "Everybody duck down! Evyan, just pretend you stalled."

We all drop down into the footwells. Evyan starts the engine and tugs on the wheel, as if she's completing the turn. A horn honks impatiently from outside.

"Yeah, yeah, asshole," Evyan says, but she fakes a smile and a friendly wave as she pulls into the lane headed back toward the main road, allowing the car to pass.

When the other car has disappeared down the lane, she turns the car in two expert moves and maneuvers it back into the same precise position as before.

This time everyone bails out immediately, pulling respirator masks over noses and mouths, and taking their bug-out bags. Bruce and Cameron head for the underbrush, along with Sofia, who asks Quinn, "Aren't you coming?"

"I'll be along in a little while," Quinn says.

When I make to get out of the SUV, Quinn holds me back, giving me a long, speculative look. I know that expression — he's planning something.

"What?" I ask, blinking.

"It's just, I'm not convinced this is going to work. The problem is, we can't be sure the lads will get out to help you push, instead of just calling ahead to Stapla for help, or summoning a tow truck," he says.

"Quinn, this was *your* idea!" My nerves are already on edge, and I'm not keen for any last-minute changes.

"Sure it was, and luckily I've thought of an improvement. Like an extra-special, secret weapon."

"Well?" I demand, puzzled. Quinn's not usually one for weapons.

Evyan's walkie-talkie buzzes, and Neil's voice says, "Nothing yet."

"Only call through when there *is* something, Neil," Evyan says.

"I'm going to need your jumpsuit," Quinn tells me.

"My jumpsuit? What the heck for?"

"Quickly," Quinn urges. "They could be along any moment now."

I unzip the jumpsuit and try to pull it off as fast as I can in the cramped quarters of the vehicle, but it snags on my sneakers. Yanking them off, I grumble, "I don't like this. I'm not wearing much underneath."

"I know," Quinn says, raising a rakish eyebrow. "I saw you this morning, remember?"

He'd come into the girls' room while I was still dressing and wearing only a sleeveless button-down shirt and a pair of really short denim cut-offs. It gets hot in the thick cotton jumpsuits, and I'd dressed with a desire to keep as cool as possible during our mission, so as to minimize any nervous sweating. Quinn came in close for a tight hug and an urgent kiss before handing me my breakfast. Both the protein bar and the carton of Jump-Juice were, I'd noted with disgust, manufactured by Tasty Plate.

"So, what's this secret weapon?" I ask, handing the jumpsuit to Quinn, who sets it on the seat beside him.

"I'll also need your hair thingamajigs," he says, pointing to the sides of my head where I've clipped back my hair back to keep it out my eyes.

I slide the bobby pins out and hand them over. "Are you going to use them to make some kind of gizmo? A distraction or something?"

"Exactly that. And a button from your shirt."

I turn over the hem of the shirt, searching for a spare button, but Quinn reaches over to the top of my blouse. The collar button is open, but instead of taking that, he tries to pull off the second button, which is fastened. It doesn't want to come off.

"Maybe if you twist it, or use your knife?" I suggest.

My face is growing warm at Quinn fiddling with the button between my breasts, and it grows warmer still when he bends over and bites the button off. In the rearview mirror, Evyan raises both her eyebrows at us.

"Do you two need to get a room?"

Quinn threads the button on one of the bobby pins. What could he possibly make with those items?

"You know what?" Quinn says, giving me another assessing glance. "I think we'll need another one."

He bites off the next button down, and my shirt, a little on the tight side, springs open. My cleavage is now clearly visible where it swells above the cups of my bra.

I frown at him and hold my hands up in a WTF gesture. "*Quinn?*"

"Right, you're good to go," he says, pocketing the bobby pins and buttons and giving my hair an affectionate ruffle. "You just need to put these on."

He extracts a cardboard box from under his seat. Inside are a pair of shoes — scarlet, ridiculously high heeled, and in my size.

"Why must I wear these?" I turn them over, half expecting to find mini-explosives glued underneath. I don't see anything, but maybe there's something hidden in the heels, or a micro-receiver stuck inside the sharply pointed toes.

"Trust me, okay?" Quinn pulls off my socks and helps me slip on the absurd shoes.

I've never worn high heels in my life — there's no point when you're practically housebound, as I was until this year, and have nowhere to wear them.

"I don't even know if I can stand in these," I say. "How am I supposed to push a car wearing them?"

"You're not." He slings the purse across my shoulders and gives the small of my back a little push. "Come on now, hurry!"

Chapter 20

Out with the old

I climb out of the SUV and stumble to the rear, where I take up my place, ready to start pushing. Or pretending to.

Evyan yells that she's received an alert from Neil.

"Good luck!" Quinn calls.

He runs up the road to where the wall ends and disappears into the undergrowth.

I place the palms of both hands on the back panel of the SUV and start to push. As soon as my legs take some of the strain, one ankle turns in the stilettos, and I curse Quinn and his crazy scheme, whatever it is. I hear the transport vehicle coming up the road, but only when a horn honks do I straighten up and turn around, smiling brightly.

Sure enough, it's one of the black Hummers that ASTA uses to transport cadets. The driver, a burly man with red hair, gestures impatiently at me to move our car out of the way. I give a helpless shrug as I totter unsteadily over to him.

When he lowers his window an inch, I pull down my mask and say, "I'm real sorry. The engine just cut out, and we can't get it going again. Do you think y'all can help us push it out of the way?"

I give him a quick smile and pull the mask back up before

anyone can recognize me. The driver closes his window without replying but twists around to say something to his four passengers. A moment later the door of the vehicle slides open, and two teenage boys step out. One has olive skin, black hair and a thin moustache — I guess this is Alejandro. The other, who must be Tyrone, looks like the poster boy for geeks everywhere. He's skinny as a rake, with thick spectacles and an asthmatic cough. He seems reluctant to help until he clocks my chest display — then he gives an enthusiastic grin and asks, "What seems to be the problem?"

"It stalled and now it won't start, and I'm not strong enough to push it out of the way," I say as I lead them to the SUV.

Soon all three of us are pushing fit to burst, but the SUV doesn't budge an inch. I turn to face the driver and point from him to the vehicle in a silent plea for him to come help. He shakes his head firmly.

It's probably ASTA policy that their drivers never leave the vehicles while they're transporting cadets. It occurs to me now that all the times we went on shooting missions, the driver always stayed behind the wheel. It's a real problem, because he's likely to be armed. Somehow we need him to get out.

Tyrone, who is breathless and wheezing from his brief exertions, pulls an inhaler out of his pocket and takes two puffs.

Alejandro grunts as he gives another push, then says, "Are you certain the parking brake isn't still on?"

I'm absolutely sure it *is*.

"And it needs to be in neutral," he adds.

"I'll check." I give a friendly smile and wobble around to Evyan's window. "They say to check the brake is off and the car's in neutral," I say loudly, then add in a desperate whisper, "The driver won't get out of the car!"

"Make him," Evyan says.

"How?"

"Just lure him out."

"*Lure*?" I repeat, not sure I heard her right.

"Yeah, flirt, tempt, attract — lure! Reach for your feminine wiles — if you even have any." She looks deeply skeptical. "And get him to come out. Why do you think Quinn dressed you like this — you're the decoy, so just try harder already."

I stare at her, horrified.

"Shake your booty, smile, show him some tits and ass!"

My mind begins plotting vengeance on Quinn, but I force myself to concentrate on the mission. There'll be time enough afterwards to make him pay. *Lure* indeed.

I make my unsteady way back to the rear of the vehicle, tell the guys the brake is now off, and on the count of three we all start pushing again. This time, I bend way over, pointing my butt in the direction of the transport driver. When, again, neither he nor the vehicle moves, it's time to engage feminine gear. I pull down my mask, stick out my chest and take a deep breath.

If only I had one of ASTA's dart guns and could just shoot the man — I'm way more confident of my marksmanship than my sex appeal. Drawing on my knowledge of movie sex goddesses, I teeter over to the driver, swinging my hips and smiling in what I hope is an appealing way.

When I get to his window, I steal a quick glance at the two cadets in the back. Dasha is completely engrossed in something on her phone, and the other girl seems to be dozing — her eyes are closed, and earbuds are plugged into her ears.

I bend down and lean forward, giving the driver a good view, then peep up at him from under my lashes, seriously hoping I don't look as ridiculous as I feel. The window lowers all the way as the driver takes in the display.

"Oh, please, won't you come help us?" I say and, noting the nametag pinned to his shirt, add, "Chuck?" I flick the nametag with a playful finger and bat my eyelashes, hoping this won't dislodge the lenses.

His eyes move reluctantly up to my face. "Sorry, we're not allowed."

"Oh, please?" I pout. I actually push my lips out like a celebrity in a selfie and pout. "It'll only take a minute." Then deciding that I may as well go all in, I say, "You look so strong that I'm sure it'll move it straightaway once *you're* pushing."

He preens, grins, climbs out and walks to the back of the SUV. Amazed that my luring actually worked, I follow and take up a position to the right of him. As we push, his eyes are on my boobs. My eyes are on his sidearm.

Evyan must have lowered the parking brake a little, because the SUV begins to inch forward.

"Yay!" I squeal, clapping my hands and taking a step back. "You see, I *knew* you could do it."

The driver pushes harder. His arm muscles bulge, and veins stand out on his thick neck. All three guys are completely focused on their task. That's when I reach into my little purse, pull out the syringe, and stick it into the driver's neck.

He grunts, and his knees buckle even as he reaches back a hand to swat away whatever he imagines stung him.

Alejandro tries to catch him, and Tyrone says, "Chuck? What's up?"

But the rest of our gang, masks pulled up high and beanies pulled down low, run up to us just then.

Cameron trains his pistol on the cadets. "Back in the transport," he orders Alejandro and Tyrone, who stare at him, eyes wide with fright. "Now!" he barks, and they hurry back to the Hummer.

Bruce is already there, his submachine gun aimed at the two girls inside. Dasha has dropped her phone and is gaping at him. The other girl, Natalie, stammers questions and begs Bruce not to hurt her.

"Shut up!" Bruce orders. He moves aside to let the two male cadets climb inside, and hands me his weapon.

I cover the four occupants while Bruce goes to help Cameron carry the driver back to the Hummer. Quinn and Sofia are well-known to these cadets, so they stay out of sight. Right now, they'll be pulling the Trojan decals off our SUV and applying the ASTA ones.

Neil arrives, out of breath from his run up the road, and tells the cadets to roll up their sleeves and hold out their arms. When he pulls out the loaded syringes, Dasha looks ready to protest.

"It's just a tranquilizer to make you sleep. You'll be fine," Neil says while I point the submachine gun straight at her.

Persuaded by either the reassurance or the threat, Dasha tucks her chin in and holds out her arm for the shot. Soon all four cadets are unconscious, and Chuck has been bundled inside the hatch at the back. Neil sits beside Dasha's slumped form, while Evyan takes the wheel of the Hummer with Cameron in shotgun.

Bruce will be driving our newly branded SUV, because no way does Evyan, with her half-shaved head and multiple piercings, look like an ASTA driver. Plus, we might need someone who knows how to shoot. Quinn, Sofia and I hop into the SUV, and I'm already sliding the door closed when Quinn yelps, "Wait!" and races back to the Hummer, which Evyan has already started backing up toward the underbrush, where she'll find someplace to hide it.

A minute later, Quinn is back, holding a clipboard with some official-looking paperwork on it.

"They'll probably want this at the gate," he says, removing one of the forms and handing the rest to Bruce, along with Chuck's ASTA nametag.

"Good thinking," Bruce says grudgingly, and then we're off.

Sofia wipes her face on the sleeve of her suit, Quinn reads the form intently, perhaps memorizing some important information, and I wriggle back into my jumpsuit and sneakers.

So far, so good. The whole hijacking couldn't have taken more than ten minutes, and it's only a minute after 9.30 am when we pull up the gravel drive and are admitted through the gates of Stapla Inc. Medical Research Facility.

Chapter 21

From here on out

As Sofia, Quinn and I crunch across the gravel parking lot toward the entrance of the Stapla building, Bruce backs the SUV into a space facing the gate, poised for a quick escape, if necessary. He's staying in the car, along with the sidearm he lifted from Chuck and the submachine gun now hidden under the driver's seat. My own weapons — the Ruger 9mm and my sniper's rifle — are stowed in a long duffel bag along with my clothing and personal essentials, in case we need to bug out, and hidden under a black blanket on the floor of the SUV.

Last time I entered Stapla, I was dragged in, blindfolded, by an ASTA goon. This time I can see the four steps leading up to the main entrance are narrow and run the length of the building, which is a five-story cube of reflective glass and steel. We take turns entering through the decon unit, donning disposable goggles and standing still for our spray of decon mist and the UV light bath.

We pass through a metal detector into a lobby with a marble-tiled floor and a trio of multicolored holograms — two of the human body, and one of a 3D Stapla logo — rotating above projecting pedestals located in the center of the space. A receptionist sits at the front desk, holding up a tablet and scanning the area around her with it.

Nothing about this scene hints at what may even now be happening on the third floor. Memories of my last visit here flash through my mind — the room with the drain in the center of its sloped concrete floor, the chair with arm restraints, Roth's slap, Sarge's smile. The pain.

I clench my fists, digging my nails into my palms until it hurts enough to claw myself back to the present.

Quinn reports to the front desk to announce the arrival of intel cadets Dasha, Natalie and Alejandro, being careful to speak without a trace of his usual Irish accent. They'll realize who we are afterwards, of course, when they scrutinize the security camera footage, but just so long as we don't raise any suspicions while we're here, we should get out in one piece.

"Hang on just a sec," the receptionist says, half standing and angling the tablet around Quinn. "Got it! It came in with you," she says, smiling widely.

I spin around, alert for trouble, but there's nothing there.

"What did?" Quinn asks.

"The repbot. Only two hundred points, but it all adds up, you know?"

Our bewilderment must show on our faces, because she says, "It's the Go! version of The Game. You know — location-based augmented reality? This is only the beta version they gave staff to test, but it's a-freaking-mazing! I can't stop playing it. I nearly fell down the stairs yesterday chasing an Alien Axis captain — that would have been two thousand points."

She giggles, and Quinn and I exchange glances. Maybe she thinks we're judging her, because her smile fades.

"Just you wait and see. It's coming out to the public on Halloween — they've got a massive launch planned. Once you start playing, you won't be able to stop either," she says with a sniff. "It's totally addictive."

"I'm sure you're right about that," Quinn says.

"Well, you're on my list, which means they're expecting you upstairs." She buzzes someone to announce our arrival and instructs us to take the elevator to the first floor. "Dr. Khan will meet you there." She pops a piece of antiviral gum in her mouth — no doubt a brand also made by Tasty Plate — picks up the tablet, and resumes her game.

In the elevator, we exchange nervous glances but say nothing. I noticed the fisheye camera up in the corner as soon as I stepped in, and I'm sure Sofia and Quinn would have, too. Besides, we have no last-minute details to clarify or remind each other of, because from here on out, we're winging it.

If we can break away to check out different areas, snoop through any documents we may find, and try to figure out what they're up to, then we will. We've each got a tiny bug hidden on us, and the plan is to plant the recording devices in different key areas.

The elevator doors open onto a waiting area with a couple of plastic chairs, a water cooler and a coffee machine on a waist-high counter. I quickly scan the walls, ceiling and corners in the immediate vicinity but see no sign of cameras.

A woman in a white medical coat is waiting for us. This must be Dr. Khan. She's tiny, five foot one at the most, with a thin, severe-looking face and short gray hair.

"Why are there only three of you?" she asks, not bothering with a greeting. "Who's missing?"

"Tyrone Davis. Apparently he spent the night vomiting and was too sick to be tested," Quinn says, handing over the forms he took from Chuck. Again, there is no Irish lilt when "Alejandro" speaks. It sounds strange to hear Quinn talk that way.

"I should have been informed. And why are none of you wearing your ID bands?" Khan snaps, glaring down at our bare wrists.

I field this question. "We were told that you couldn't wear metal in the MRI scanner."

"Yes, but we remove them here. I don't like this at all. How do I even know you are who you say you are?" she asks, tilting her head and pinning me with the sharp gaze of her black eyes. She's like a crow, searching for the softest place to peck.

"Uh ..." I can't think what to say, but Quinn smiles charmingly and says, "Who else would we be?"

"Hmm. I'll check later."

Uh-oh.

"Right now I need to get you to your first tests."

"Natalie? That's you, is it? You're up first for the FMRI. Down that hallway, on the right-hand side, you'll find a changing booth. Everything off please, and into the garments provided. You two, come with me."

"Bye, Natalie, have an amazing time," Quinn says.

Amazing. That's our code word for when we've planted a bug.

"I'll try my best," I reply.

Dr. Khan marches off in the opposite direction, with Sofia and Quinn in her wake. Behind his back, Quinn crosses his fingers, wishing me a silent good luck.

I spin on my heel and head off down the hallway Dr. Khan indicated. The floors are lined with pale-gray linoleum, and the white walls are studded with framed photographs of beautiful scenes — the seashore at sunset, a fat yellow moon poised behind the Eiffel tower, wild horses galloping along a beach. I think the prints are supposed to make the visitors here feel relaxed, but they only serve to remind me of the freedoms we've lost. Again, I don't see any sign of cameras.

In the changing stall, I remove all my clothing except my facemask and slip into the disposable panties and the cotton gown provided. There are no buttons or zips on the gown — it fastens at the side with cotton ties. There is absolutely nowhere that I could squirrel away the bug I'm supposed to plant, unless I hide it in my mouth, but then it would surely show up on the scan of my head. Besides, it might not work if it got wet. I leave it with my clothes for now. Maybe I'll get an opportunity later.

A medical technician with zebra-patterned hair comes to fetch me. As we pass down the hallway, I peer into the rooms on either side. Some look like offices with desks, computers and filing cabinets I wish I could search, while others are fitted with examining tables and medical equipment. We stop outside a pair of sliding doors labeled *Neuroimaging*. Big notices warn that the room beyond is a high magnetic field zone.

"Wait here," the technician tells me. He sticks his head into the room behind him and says, "Andy, your first customer is ready," before strolling back up the hall.

"I'll be right there," a male voice calls from inside the room.

Chapter 22

Out of bounds

I creep forward to look inside. It's a long, narrow booth with a glass front overlooking a room dominated by a huge machine, which I assume must be the scanner. A plump man with a comb-over of thin blond hair keys something into a computer in a bank of medical equipment with switches, digital controls and blinking lights. This must be the cubicle where the MRI operators sit, and it would be an excellent place to hide my bug.

With a final keystroke, the man stands up, and I take a quick step back out of sight.

"Oh, hello, there," he says when he emerges from the room. "You must be Natalie? I'm Dr. Holmgren, your radiologist for today. We'll be doing an FMRI — a functional magnetic resonance imaging scan —of your brain in just a few minutes."

He looks me up and down while explaining what to expect and what I'm supposed to do. Then he hands me a face-cleaning wipe, saying, "You'll need to take off all that pretty makeup. Some brands can heat up unpleasantly in the scanner. Before I take you inside, we need to go through this checklist. Firstly, any metal in that facemask? No? Okay then, are you wearing a pacemaker, or any implants, metal screws, plates, pins, joints, cochlear implants, false teeth?”

“No.”

“Or” — he gives me a sly smile — “an IUD?”

“No.”

“Are you sexually active?”

What the actual? “*Excuse me?*”

“I need to know if you might be pregnant.”

“I’m not,” I say firmly.

“No watch or ID band, good,” he says, scanning my wrists. “But you can’t go in with that.” He strokes the single silver loop in my right ear, the matching twin of Quinn’s. I jerk my head back from his fingers — this man is giving me the creeps. When I hand him the earring, he drops it into a pocket of his white lab coat, saying, “Remind me to give it back to you before you go — there’s an intercom connecting us, so we can communicate easily. Right, where were we? Any permanent tattoos on your head?”

“No.”

“Any piercings in secret spots I can’t see?” He gives me a knowing look and licks his lips.

“No.”

I feel like I need a shower.

“And, last question, are you claustrophobic?”

I shake my head.

“Then we’re ready to see how your brain is wired and how your blood-flow and oxygenation functions in response to different stimuli,” he says brightly, sliding open the heavy door to the imaging room and leading me inside. “At the end of this, we’ll have a comprehensive brain-print of your neural structure and functioning. And because we also want to monitor your skin conductivity and heart rate to measure your levels of *arousal,* this needs to go on your finger.” He leers at me as he clamps a monitor on my right forefinger, then picks up a band like the one I had to wear during the polygraph test. "And this goes around your chest."

"I'll do it," I say quickly and fasten the band in place.

"Right, hop onto the bed, and on your back please." I swear he loads the words with a double meaning.

I climb onto the narrow table protruding from the huge ring of the scanner and lie down on the cool, padded cover, tucking my cotton robe tightly around me so that Dr. Creepy won't get to see any more of me than he has to. He lifts my left arm and gives the inside crook of my elbow a little tickle and a pat before wiping it with something cold and wet.

Then he holds up a filled syringe and says, "Time for penetration!"

Ugh! It takes everything I have not to run away. I swear, if he touches me anyplace he shouldn't, I'm going to take him down.

"What is that?" I ask, jerking my chin at the syringe.

"Contrast fluid, for the scan."

While he injects the contents of the syringe into me, and I feel the burn hitting my veins and traveling up my arm, I distract myself by reviewing the incapacitating moves Charlie taught me back at ASTA. It would give me great pleasure to inflict some grievous bodily harm on this pervert.

"Now the most important thing is for you to lie absolutely still once we begin. No crossing your arms or legs, and no moving, no matter where it itches!" He gives an irritating titter of a laugh. "Oh, and I always insist on protection — it can get quite noisy when the scan begins." I stuff the foam plugs he hands me into my ears. Unfortunately, they don't entirely muffle the sound of his voice when he says, "Have fun now. I'll be watching you every moment, don't worry."

He leaves the room, sliding the heavy door closed behind him, and a minute later, the table I'm lying on moves backward, sliding my head deep into the white tube of the scanning ring.

I spend the next half hour lying on my back while the scanner bangs loudly around me. I hold my breath when the doctor instructs me to, and don't move any part of me except my fingers, which twitch involuntarily from time to time. My contact lenses grow increasingly uncomfortable, and I have to fight the urge to pluck them off my eyeballs and flick them away.

For part of the scan, I'm shown a succession of pictures on the screen above me — first images of day-to-day things like chairs, puppies, trees and refrigerators; then more upsetting pictures of rabid plague victims, mutant rats, a pregnant woman in obviously painful labor, a man wearing a checkered headdress and brandishing a machine gun.

I don't like watching these, but I can't turn away, and Holmgren tells me not to close my eyes so, in order to keep myself calm, I fall back on the deep breathing methods I always use to steady my nerves before a sniping shot. I wonder what's happening in my brain as I view these disturbing images.

Next I'm presented with a series of math problems and incomplete number and picture patterns. Holmgren instructs me to try to calculate the answers in my mind. After that, I watch several scenes taken from The Game — some of coded messages, or a bunch of images where I need to find the common element or predict what will happen next, and then others of scenes where repbots scurry around and Alien Axis soldiers hide behind abandoned trains and cars.

I recognize some of these scenes from ones I've played as a sniper. Without intending to, I fall automatically into the old reconnaissance patterns of scrutinizing the environment, searching for targets, and picturing the perfect shot setup. I'm a little shocked at how much I enjoy this part of the scan. I even feel a longing to play The Game again.

The sudden thought that what I've just watched might be laced with subliminal ads shocks me out of the pleasantly relaxed state I'd slipped into.

Finally, I'm shown a series of photographs of famous people, including President Hawke. They're obviously checking how my brain reacts when I see him versus other people I recognize. Are those subliminal pitches for him still working on me?

At last it's over. The bed emerges from the scanner, and I scramble off and hurry out of the room and back down the hallway before Holmgren can come near me again. Back in the changing booth, I slip into my clothes, and when I inspect my appearance in the mirror and notice what's missing, I get an idea. I pry the tiny bug out from behind the silver intel badge, switch it on, and carefully peel off the cover to its sticky backing. Then, holding it carefully between my fore and middle fingers, I march back down the hallway to the MRI unit and straight into the operator's booth.

Dr. Creepy looks up in surprise. "You can't be in here," he says, half rising.

"Sorry." I smile innocently at him. "I forgot to get my earring back."

He mumbles something indistinct, but fishes it out of his pocket and holds it out to me. As I step forward, reaching out to claim the silver hoop with my left hand, I pretend to trip. I stumble against the control console, steadying myself with my right hand on the edge of the counter, curving my fingers underneath and pressing hard for just a moment. Then I'm upright again, murmuring apologies and scampering out of the room.

Mission accomplished.

Quinn and Sofia are already waiting, sipping on cups of coffee, when I get back to the waiting area. Their tests must have been shorter than mine.

"How'd the MRI go?" Quinn asks. His hair looks sticky and is standing up in all sorts of crazy angles.

I'm about to reply when Dr. Khan walks up, checking off something on a clipboard, and I have to rethink what I was about to say.

"Okay, I guess. The scanner was loud and uncomfortable, but the control booth looked amazing," I say. "Maybe I'll study radiology one day."

Khan gives a dismissive snort as if she highly doubts the likelihood of that ever happening. Maybe she's already seen my results and knows I haven't got the smarts for a career in medicine.

"How were your tests?" I ask the other two, pouring myself a cup of coffee.

"I didn't much enjoy the EEG," Quinn says. "Can't say I found it amazing at all. They stay with you and videotape you the whole time, and I got a little camera-shy."

So he didn't find a way to plant his bug? Sounds like he's also warning me that I'll be under constant observation during that test. I take a sip of coffee. It tastes bitter and burnt.

"The computer-based testing wasn't much fun, either — just working by myself in a boring little room. Not very interesting," Sofia says, giving her head a miniscule shake.

So she didn't want to waste her bug on a room where only testing happens?

"Ah, here's the tech to take you to the CBT room, Natalie. Alejandro, you'll be doing the FMRI. Wait here — the tech will come back to take you there. Dasha, you come with me to the EEG room."

"Which way is the bathroom? I need to go," Quinn says.

"The tech will take you," Khan replies.

"Oh, that's okay. I've been going alone since I was a little boy."

I giggle, but Khan is not amused.

"Wait for the tech," she enunciates. "You are not to go wandering around on your own."

"Sure, but I hope he comes soon." Quinn crosses and uncrosses his legs as if in discomfort.

Khan and Sofia set off down a hallway, with the zebra-haired technician and me following behind. This time I'm the one who crosses my fingers behind my back, because I bet that as soon as we're out of sight, Quinn will be up and searching for a good spot to plant his bug.

The CBT room is a tiny office with nothing more than a desk with a PC, keyboard and mouse, and a chair where the tech tells me to sit. He enters my assumed name and intel cadet category into the system and reads a set of instructions off a printed card.

"You are now about to complete a computer-based testing program which measures your performance on tasks of recall, recognition, response times, speed and accuracy. Please try to do your best on every task. The full program should take you approximately one hour to complete. Click the start tab on your screen when you are ready to begin," he reads, sounding seriously bored. How many times has he done this?

"I'll come check if you're finished in an hour from now," he adds before leaving the room and closing the door behind him.

Here goes nothing, I think, and click *start*.

Chapter 23

Out of my depth

The program is a mix of straight-up timed tests interspersed with sniping, intel, code-breaking and programming sections from The Game, which a pop-up window announces with a message reading: *And now for some fun! To give your brain a rest between tests, please enjoy gaming for a few minutes. The program will redirect you to the next task in a short while.*

A rest? Yeah, right. I'm damn sure they're also testing how well we perform on The Game tasks.

I obviously fail at the programming sections — I couldn't write a line of code if my life depended on it. And with the puzzles and codes and pattern-prediction tasks, I'm so out of my depth that I have to look up to see bottom. I really do try my best, because I'm supposed to be a brainy intel cadet, but I'm pretty sure I fail most of them.

I make a deliberate effort to screw up when I play as a sniper or do tests I think might be related to those skills. Hopefully they'll think I'm an all-round dud, rather than an intel cadet who performs suspiciously well at entirely the wrong subsection of tasks.

I finish in forty-five minutes flat — I guess because I flunked out of so many tests without getting to the end of them — and I'm determined to use my fifteen-minute window of opportunity before the tech returns to do some snooping.

I turn the handle of the door, easing it open a few inches to check the hallway. One way is clear, but the other is not. A gray-haired man in a dark business suit is leaning against a wall, talking on his cell phone. Looking directly at me.

"Hold on," he tells the person on the other end of the line. "Yeah?" he asks me.

"Uh, I'm finished with the tests," I say.

"Just wait inside the room. Someone will be along shortly, I'm sure."

"Okay," I say.

I duck back inside, leaving the door open a crack in the hope of overhearing something useful in his conversation, but a moment later, someone on the other side closes the door firmly. I wait an impatient few minutes and try again. The man is still in the corridor, still talking on his phone, but this time his back is to me.

He's not saying much. Mostly it's just "uh-huh" and "yeah," and one "the more data we collect, the more we'll know how well it's working." So I decide to try sneaking down the hall in the opposite direction. I've taken only three steps when he says something that makes me halt mid-stride.

"I understand the urgency, Roberta, truly I do. No one knows better than me that the thirty-first is only two weeks off."

My mind jumps straight to the only Roberta I know. Could he possibly be talking to Roberta Roth? Probably not. There must be loads of people in the world with that name. Still, it's enough for me to turn around and listen hard.

He says, as if in response to a question, "From the abundance or paucity of neural connections in localized regions."

The reason I hear each word clearly is because as he

speaks, he turns around.

Glaring at me, he covers the bottom of the phone with the palm of a hand and says, "Well, what now?"

"Shouldn't I be moving on to the next test?" I ask.

"I told you to wait in the room," he says, clearly irritated.

"Okayyy. Chill!" I draw out the words and inject my tone with heavy teenage snark. "Sorry for trying to be helpful."

I return to the room, and this time I stay put until the tech arrives.

"You finished early," he says. It doesn't sound like a question.

Maybe when the program ended it notified him somehow. Or maybe the suit in the hallway did.

Sofia's seated in the waiting area when I get there, but there's no sign of Quinn, and we have no chance to talk before Khan arrives to take me to my next test which, she tells me, she will administer herself.

In the EEG room, Khan cleans spots on my scalp with alcohol swabs then applies some kind of gel glue to a bunch of wired electrodes and sticks them to my scalp. This must be the source of Quinn's wild hair.

"What are those for?" I ask.

"An electroencephalogram measures the electrical activity in your brain. Sit here, please."

Khan attaches me to a machine and seats me in front of a PC. She switches on the camera in the corner and sits on a chair behind a desk opposite me, from where she issues directions and presumably observes my brainwaves on the sophisticated setup in front of her.

The EEG is the quickest of all the tests I've had this morning. The tasks are similar to the ones in the previous test, though there are way fewer of them, and I only have to play one unit of The Game — as an intel agent. I must be flunking again, because Khan looks increasingly perplexed. At one point, she actually stops the test and pins me with her beady crow's eyes.

"Are you doing your best?" she demands sharply.

"I'm trying, but I'm not feeling well, and I have a bad headache," I say, squinching my eyes as if in pain. "Maybe I'm coming down with Tyrone's bug."

"We're nearly finished. Just … try harder."

I blunder through a few more puzzle-solving tasks, and then I'm told to breathe deeply and quickly.

"Do you want me to relax?" I ask.

"I want you to hyperventilate."

"Oh."

I puff and pant for a few minutes while she leans forward and stares hard at her screen. After that she gets me to close my eyes for a few minutes and then to keep them open while a strobe light flashes on and off rapidly.

"Right, we're done," she says and helps me pull off the electrodes.

My hair feels gummy with the residue of the gel, and I try to smooth it down on the walk back to the waiting area. This time neither Sofia nor Quinn is there.

"Wait here, please," Khan says. "The others will be another ten to twenty minutes. Grab yourself a cup of coffee and have something to eat while you wait."

She points to a tray of sandwiches. My stomach growls loudly at the sight and I realize I'm famished.

"Tell Kenny to come call me when the others are finished. I'll be in the staff room up the hall," Khan says.

"Who's Kenny?"

"The technician with the striped hair."

"Okay, sure. See you later."

I grab a cheese and tomato on rye bread and munch while I watch Khan walk down the long hall and enter a room at the far end. I swallow the last bite of my sandwich then, moving as silently as I can, I walk up the corridor after her. The door of the first room along the hall is open, and the clicking sound of keyboard keys tells me there's someone inside who might spot me when I pass. I hesitate. I can risk being discovered, or play it safe and turn back now.

Screw it. If I'm discovered I'll just say I needed the restroom, too.

I take a quick step past the doorway and pause on the other side, listening, but the clicking continues uninterrupted. I pass two offices, both with their doors closed, and then pause outside a room with an open door labeled *Synapse Meeting Room*. There's no sound except laughter — and that's coming from the room beyond this one, the one which Khan entered. I would very much like to hear the conversations that are going on in there right now.

Ready to make excuses, I risk a glance inside the meeting room, but it's empty, and I sneak closer to my target room. When I'm almost outside the open door, I crouch down with my back pressed to the wall — so that I can monitor both directions — and pretend to tie the laces of my sneakers while I eavesdrop.

I hear a man's voice, possibly the suit from the hallway earlier, but it's too low for me to make out more than a couple of phrases: "individual capabilities" and "neuroimaging".

Now Khan speaks, loud and clear enough for me to hear every word. "There are some surprising results from today's measurements. One of the candidates doesn't fit the expected pattern at all."

Oh, crap. I bet that's me, with my brain which is useless at doing intel tasks.

"It's unprecedented in our testing of the specialists so far," she says.

The man mumbles again. I catch a word I think is "concerning" but might be "discerning" or even "returning".

"Indeed." Khan again. "It might mean there are exceptions who are unresponsive to current development protocols. Or that there may be errors in selection tests. Or both, I suppose."

She sounds worried. Obviously intel cadets who were recruited through The Game because they were gifted at discerning patterns and making sense of seemingly unrelated information, and who have been trained to further develop those skills at ASTA, have one type of brain, and I have another, completely different kind.

"Excellent visual-spatial abilities, no seizure patterns in the EEG," she continues, "but substandard performance in many of the specialized tests. Those neural pathways are simply not as developed as they should be given the measured levels and categories of programmatic exposure."

Another woman speaks. Her voice rises at the end, so I gather she's asking a question, but she talks too softly for me to hear what it is.

"The amygdala activity was, if anything, *under*-reactive to distressing stimuli," Khan replies. "Overall, that subject shows general hyp*o*-arousal of the sympathetic nervous system compared to the norm group's median. In fact, no other testee has calmed themselves down so quickly after the stress cues. Well, except for a couple of the specialists in the sniper unit. And we all know they verge on being sociopaths, so that type of response isn't atypical for their category of brain. I mean, it's what makes them perfectly suited to their jobs."

The soft female voice says something, and they all laugh.

"I'll tell you what else is strange — all three of today's subjects show reduced responsivity in the desired direction to supraliminal presentation of images of target number one."

Number one. Could they be talking about Hawke?

"I wonder if they have enough game time at the training center?"

"I'll take it up with the task team. Maybe when the new Go!Game comes out, they can all get it." That's the man speaking again, and I can hear every word, which tells me he has probably moved closer to the door and may come out at any moment. I cannot risk him catching me a third time.

I spring up and sprint back down the hallway, flinging myself into a chair just in time. At the far end of the hall, Khan and the suited man are just coming out of the room.

When they get to the waiting area, the man summons the elevator and gives me a long, evaluating look while he waits.

Khan looks at me with more concern than she's shown all morning. "You're looking sweaty and clammy. I think you may indeed be coming down with something."

Chapter 24

Out on a limb

The trip back to Neil's house is noisy with chatter and slightly hysterical laughter as we come down from the excited high of the mission. I waste no time in removing and disposing of the irritating contact lenses. We collect Neil, Cameron and Evyan from their hiding place in the undergrowth and fill them in on the details of what we accomplished.

Quinn managed to stick his bug under the desk in Khan's office ("It very helpfully had her name on the door"), while Sofia stuck hers under a basin in the ladies' restroom ("Hey, you'd be amazed what secrets get traded in restrooms," she says, exchanging a knowing smile with me). Bruce says someone from inside the building came out to bring him some coffee and snacks, and checked his paperwork, but seemed to be satisfied. I tell them what I overheard, and we all pitch in, trying to make sense of what it might mean.

"It means they're poking around in our brains, man, like we're lab rats or something. I don't like it," Bruce says. It's what we're all thinking.

But still, we're pleased with our success.

"We got in and out of bad guy central. The nation's most wanted were right under their noses, and they didn't recognize us," Sofia says.

"And we should get some good stuff from the bugs," Quinn adds. "How long will they stay live and transmitting, Neil?"

"They have a twelve-day battery life."

"How cool is that!" Sofia says.

I'm not as giddy with success as the others. If they haven't already discovered that we swapped out with the real intel cadets, they soon will — Dasha, Natalie and Alejandro should be coming around about now. It won't take them long to figure out what happened, and when they do, they're surely going to ramp up the hunt for us even more.

When we arrive at the house, Beth greets us with obvious relief, not even complaining when we all dump our bug-out bags in a messy pile at the bottom of the stairs and head in a noisy throng directly for the kitchen in search of a late lunch.

Sofia goes to update Robin on the mission and returns from the basement, saying, "I'll make him some lunch and take it down. He says he's too busy to come up and join us right now."

Translation — he's still sulking at not being allowed to come with us to Stapla.

We've just hauled smoked ham, mayo, pickles, lettuce and a six-pack of sodas out of the fridge when a buzzer sounds.

"There's someone at the gate," Neil says, sounding alarmed.

In the two weeks we've been here, I've never heard that buzzer once. Neil doesn't encourage visitors.

Quinn and I follow him to the front door, where the control panel for the property's security systems is. The monitor with the video-feed from the end of the driveway shows a vehicle idling outside the front gate. A hand protrudes from the driver's window, repeatedly pressing the buzzer, but my attention is riveted by the vehicle itself. Huge, black, sitting high on enormous tires, with roof-mounted lights and a front bull bar big enough to ram through any gates — it's an armored car for a tactical response team.

"Bug out!" I scream. "Bug out now! We've been followed."

"Enemy at the gate!" Neil shouts, manically punching at the keypad. I assume he's doing whatever he can to arm the systems and keep the gate locked.

Everyone rushes into the entrance hall, Bruce and Cameron cocking their firearms, as a deep male voice comes through the intercom. "Open these gates now. Your property has been designated for a security search under Emergency Regulation 2021.3.7A."

"Go through Neil's room and through the trees!" Beth yells. "The bug-out vehicle is beyond the last tree."

Robin! I need to get him from the basement.

"Open the gate immediately! We have legal access to this property," the man's voice commands.

Evyan and Neil snatch their bags and run up the stairs after Beth. Bruce and Cameron follow suit but take up positions on the landing of the first floor, covering the entrance with their weapons.

"No!" I yell at them. "Just go! We don't want a firefight we can't win."

I seize my duffel bag and run for the basement door, but stop when I realize that Quinn and Sofia are following me.

"Go, both of you. Go!"

"But what about Robin?" Sofia asks.

"I'm not leaving you," Quinn says.

"I'll get Robin. Quinn, please get her out of here." I slip my arms through the straps of the bag so that it sits on my back. I need my hands free.

Quinn looks like he's about to refuse.

"Have you still got your knife?" I ask him.

"It's in my bag."

"Cut the rope ladders on the trees, so they can't get up from the yard and follow us," I tell him.

"We said we'd stick together. I'm not leaving you," he repeats.

"You're not helping me!"

I hear a loud bang and crashing noises coming through the intercom system. They must have rammed through the gate.

"They're here. Please, run!" I wrench open the door to the basement and scream down, "Robin! Come quickly, there's a SWAT team, we've got to go — now."

Sofia takes a step back, but Quinn stands firm. Time to play dirty. "Look," I say, pointing up the stairs to where Bruce and Cameron still crouch, weapons at the ready, "the boys are covering me. I'll be safer and can move faster without you two."

With a last unhappy look, Quinn grabs Sofia's elbow and steers her back to the stairs. I scramble down into the basement, yelling at Robin all the while. He's seated in front of a computer monitor, wearing noise-canceling headphones.

"Robin!" I yank the headset off. "They're here, they'll be inside at any moment!"

"Who? What —"

"It's an intercept team, we've got to go now!"

He leaps up, and I grab a fistful of shirt, trying to drag him to the stairs.

"No, wait!" He pulls free and gathers up a laptop awkwardly in his left hand — his right is still immobilized in the sling. "We need to destroy this stuff first."

He runs to the bio-hazard incinerator at the far end of the basement, chucks the computer into the chute, then returns for another.

"We've got to go, Robin! We don't have time for this.

They'll capture us."

Even as I say the words, we hear a series of battering thuds coming from the ground level. They're already at the front door. It's reinforced with a steel core, but it won't keep them out forever. In another minute, we'll be trapped.

"We can't leave this for them to find," he says, running back for another load. "They can't find out what we know, or it'll all be for nothing. Help me, why don't you!"

"If they capture us, they'll find out everything we know anyway, trust me on that one," I retort, but I shove Robin aside to lift the biggest computer box with both hands, hurtle across the basement and heave it into the incinerator. There are another two that need the same treatment. Meanwhile, Robin has opened the zipper of a laptop bag and is sweeping the bottom half of his slinged arm across his and Neil's desks, brushing external drives, flash disks and thumb-drives into it. I grab the bag from him and run to dispose of it too, when he cries, "No — we need to take that with!"

"Have we destroyed everything important?"

"Yeah, that's everything, I think. I hope."

"Then let's get out of here."

As we run up the stairs, we hear a splintering crash that can only be the front door caving in.

I curse.

"What now?" Robin whispers, his face pale in the dim light of the basement.

"When I say *go*, run upstairs to Neil's room and out through the trees."

I help him put the computer bag on over his shoulders, then crack the door open a slim inch and peep out. Four tactical team members, dressed from head to toe in black and wearing helmets, Kevlar vests and full-face respirators, are in the entrance hall. They crouch in back-to-back formation, scanning all around and above them with their assault rifles at the ready.

I glance up at the landing, but either Bruce and Cameron have left with the others, or they're well hidden.

Using hand signals, the tactical team leader issues orders to the others. One is to go back out of the front door and check the area front and back of the house. The other two are to investigate the ground floor to the north of the entrance hall. He points one in the direction of the kitchen and the other toward the living area. He'll check the south side, and then they'll meet again in the hall and go upstairs together.

They split up. I pull the door to the basement closed silently.

"It's now or never." I breathe the words to Robin.

He nods.

I tense and raise my Ruger as the heavy tread of the soldier approaches the door, but his footsteps jog past. I force myself to count to five before opening the door, checking and whispering, "Go!"

Robin and I race up the hall, swing around the bannister, and hurtle up the stairs. We've just reached the landing when there's a shout from below.

"You there — stop!"

I thrust Robin ahead of me into Neil's room as I drop down. A gun cracks, and a round whizzes over my head. Keeping low to the ground, I leopard-crawl out of the direct line of fire, scramble to my feet, and dart through Neil's doorway.

Robin is already out on the wooden bridge that leads to the first tree. Bruce waits for me at the balcony. He has his submachine gun in one hand and a black cylinder-shaped object in his other. Can it possibly be a grenade?

"Go!" I yell, crossing the room.

Bruce pulls the pin out of the object, flings it over my head to the doorway behind me, then turns and runs. I'm hard on his heels. There's shouting from behind us and the honking of geese from below. As I reach the first tree, there's an almighty bang and a flash of blinding white light from the rear.

"OOH-RAH!" Bruce roars from the tree ahead of me.

"What was that?"

"Stun-grenade!"

There's no sign of the others as Bruce and I race through the web of interconnected trees. They must already have descended the last tree and be waiting in the bug-out vehicle. I run across the next bridge to the platform where Quinn and I cuddled and cloud-watched, noting with approval that my pirate has done his job — the rope ladders of both this tree and the one ahead have been severed and now lie in useless piles at the base of the trunks.

Gunfire pulls my gaze downwards as I leap onto the small platform of a maple tree. The soldier who was deputized to check the yard is surrounded by a gaggle of angry geese who honk and hiss at him and peck at his legs. He fires off a few more rounds, and two geese collapse in shivering heaps of feathers. He runs ahead to the horizontal monkey-bar ladder which connects the next two trees in the tree-maze, springs up to catch hold of a bar, and starts pulling himself up. I slingshot myself around the trunk of my tree, leap onto the ladder and jump onto his hands.

There's a crunch of bones beneath my sneakers. The soldier screams and drops his firearm. As soon as I move off his fingers, he falls to the ground, cursing loudly. I scamper through the last few trees and swing-bridges like a fleeing monkey. Quinn is waiting in the last tree, on the huge branch that extends over the electrified perimeter fence. Through the pine needles and branches, I can see Bruce and Cameron standing beside a dark-blue panel van.

"Go!" I yell to them and to Quinn as I approach. "I'm

right behind you."

"You first," Quinn says. "I need to cut the rope so they can't follow us." He gestures to where a single rope, knotted at regular intervals, is tied to the branch at his feet and dangles down to the ground more than ten feet below.

"Okay," I pant.

I stuff my sidearm into my waistband, seize the thick rope with both hands and half-clamber, half-slip down the rope. It's only as my feet touch the ground that I realize the obvious flaw in this plan.

"How are you going to get down?" I call up to Quinn.

The trunk of the pine has no knotholes or protrusions for footholds on a downwards climb. And it's way too high to jump. The rope slithers into a useless pile at my feet, and I crane my neck up to see Quinn replacing the knife into a sheath on his belt.

Quinn meets my gaze. He gives a shrug and a twisted little smile.

"Damn it. Quinn!" I shout up at him. "Bruce, Cameron!" I call them over, intending for us to make some kind of landing net with our hands, but Quinn glances over his shoulder, panic on his face. They're *coming*.

"Love you, Jinxy," he says.

And jumps.

Chapter 25

Out for the count

Quinn hits the ground with a sickening thud that resonates in my chest. His head actually bounces against the hard earth. For a moment, I stand frozen with horror, staring at his unmoving body.

Bruce and Cameron push me aside, scoop Quinn up and carry him, head lolling, arms and legs dangling lifelessly, to the van.

"Blue!" Bruce's shout shocks me out of my paralysis. And I follow.

Before I've even closed the doors of the van behind me, we're speeding off with a screech of tires and a cloud of dust from the dirt road. I try to grab the handle of the door banging wildly at the back of the van, but Cameron gently sets me aside.

"I'll get it," he says, and I drop to my knees beside Quinn.

I'm swamped by a wave of déjà vu.

Again. Again I'm in the back of a van beside someone I love, someone who's seriously injured. And what was it all for? What did we learn? *Nothing.*

Beside me, Robin is holding Sofia tight.

"They were suspicious of us from the get-go. Khan said she was gonna check on us. We should never have gone through with it," Sofia sobs. "And how did they track us back to the house?"

I can't think about that now. I can't think about anything except Quinn. I'm trembling all over, and cold with dread — more panicked and terrified than when the soldier pointed his weapon at me, more fearful than the moment before they started torturing me. I'm too scared to check if he has a pulse. Can't imagine what I'll do if he hasn't.

"Is everybody okay back there?" Beth asks from up front, where she's sitting with Neil and Evyan.

I can't form words. My mouth is as dry as ash. I look a mute appeal at Bruce, who sits on the other side of Quinn's crumpled body.

"Doc, can you come check him? He fell pretty hard," Bruce says.

Cameron holds up a hand to steady Beth as, swaying with the wild movement of the van, she clambers between the seats and climbs over storage boxes and bug-out bags. Crouching down beside Quinn, she places two fingers over the pulse-point on his neck.

I wait. For seconds longer than years, I wait.

At last, she nods. Relief shudders through me in a trembling wave.

"How's Quinn?" Evyan asks from up front, her voice catching as she says his name. I remember that she cares for him, too. "Is he —"

"He's alive," Bruce says.

I want to lift Quinn's head and cradle it in my lap, but I'm scared to move him. What if his neck is injured? I don't even want to think about what damage might have been caused by lifting and carrying him to the van, by the bumps that jolt us as we speed God-knows-where.

Beth lifts Quinn's eyelids and shines a small flashlight into first one eye and then the other. Clearly trying not to move his neck, she feels around his head with both hands. And winces.

"What?" I say.

"He's banged his head badly. There's a big lump swelling behind his temple here on the right."

"Will he be okay?"

He's got to be okay. He's *got* to.

"We need to keep him as still as possible. I'll be able to check him out better when we're not moving," Beth says noncommittally, and my heart sinks. She holds Quinn's head stable as we race through the streets.

"But how did they track us?" This time it's Neil who's demanding an answer. "Could they have implanted any of you with something?"

I think back but can't figure out how they could have done that. Unless …

"Check your hair," I tell Sofia.

I run my fingers frantically through my hair, feeling for anything that might still be stuck to my scalp, and then do the same with Quinn using as light a touch as I can.

"Nothing. You?" I ask Sofia.

"Me either," she says.

"Maybe they planted a tracking device on the SUV when that guy came out to check my papers," Bruce says, sounding guilty.

"Oh God," Sofia gasps. "They could've planted them on our clothes while we were in the MRI!"

She rips off her jumpsuit, and I do the same. Cameron removes the sharp hunting knife from the sheath at Quinn's waist and slices up the arms, legs and torso of his jumpsuit. He and Bruce very gently roll Quinn onto his side so that I can tug the remains of the garment out from under him, then almost tenderly lay him back down again. Cameron eases a buckled strap from one of the backpacks out from under

Quinn's hip. Bruce removes his own jacket and covers Quinn's chest with it.

I feel a pang of something, love maybe, for these two friends, kinder than I deserve, who have stood by me, as loyal and steadfast as family. Maybe this is what Sarge meant when he said, "Squad before blood."

Sofia gathers all three jumpsuits into a bundle and tosses them out of the passenger window, while Evyan asks, "Where to? Just where the hell am I supposed to be driving us to?"

Nobody volunteers an answer. Bruce and Cameron look at me expectantly.

"*Where?*" Evyan yells, banging a fist on the steering wheel.

I can think of only one place.

"Tallulah's," I say. "Take us back to Tallulah's."

Chapter 26

Outpatient

Tallulah, looking strained and distressed, makes no protest and asks no questions, even when Beth asks her for a stretcher or a long plank on which to carry Quinn. She directs Evyan to park the van in the back alley, sends a teen boy to fetch an ironing board, and goes ahead to prepare a room on the ground floor.

Bruce and Cameron help Beth strap Quinn to the ironing board by fastening their belts around his chest and hips, then carry him inside, while Beth holds his head stable. I trail uselessly behind, my eyes fixed on Quinn's white face. I've never seen his dark golden skin so pale.

Neil brings Beth's medical bag to the room where we place Quinn, still on the board, onto the bed, and Beth immediately rolls and folds a towel around his head to keep it still. She extracts a stethoscope, a tiny rubber hammer, and a blood-pressure cuff from her bag and begins examining Quinn — checking his breathing and pulse, squeezing the nails of his fingers and toes.

When I start peppering her with questions about what she's looking for, and what she's finding, and what that means, she orders me out of the room. I leave, but I wait right outside the door, gnawing a thumbnail to the quick. It's the nail that was ripped off when I was tortured at Stapla, and although it's grown back, it hasn't been quite right since. A bit like me.

When Beth emerges, looking grave, I ask, "How is he?"

She sighs and rubs a hand behind her neck. "Well, his signs are stable, reflexes are normal, and I don't *think* there's internal bleeding, though I can't be sure without a CAT scan. There's no leakage of blood or cerebrospinal fluid at all events."

"But?" I whisper, because I can hear the unspoken word in her tone.

"But I don't like that he still hasn't regained consciousness."

"What does that mean?"

"Can you contact his family?"

"Why?" I ask, about a millimeter from freaking out. "What for?"

"We need to make a decision about whether to move him to a hospital, even if that means probable capture. And also because ... well, just in case he ... deteriorates."

Oh God. I can't catch my breath. I stare into her eyes, wildly searching for some hope — or for the awful truth that she may be keeping back from me.

"Can you contact someone from his family?" she repeats, speaking slowly and calmly, as though suspecting any hint of urgency would trigger the hysteria that threatens to erupt in me.

I nod several times, not trusting myself to speak.

"Do that now. And see if you can find a cold-pack or some crushed ice."

I run to Tallulah's office. She takes one look at my face and enfolds me against the soft warmth of her bosom.

"There, child. That boy is strong. He'll come through fine, don't you fret now."

Her motherly kindness loosens the tight knot of terror inside me, and I burst into tears, sobbing out my fears and my doubts. My guilt.

"I d-don't know what to do," I hiccup. "If we take him to a hospit-tal, they'll seize him. But if we don't, he might get worse. He might d—"

"Hush, now. He'll be okay, you'll see." She kisses my forehead and rubs my back, wipes my nose on her apron. "Is there anything I can do to help? Can I make you some tea?"

I want to stay in the comfort of her embrace for a while longer — forever — but I fight the temptation. I can't be weak when Quinn needs me. I can't give in to the fear and fatigue that threaten to tug me down into despair.

"We need an ice-pack for Quinn's h-head. And can you get a message to Connor? The doctor wants his family notified."

"Leave it to me. Y'all go sit with your man and try not to worry."

I spend the night at Quinn's side, watching his still form constantly, holding bags of frozen peas and crushed ice against the side of his head until my fingers ache from the cold. Beth pops in at intervals and my answer to her repeated question — "Any change?" — is always, "No."

Cameron brings me a cup of chamomile tea and some buttered toast. Bruce comes in, paces up and down the room for a few minutes, then gives my shoulder a squeeze and says, "Sorry, Blue, this sucks," before leaving with a muttered comment about *really* needing to shoot something.

Evyan comes in, holding a blanket. "Tallulah said to give you this."

She offers to sit with Quinn while I get some sleep. When I refuse, she nods glumly and sits beside me silently for a long while before leaving for bed.

Halfway through the night Tallulah comes in to tell me

that she's managed to get a message to Connor.

"He's on his way," she says, rubbing a hand over her eyes. She looks exhausted. It must be putting an enormous strain on her to have all these outlaws coming and going from her shelter.

"Thank you for all your help, Tally. And … I'm sorry for all the extra work and worry. I just didn't know where else to go."

"You're far from being my biggest worry, hun," she says, and leaves.

I talk to Quinn through the night, alternately telling him how much I love him, how I know he's going to get better, how I can't wait for us to hold each other again, and furiously ordering him to wake up, threatening him with death if he leaves me. And I pray. I pray like I haven't for years, begging a God I'm not sure exists to save Quinn.

The black night sky is just lightening to a dull gray when the door opens again, and in steps Connor O'Riley.

"Hi." My voice is hoarse and unsteady.

I'm not quite sure what to say to him. The last time I saw him, he told me he planned to make it his life's mission to get and keep Quinn away from me.

Connor walks to the head of the bed and curses as he takes in his brother's appearance. Then he scowls at me.

"What did you do to him this time?" he demands.

"*I* didn't do this — he fell!" I say indignantly. "Actually, he jumped."

"And was he by any chance trying to save your skin at the time?" He takes in my guilty expression and says, "Aye, I thought so. You've brought him nothing but bad luck."

I bite my lip to keep from giving him a piece of my mind — I know his anger springs from fear for the person we both love.

Connor flings himself into a chair. A muscle pulses in his

jaw, and his eyes never leave his brother's face. I perch on the end of the bed, rubbing Quinn's feet through the bedclothes. We sit in an uncomfortable silence for long minutes.

"How are Zonia and the rebels?" I ask eventually.

"Zonia's dead."

"*What?*"

"Zonia's dead. Darius, too. They were shot by guards in a raid at Hawke's compound."

"That's … Oh, Connor, that's terrible!" My words sound inadequate. "I'm so, so sorry."

He makes a contemptuous sound. "Please don't pretend like you gave a rat's arse about either of them. If you cared about the rebels, then you should've stayed and helped us."

"Connor — let's not fight, please. We need to decide if we're going to take Quinn to hospital for treatment."

"No," he says flatly.

"The doctor says he should get a scan."

"Not. Happening." As he gets angrier, his Irish accent gets stronger. "If he falls into their clutches, he's dead anyway."

"But what if he needs —"

"You have no say here. You're not family."

I'm trying to stay civil, but his complete dismissal of me rankles.

"I *love* him."

"Aye, so you say. But for someone who supposedly loves him, funny how you're forever endangering him. You're as bad as your name — a real jinx to our family."

A moan from the bed snaps our attention back to Quinn. His head is moving from side to side on the pillow, despite the rolled towel.

"Look! Surely that means his neck is okay?" I ask, hope rising.

One of Quinn's feet jerks under the covers, and his

fingers twitch.

"Quinn. Quinn, how are ya?" Connor asks, bending over his brother.

Quinn opens his eyes, blinks blearily and stares up at us with an unfocused gaze.

"You're awake!" I say, half-laughing with the relief of it.

"Was I asleep?" Quinn asks, looking like he suspects he still is.

"You were unconscious, for ages." I check my watch. "For over twelve hours. I was so worried!"

Connor snorts at this. He tells his brother, "Don't move. I'll go get the doctor."

Chapter 27

Out of my mind

When Connor leaves the room, I seize the opportunity to move into the spot near Quinn's head.

"I'm so glad you're back," I tell him, tears pricking my eyes.

He yawns widely and looks around the room. "Where am I?"

"At Tallulah's." At his blank look, I say, "We brought you to the Inner City Teen Shelter — we're all here."

"Doctor," he says slowly, as if Connor's words have only just registered. "Am I in the hospital, then? Are you my nurse?" Quinn looks at me again, and this time he takes in the whole of me, including the stupid cut-off shorts and half-unbuttoned shirt I'm still wearing. A slow, sexy smile spreads across his face. "You don't look like a nurse."

Uh-oh. This can't be good.

"Quinn?" I say, nervously.

"That's my name, is it?"

"*Quinn?*"

"Yeah, it feels like my name. Wasn't there an old song about the Mighty Quinn? And what's your name, my sweet?"

"*Quinn!*"

I stare at him in horror and then lay my hand on his forehead, as if testing for fever could tell me something about his confusion. Quinn takes my hand in one of his, rubs it against his stubbly cheek and smiles at me.

Connor comes into the room, saying, "The doc's on her way."

"Now you," Quinn says, pointing the forefinger of one hand at Connor while still hanging onto my hand with the other, "I remember. You're Connor, and you're my brother, right?"

He beams up at me, clearly proud of himself for getting this right.

"What's he on about?" Connor demands, glaring at me as if I did something to Quinn while he was out of the room.

"He doesn't remember who I am!" I say, my voice high with panic.

Connor gives me an evil, satisfied smile and then tells Quinn, "Yes, I'm your big brother."

"Right," says Quinn. He plays with my fingers while he hums a little tune, then suddenly looks up at me, a look of alarm creasing his features. "Wait, you're not my sister, are ya?"

"No!" Connor and I say at the same time, both horrified for different reasons.

"Faith, that's a relief! If we were related, it would be very wrong for me to have such thoughts as I've been having about you, darling," Quinn says, giving me a rakish wink.

At that moment, Dr. Beth comes in the room.

"Good! You're awake," she says, smiling at her patient.

"Am I though? It rather feels like I'm dreaming."

"There's something wrong with him," I tell Beth. "He doesn't remember me."

"Ah, so I know you, do I? That pleases me." Quinn seems utterly unconcerned about his patchy memory.

"What's your name?" Beth asks.

"They call me Quinn," he says, waving a hand at Connor and me.

"And your surname?"

He rolls his eyes up to one side, then the other, clearly thinking hard. He shakes his head, then grabs it with both hands.

"Devil, but my head hurts! I think it might be cracking open."

"Can't you give him something for the pain?" I ask Beth.

She opens her medical bag, half fills a syringe with clear liquid from a small glass vial, and injects Quinn in his upper arm.

"So you're the doctor, are you?" he asks her.

"I am. Can you tell me what day and date it is?"

"I'm not sure. Sunday, perhaps?"

Today is Wednesday.

"Do you know who the current president is?"

Quinn gives a low whistle. "Ah, now that's a hard one." He slides me a sideways glance. "Do you know?"

I swallow hard and nod.

"Would you mind telling her" — he jerks a thumb at Beth — "she wants to know. She's full of questions. It's making my brain ache. Also, I'm damned uncomfortable." He wriggles and feels with his hands along his torso. "Why am I tied down?"

"To keep you still," Beth says, pulling aside the bedclothes.

"I'm not a madman, am I? Is this a loony bin?"

"What's the last thing you recall?" Beth moves down to his feet and pulls off his socks.

Quinn screws up his face with the effort of trying to remember.

"It's all mixed up. Like a dream. Just flashes and … Wait

— did you leave home?" he asks Connor.

"Yeah, a while ago now."

"There's dogs. And a cat?"

I try not to be mortally offended that Quinn remembers his pets, and not me.

"Yes, that's right. Surely, Goodness and Mercy," Connor reminds him.

"Ow!" Quinn jerks his foot away from Beth. "Did you just stick a pin in my toe?"

"His reflexes seem okay," Beth says and pricks a toe on his other foot.

"Stop that, woman! Can you make her stop hurting me?" he asks me in a pitiful voice. Then, in a much happier tone, adds, "Those eyes, though — the color of sapphires — I know those eyes!"

I smile encouragingly at him.

"Did we kiss?" he asks me, smiling again. "We did, didn't we?"

"Yes." Please let it be coming back to him.

"Your name, I know it — almost. It's like a whisper just too soft to hear."

For the first time, Quinn looks concerned.

"Don't strain yourself trying to remember her name. Of all the things you've forgotten, that's the least important, trust me," Connor says. "How's the pain? Still bad?"

"It's a bit better." Quinn sighs deeply and closes his eyes for a moment.

"He's got some post-traumatic retrograde amnesia," Beth tells Connor and me. "Usually it clears up in a few hours or days."

"Usually?" I ask.

"There may be bits he never recollects."

From the nasty look Connor shoots me, I can tell he hopes I'm one of those bits.

Quinn opens his eyes and says, "I can't get it all straight. Where did you say I was?"

"Don't worry if it's all a little confused now," Beth says. "Falling out of a tree and landing on your head will do that to you."

"I fell on my head?" Quinn opens his eyes, looking more amazed than concerned.

"Yeah, thanks to her," Connor says bitterly, pointing at me.

"Did you push me?" Quinn asks me.

"No!"

"You can count yourself lucky she didn't shoot you again," Connor snipes.

"*Again.* You shot me before?"

"Aye," says Connor.

"Define 'shot'," I say, looking down at my toes.

"A beautiful lass who has both kissed and shot me — I think I should know your name," Quinn says.

"Jinx. You call me Jinxy."

"Whoa, hold the phones — something came back there. Jinxy. *Jinxy.* Yes … I remember that name. Are you …? Hmmm. Did you have blue stripes in your hair?"

"Yes!"

"And did I give you that earring?"

"*Yes.*" Tears of relief well up in my eyes and spill over. "It's the pair of the one in your eyebrow."

He lifts a hand to feel for the earring, and I notice that it automatically goes to the correct brow. "Ah, yes. Yes."

"It'll start coming back in bits and pieces. Just relax and take it easy," Beth tells him. "And don't worry, most people get almost all of it back."

"I'd like to get all the memories of *you* back." Quinn grins at me again.

"Huh, you wouldn't if you knew what she'd done," says

Connor.

The thought flashes across my mind that Connor's mad Quinn is paying more attention to me than to him.

"What's that then?" Quinn asks.

"She betrayed us. She shot us both."

"For the hundredth time, they were *tranquilizer darts*!"

"She abandoned the rebel movement when we needed her most."

"I haven't abandoned the rebellion. I just don't agree with your methods, and I won't be your pawn."

"And she inveigled you away from our cause, too."

"I did not! Quinn's an adult. He makes his own choices."

Quinn's frown deepens as he glances from me to Connor and back again.

Beth waves an impatient hand at us. "Will you two give it a break! This hostility is not conducive to rest and recuperation."

Connor can't seem to resist getting another jab in, though. "Bottom line, brother, she's a jinx alright. She's not to be trusted."

But Quinn has taken my hand again and is smiling up at me dreamily — though that may just be the pains meds kicking in.

"Oh, I don't know, brother. My head might not remember her, but I feel like my heart does," he says.

I stare back into his gray eyes and try to put all the love I feel into my own.

"I've got a good feeling about you," Quinn says and pulls me down for a kiss. When he lets me go a moment later, he says, "Jinxy, lass, will you do me a great favor?"

"Anything."

"Will you tell me why I'm stretched out like a starched shirt on an ironing board?"

Chapter 28

Out of luck

October 18

After a long, hot shower, I surrender to my bone-deep exhaustion and allow myself to sleep for a few hours. I want to lie beside Quinn, but Beth says not to in case I jostle him. So I find a bed in another room in the shelter and collapse on it, but only after Cameron swears he'll stay with the patient. I wouldn't put it past Connor to try to smuggle his brother out while I'm asleep.

I wake up mid-morning, brush my hair and teeth, and go check on Quinn.

"How are you?" I ask him, noting with pleasure that he has some color in his cheeks and his eyes are properly focused.

"I have the mother of all migraines, but other than that I feel fine. Hungry, though. Famished!"

"And your memory?"

"It's mostly all come back, though it's pretty jumbled." He runs a hand through his hair and winces when it touches the lump on the side. "I remembered the time when you darted Connor and me."

I'd been hoping that one would stay lost in the amnesic

void.

"But I also remember … did we canoodle up in a tree?"

"Yes, we did. Do me a favor — hang onto that version of me, okay?"

"I still don't remember anything after we left Stapla."

"Well that's a damned shame, O'Riley, because some pretty significant things happened after that."

"They did?"

"Oh yeah. For one thing, you told me you loved me."

He smiles his slow, sexy grin. "I do indeed."

"And for another, you promised to give me daily back massages."

He takes one of my hands in his and starts playing with my fingers, sending tingles up my arm.

"I did?"

I nod, straight-faced. "And then you vowed to keep me in the style to which I've grown accustomed."

"Which is?" he says, looking worried.

"Chocolate muffins."

"Ahh. Well, I'll do my best, lass."

"And lastly …"

"There was more?"

"You committed to be my slave for life."

"You've already enslaved my heart, wench, what more do you want?"

"All of you."

"Done!" he says, flourishing his hand like a king passing a royal decree. "*Now* may I have something to eat?"

With a giggle, I plant a quick kiss on his lips and promise to return with food.

"Bring lots, Jinxy. I could eat a horse."

I follow the smell of cinnamon and butter to the kitchen, where I find Robin and Sofia at the scrubbed wood table, eating freshly baked cinnamon rolls. Two teen boys, pouring themselves cups of coffee at the machine in the corner, look up when I enter. The one elbows the other, who grins at me, and then they saunter out, suppressing laughs.

I fill Robin and Sofia in on Quinn's much-improved condition and ask, "Where is everybody?"

"Beth is catching some shuteye, I think," Robin replies. "And Bruce and Cameron were in here earlier, washing dishes."

Ha! Wish I'd seen that.

"Evyan helped Tallulah make breakfast and bake these beauties." Robin sinks his teeth into a roll and closes his eyes in pleasure.

"Here" — Sofia hands me a plate of the rolls — "I had to fight Carlos off to save these for you and Quinn. If you're looking for Bruce, Cameron and Evyan, they're in the games room now."

"They're not playing The Game, surely?" I ask around a mouthful of sweet pastry.

"No, I think Evyan's teaching the boys how to pick locks," Sofia says.

I wonder if Connor has told her and Neil about Zonia and Darius yet.

"She'd better not be teaching the teens in the shelter how to pick locks. Tallulah will kill her if she leads the 'lambs' astray," I say.

"Speaking of unlocking things, we need to get back to work," Robin says.

"Work?"

"We've set up the equipment we were able to bring — Neil had a bunch already stashed in the van — and we've recovered what we stored in the cloud and from the storage devices I brought. Last night, Neil jumped straight back into that other layer of encrypted code. He says he's finally getting somewhere."

"Are you helping him with that?" I ask, placing three rolls on a plate and adding some wedges of cheese I find in the refrigerator.

"Nah, I'm on black hat duty. Cyberwarfare," he adds when I give him a blank look. "With the help of my right-hand woman here," Robin says, breaking off a frosted piece of pastry, and feeding it to a blushing Sofia, "I'm creating some truly evil malware — malicious software — which I plan to upload into The Game to create a lethal cyber infection."

"Will it destroy it?"

"Oh yeah. It's Neil's and my job to write the malware, but it's your job to figure out a way to get into PlayState to upload it manually."

"Sure, no problem. I'll figure out something this afternoon, shall I?" I say sarcastically.

Robin finishes his last bite of food, then rinses off his and Sofia's plates in the sink and stacks them on the drying rack, while she wipes the table free of crumbs, covers the remaining cinnamon rolls with a tea towel, and places them on top of the fridge. If she's trying to hide them from Carlos, she'll need to do better than that.

"Before you go," I say, when they head for the doorway, "have we picked up anything useful from the bugs at Stapla?"

"Bad news there, I'm afraid," Robin says, grimacing.

"What now?"

I'm so tired of bad news. I feel like a punching bag that's spent the last four years being pummeled with blow after blow of bad news. When will there be good news?

"They obviously knew pretty soon after we left that we weren't the real cadets, and they must have called security services immediately for a sweep, because the bugs stopped transmitting about an hour after we left."

"We only got an hour? After all that effort and risk?"

"'Fraid so."

"Was there *anything* on it?"

"Not much. The doctor said something about a new protocol coming out in the Go!Game — probably new ads — and another woman with a really quiet voice may have said something about synaptic enrichment, whatever that is," Robin says. "Oh, and she — the quiet one —"

"Isn't it always the quiet ones?" Sofia sniggers.

"Is doing the dirty with some guy in a cubicle in the ladies' restroom," Robin says.

"With Kenny," Sofia adds.

"Oh right, how could I forget? *Kenny, oh Kenny, yes, Kenny, yes!*" Robin mimics a high, breathy voice, and he and Sofia leave the kitchen, laughing.

I'm not laughing. I'm disappointed, and frustrated enough to scream. The mission was a complete waste of time — all we achieved was plunging our group into an even worse situation. We've lost our comfortable base, and we're endangering Tallulah just by being here. Plus, Quinn could easily have broken his neck, and we all could have been shot or captured.

I pour two cups of coffee, adding milk and sugar to Quinn's, grab the plate of food, and am on my way to take it to him when Carlos runs up, telling me Tallulah wants to see me in her office.

"Okay, you take this to Quinn, the sick guy. You know where he is?" Carlos nods vigorously, but there's a greedy glint in his eye when he takes the plate that makes me add, "And Carlos? That food is for *him* — all of it. If you steal any of it, if you as much as take a lick at the frosting, I'm going to open a can of whoop ass on you."

He nods solemnly, his eyes wide and his lips pinched together as if to trap his wandering tongue safely inside his mouth. Perhaps he remembers that I have a gun.

"Good. Now off you go."

He walks off with his face lifted high as if averting his eyes from the temptation of the pastries.

"Close the door, hun," Tallulah says when I enter her office. "I don't want to be interrupted or overheard."

She looks dog-tired. There are dark rings etched under her bloodshot eyes, and her voice sounds hoarse. She runs her hands up and down her arms as though chilled, even though it's warm as toast in her office.

"Tally, we've brought a heap of work and worry to your door, I'm so sorry. I'll make sure we have a meeting today and figure out our next step, and where we can move our operation to."

"There's no rush, you can stay awhile," Tallulah says. "But I'm afraid I have to go."

"Oh," I say, taken aback. "Sure, of course. Is there somewhere you can go and get some rest? We'll take care of the kids for you until you get back."

"Kid, where I'm going, I ain't coming back." She scrubs her hands over her face as if to rub out the wrinkles.

"Tallulah?" I say, worried. What on earth could make this generous woman, who loves and protects her charges so fiercely, decide to abandon them? "What's wrong?"

Chapter 29

Checking out

Tallulah takes a deep breath and blows it out slowly between pursed lips.

"Are you sick?" I ask.

"Yeah, you could say that." Tallulah gives a sad smile. "Jinx, I got rat fever."

I sit, speechless with shock and horror, while Tallulah tells me how, on the day before we all descended on her, she was bitten by a dog.

A stray dog.

"I was mopping the kitchen floor, and when I opened the back door to toss the water into the alley, this crazed dog jumped up and bit me on the leg." She lifts the hem of her dress, and I see a gauze bandage wrapped around one thigh, stained where blood and pus is seeping through. "And I'm starting to feel real sick."

"Maybe it's not the plague. Maybe it's … ordinary rabies, or something."

"Somehow, I don't think so. But either way, I'm screwed."

She's right.

I want to scream my rage, howl my pain and sadness, but then she'd feel the need to console *me*. And that's not the direction the comfort should be flowing here. There'll be time enough for me to lose it later. Afterwards. Right now Tallulah needs me, so I need to stay calm.

"What can I do? How can I help?" I ask her, pushing the words past the lump in my throat.

She opens a drawer at her desk and pulls out a blister pack of strong painkillers.

"I've thought it all through," she says, punching four tablets through their foil seal. She hesitates before swallowing them with a gulp of water. "The headache's a killer, and it's getting harder to drink the water."

It was the same with Nicky, back in the rebel camp in the woods. After a few days, she simply refused to drink any more. I'm terrified that Tallulah will ask me for the same favor Nicky did. I can't do that again.

But Tallulah has a different plan in mind.

"I'm going to drive myself to the hospital today. My car is waiting out front. Community General has a plague unit — I'll go there. They can do what they like to me once I'm inside, but I'm not dying on the streets like that poor man who came in here with his bleeding eyes and broken mind. And I'm not risking my little lambs, or you kids, by staying here any longer. I'm not sure how much time I've got before my brain turns to mush and I become dangerous, but I want to be far away from anyone I could hurt by the time that happens."

I take one of her hands and hold it tight. There are no words that can help. None that I can summon anyway.

"Now I know you can't move your man yet, and that y'all need to stay under the radar, so I won't tell them at the hospital who I am or where I'm from."

"They'll pressure you," I warn.

There are compulsory reporting requirements and contact-tracing procedures for plague patients in Q-bays and biocontainment units.

"Honey, about the worst thing that can happen to a body is already happening to me. I ain't going to be scared into telling on you by a bunch of white-coats. And in a few more days they won't be getting any sense out of me anyway. Y'all will be safe to stay here for a while yet. Just take care of my kids, okay?"

"Of course."

"For now, tell them I've gone visiting family. Come to that, might be safer to tell everybody that story. But when you and your team move on, call the authorities on this number" — she hands me a card printed with a name and number of the social services regional manager — "and let them know I'm gone and they should send someone to come take over. And see here?" She lays a trembling hand on an old wooden cigar box on the bookshelf behind her. "I've written goodbye letters to each of my kids here at the shelter and put them in here for safe-keeping. You make sure they get them before you light out."

"I will. I promise." My voice cracks on the last word, and I swallow hard, determined not to burden her with my grief.

"I'm leaving my will, such as it is — Lord knows I'm no millionaire — on the desk for the authorities to find when they come, but this package is for my sister." She hands me a large padded envelope with an address scrawled on the top. "It's just a letter and a few odds and ends that I know she'd like to have. My mother's wedding ring and some photos of us when we were just scrawny li'l girls. Things like that. She'd want to have them, but if those disposal techs get a hold of it, they'll just incinerate it all." She pauses, seemingly tired from all the talking. Her eyes move to the glass of water then flick away. She gives a rasping cough and says, "One day, when it's safe and the post starts up again, will you send that to her?"

"Yes."

I will. I will get this package to Miss Edna Clark of

Warrior River Road, Tuscaloosa.

"Come, child, you give me a hug and then let me slip out. I don't want any fuss, you hear?"

I put an arm around her slumped shoulders as we leave the office, and leave it there as we walk down the hall. At the front door, she pauses and says, "Oh, I forgot to tell you — I've got a bunch of candy stashed in the filing cabinet in my office. If you're still here by Halloween, the way we do it here is the kids try to make some kind of costume. Then I give the older teens bags full of candy and the little ones go knocking at their bedroom doors, trick-or-treating. It gets a little loud, but they love it. You'll remember?"

I nod then pull her into my arms and hold her close.

"You are a magnificent woman, Miss Tallulah," I say fiercely. "You have saved lives and given hope and so much love to so many people."

She sighs, pulls back and wipes the tears streaming down her face with her apron. As she opens the front door, Carlos bounces down the stairs. He gives Tallulah a curious stare.

"Where you going, Miss Tally?"

Her gaze meets mine. What to say? Luckily, Carlos doesn't wait for an answer.

"Can I have a cookie, Miss Tally, can I?"

"Carlos, you can have them all!"

He squeals with delight and runs away to the kitchen. Tally's arms half rise from her sides — I know she wants to hug him tight one last time. But she won't. She'll leave this house and drive herself to the hospital, where she'll suffer and die alone.

"You take our love with you — remember that," I say in a choked whisper as she passes out the doorway.

She gives me a little wave, and then she's gone.

I stand unmoving in the doorway — as still as a deer in the woods, as still as the hunter with his crosshairs poised over the target of her eye.

It takes mere seconds for my tears to clear and hot anger to flood me. My body contracts into a hard, concentrated missile of rage. My eyes narrow, my muscles tighten, my jaw sets. My heart thuds my need to wreak havoc. My hands prickle with the urge to destroy.

This war! *This* war!

I slam the front door closed with all the strength in my arm and all the fury in my heart. The loud bang reverberates through the house. Down the hall, Bruce sticks his head out of the games room.

"Blue?"

I don't know what the expression on my own face is, but his is a mixture of curiosity and concern.

"I am going shooting. Are you coming with?" I say.

"Hellz to the yeah!"

In my room, I blow my nose and clip my hair back from my face. I retrieve my weapons from the closet where I'd locked them and assemble my rifle. Running a hand over the smooth curves of its stock and checking the internal magazine is fully loaded, I feel calmer already. Snatching up the new suppressor and extra ammunition, I head downstairs, and I'm fitting it to the end of the barrel when I pass Quinn's room.

His door is open, and he must catch a glimpse of me as I pass, because he calls, "Jinxy?"

My feet do not slow or stumble, and I do not reply.

In the games room, the boys are already waiting for me. A couple of teens are seated in front of PC's. They're wearing their virtual reality headsets and are lost in The Game. Evyan sits cross-legged on a low coffee table in the middle of the room, her gaze moving from Bruce and Cameron to me.

Bruce is grinning from ear to ear, like Christmas has come early; Cameron's expression is more inscrutable. He hands out protective gear, and we slip on the disposable PPE suits, pull up the hoods and fit on the face masks. We strap on our weapons.

Evyan eyes our arsenal and demands, "And where are you three going?"

Ignoring her, I set off down the hall to the kitchen, where the back door that leads onto the alley is. Bruce and Cameron fall into step behind me.

"Wait! Have you spoken to Quinn and Connor about this?" Evyan says.

Bruce snorts in derision.

Last time I left the shelter, it was via the front door. I was acting out of love, desperate to save Robin, and Quinn and I were on the same team. Last time I was ready to risk myself to save my brother. This time I'm ready and willing, eager even, to kill anything — *any*thing — that looks dangerous. This time, the back door seems more appropriate. My motives are less pure, my actions will be a lot less noble, and Quinn would never join me in this mission.

And — right now? — I couldn't care less.

We unlock the back door and step out into the alley behind. It's a blustery day. Gusts of wind kick up swirls of dust and dry leaves, but there's no rain or clouds to hide us. The sun will be shining its full brightness on what I'm about to do.

"Hey, stop! Where are you going?" Evyan calls after us.

It's Cameron who replies.

"Hunting."

Chapter 30

Falling out

Evyan is waiting for us when we return, several hours later.

"Where did you go?" she asks me.

"What are you, my mother?"

"Believe me, I have no desire at all to be genetically related to *you*," Evyan sneers.

"Sorry. Forgot who I was talking to. My probation officer, then?"

"What were you doing out there?"

"Making the world safer for freedom."

"Quinn's been asking for you. But I guess you were having too much fun with your boys and your toys to care about how he's doing."

I give her a hard, flat stare.

"Do not mess with me today, Evyan," I say slowly. "I am capable of anything."

Bruce cackles delightedly. "I'd back off if I was you, Goth-girl. The ice-maiden is back. And she is le-thal!"

Evyan looks set to continue the argument, but Cameron distracts her by asking if she knows how to crack a safe, and I use the moment to slip out of the room.

In the bathroom, I lather up a squirt of germ-killing liquid soap and wash my hands three times. When Robin and

I were little, Mom used to make us sing a song while we scrubbed, to make sure we did it for long enough to be thorough. Now, as I rub the lather over and over my hands, the old jingle comes back to me. *If you're dirty and you know it, wash your hands.* I push the suds between my fingers, into my knuckles and the creases of my palms. *If you're dirty and you know it, then your hands will surely show it.* I clean under my nails, watching the stained water swirl down the drain. *If you're dirty and you know it, wash your hands.*

My eyes, in the mirror, are shuttered — inviting nothing, revealing nothing. My lips are narrowed. I look … hard. And I'm grateful for it, because it's the hardness that's holding me together.

I'd like to avoid Quinn, but Beth finds me and tells me he's asking for me.

"Try to keep him calm, okay?" she says, anxiously scanning my face.

When I enter his room, Quinn is standing, somewhat unsteadily, beside his bed.

"Look, Ma, no ironing board," he says, beaming proudly at his achievement.

"Very good," I say.

I try to give him a smile in return, but there isn't one to be found anywhere inside me. His brows come together in a frown, and he sits down heavily on the bed.

"Where were you?"

"I was out. I needed to think, to clear my head."

"You mean you needed to kill something," comes a deep voice from behind me. It's only then that I see Connor is also in the room, slouched up against the back wall, chewing on a match. "Maybe even someone."

Quinn shoots his brother a sharp, enquiring glance.

"She went out shooting with those two thugs. Evyan told me," Connor explains.

Thanks, Evyan. Glad we're all on the same side here.

"If I remember correctly, you didn't have a problem with me shooting when you were the one choosing the targets," I bite back.

"So what were your targets today?" Quinn asks. His tone is completely neutral, but I still feel judged.

"A dog, and … other plague vectors," I reply.

"Such as human beings?" Connor demands.

"We're at *war*! The plague, and the people spreading it, are the real enemy, don't you get that?" I say, looking from Connor to Quinn, wishing I could make them understand. "So what if PlayState is selling us gloves and games and politicians? We've wasted so much time on your precious 'second war' — putting all our energy into trying to uncover grand conspiracies, and track the money trails, and find out what ASTA's doing. But all the while, terrorists have continued their attacks, and the plague keeps killing people. That's the first war. That's the *real* war."

"Are these Bruce's ideas?" Quinn asks.

"What? Jinxy has a thought bouncing around in her empty head, so someone else must have put it there? I'm quite capable of having my own ideas, thank you very much," I say, outraged.

"Sorry, I didn't mean —" Quinn begins.

"Then if it wasn't that oaf who inspired your grand mission of death and destruction," Connor sneers, "what did?"

"Tallulah. That's what."

They stare at me blankly. Clearly they weren't expecting that response.

"Tallulah was bitten by an infected dog. She caught rat fever and is, at this very moment, likely lying in a plague ward at Community General, waiting for the most horrific death possible."

"Oh, Jinxy," says Quinn, his face creased with pain and concern. He holds out a hand to me and I take it, hold tight.

I look straight into his eyes as I speak. "All these deaths, Quinn. Tallulah and Nicky and my father." My voice breaks on the last word. "And the killings — Sarge and Zonia and Darius — it's all because of the plague. Can't you see that?"

"And you think you're going to stop the plague by running out with your pals and killing a few rats, cats, dogs and M&M's every now and then? That's going to end the 'first war', is it?" Connor says, his voice dripping with derision.

"*Connor*," Quinn warns.

"It's better than sitting around doing nothing while people die! What's *your* war doing to end the plague?" I challenge Connor.

"Oh, it's 'your war' again now, is it?" Connor says. He turns to Quinn and adds, "I told you she wasn't on our side."

"Connor, will you please shut up," Quinn snaps. He takes a calming breath and then says, "Jinx, I don't think the government *wants* to end the plague, not really, not completely. As long as it continues, they'll stay in power and make more money." His voice is calm, but intensity lights his eyes and, as always when he's with his brother, his accent is stronger. "But just imagine what could happen if people stopped playing The Game, stopped getting brainwashed into buying and voting and living in ways that profit the government and its cronies? If everyone knew the real, rather than the exaggerated risks, of contracting the plague? If all that money and manpower was put into finding a cure or a vaccination? Think!"

"I'm done thinking," I say stubbornly. "I never was a thinker."

"You never were a killer, either," Quinn says gently.

"She never was a *rebel*, that's for certain," Connor says.

"*Connor!*" Quinn stands up suddenly, fists clenched,

looking ready to hit his brother.

"Well, the rebellion's all yours now, Comrade Connor. I quit." I spin around and leave the room, chin held high.

But just a few paces outside, I slump against the wall, pressing the heels of my hands into my eyes to force back the tears that threaten. I hate fighting with Quinn. Especially when I agree with him. Because he's right — about the warmongers and profiteers — I know that. And he's right about me, too. I never was a killer. I never wanted to hurt or shoot a living creature. I just happened to be stupendously good at it. And it was my ticket out of the claustrophobia and endless boredom of home.

But the thing is, *I'm* right, too. Freedom isn't a place, it's a state of being. We'll never be free as long as the plague thrives, and I don't know how to fight it any other way than with my gun and my sharp eye and my steady hands.

Raised voices from the room yank me out of my miserable thoughts.

"What do you mean by that?" Quinn is saying.

"I mean, that's *her* decided then. What's our next step, d'ya think? Where should we go from here?"

"*Our*? *We*? We — who?" Quinn says.

"You and me, obviously. And Neil and Evyan if they're willing to recommit to the rebellion. We'll find another rebel pod and keep fighting!"

I take a step closer to the doorway, needing with every fiber of my being to hear Quinn's response.

"There's something you don't seem to understand, Connor. Jinxy and me — we're one. We're like *this*," I hear Quinn say, and I can imagine him holding up fingers twisted together. "And I'm not going to leave her to go swanning about with you and your rebels. Especially not when I can see how hard she's hurting."

Connor must snort or pull a face at that, because Quinn

continues, "She *is*. She puts on a tough act, but the pain is almost crushing her, I can tell."

He knows me so well. He sees right through to the real, damaged me inside.

"*Crushing*? Are you yanking my chain, boyo? The only crushing going on with her is the rekindling of her affections for that brute, Bruce. Evyan's told me all about them."

"That's rubbish. You're talking bollocks, now. The only thing between them is friendship."

"Are you so certain?" Connor's voice is taunting.

"Yeah, I'm absolutely sure," Quinn says firmly.

You tell him, Quinn.

"I don't trust her — never have. And he's a total *cúl tóna*."

Cool toner? What's that?

"*I* trust her. And she trusts him. And that's good enough for me. I'm lucky to have her. And Bruce isn't a dickhead. He's strong, loyal, brave, and he can protect her better than I ever could. What makes *me* such a catch?"

"Now *you're* the one who's talking bollocks."

Finally, I agree with Connor on something.

"Look, they called you because they thought I might die from that knock on my noggin. And you came because you care. And I appreciate that, I really do. But as you can see, I'm good and getting better. So you're free to go, now."

"Are you sending me away, Quinn? Are you choosing *her* — that fecking little gun-toting blonde — over me? Over family?" Connor's voice is full of shocked disbelief.

My heart is pounding so hard I want to tell it to hush. Quinn's next words will be do-or-die for our relationship. Everything is on the line.

"Yes," I hear him say. "I choose Jinxy."

My heart swells with love and hope. He chooses me. *Me.* He doesn't agree with everything I believe, he doesn't approve of everything I do, but he chooses me. I have never loved him more than I do at this moment.

I punch the air in victory, trying to make no noise because Quinn is speaking again.

"The question is, what do *you* choose, Connor? Because you can either accept her as a permanent, as a *beloved* part of my life, and treat her with respect, or you can bugger off and do whatever makes your rebel heart happy somewhere else."

Connor bursts out of the room and clocks me standing in the hall. With a furious glare at me, he storms off. *Don't let the door hit you on the way out,* I think, giving his departing back a grin and a cheerful waggle of my fingers. Then I go back to the man I love. I am permanent and beloved in his life.

And he is in mine.

Chapter 31

From the inside out

October 24

This morning, most of the kids in the shelter are in the games room, playing at the computers and chattering excitedly about the Go!Game, because today PlayState announced the nationwide release that will be happening in one week's time. No less a personage than Alex Hawke, president of the Southern Sector, will be visiting PlayState on Halloween to launch the release.

There are amazing trailers on the web and in The Game of what the new version will look like. They show kids in their houses hunting repbots in closets and drawers, finding and capturing tiny spy drones hiding in robes hanging behind bedroom doors or inside microwaves, shooting Alien Axis Army soldiers breaking into houses via windows and decon units. Honestly, it looks awesome. Come Halloween, every kid in the country is going to be addicted within minutes, even without any subliminal messages.

This Halloween, get ready to fight real monsters! The advertisements chime.

Robin is gearing up to do just that. He's been working

day and night, along with his secret team of virtually connected hackers, to create the perfect takedown of The Game. He says their plan, which they're calling Operation Black Hat, is to upload malware into PlayState's main centralized servers, implanting it into the new version of The Game.

It's six days since Tallulah left, eight days since she was bitten. The average number of days from infection to death is thirteen. By now her skin will be covered with a rash of bleeding spots, her eyes will be red, perhaps already bleeding, she'll be drifting in and out of consciousness, making sense in neither state. She'll have started the rocking or head-banging, and might already be coughing up great clots of black blood and hemorrhaging from her every orifice. That's if she's still alive. She may be one of victims who goes quickly.

Or they may have euthanized her already.

And here at the shelter, her precious lambs are excitedly playing games, counting the days until they can immerse themselves in more virtual reality, and thinking up costumes they can wear for in-house trick or treating.

Quinn beckons me from the doorway. In the week since Connor left, Quinn has recovered well. He swears he's feeling fine, apart from the headaches which come when he gets tired.

"Neil's calling a meeting of all of us. And now would be a good time while they" — Quinn tilts his head toward the kids clustered around screens — "are distracted."

"Has he found out something?"

"Yeah, and Beth says it's big."

I fetch Robin and Sofia, and we join the others in the kitchen, who're sitting around the big wooden table in the center and leaning against walls and the huge refrigerator. Evyan perches on the counter opposite me, kicking her black-booted feet against the cupboard beneath in a random, irritating rhythm. Neil confirms that everyone is present and closes the door to the hall.

"You're all very young," he says, earning an eye-roll from Evyan. "Too young, some of you, to remember the way the world used to work for teenagers."

"Dude, I remember fine — I was already fourteen when the plague started," Bruce says.

"And that's about the time you would have started thinking about what career you wanted to pursue when you left school."

"I was going to run a hunting-supplies store with my uncle up in Montana."

"Figures," Evyan says.

"What were you going to be when you were big, Goth-girl? A car thief? Cat burglar?"

"I planned to become a mechanic, for your information."

"Oo-ooh, a grease monkey," Bruce mocks. "What were you going to do, bro?" He elbows Cameron.

"Maybe cattle ranching."

"Aren't we getting off track here?" Quinn asks.

"Not really," says Neil. "Did you have an idea of what you wanted to do when you left school?"

"I thought … well, when I was younger, before the plague, I figured I might like to study architecture," Quinn says.

"I never knew that," I tell him.

"I guess it's not something we talk about," Quinn replies.

"Exactly!" Neil points a finger at him. "Jinxy, Robin — you're the youngest here. What were your career plans?"

Robin and I exchange glances, shrugging at the same moment in exactly the same way.

"Don't know, never really thought about it," Robin says.

"We were only twelve years old when the plague started and everything changed," I add. "And after I started playing The Game, that's all I really wanted to do."

"And that, in a nutshell, is what I've figured out from the code I've analyzed," Neil says, sitting back in his chair, slapping his hands on his thighs and looking smug.

There's a moment's confused silence, then Bruce says, "Dude, you're going to have to connect the dots here. I dunno what you're trying to say."

"Let *me* try to explain," Beth says, with an exasperated glance at her brother. "When teens hit fourteen or fifteen, schools generally kicked into gear with career guidance — they'd organize career exhibitions, guest speakers, maybe even psychometric testing and college visits. Teens could do specialized programs during their summer vacations — space camp or theater school or robotics retreats. At some schools, kids had to do community service hours at different places — hospitals, animal shelters, garden centers — or do job shadowing."

"I got to do that once," Sofia says, smiling wryly. "I went to a hospital and shadowed a gastric surgeon. Ran out of the operating theater and hurled up and down the length of the hall. Crossed that one off the list pretty quick."

"I thought it might be cool to be a butcher — got a job at World of Meats one summer. But no way, man, it was disgusting! And the *smell*." Bruce shudders.

"Nobody cares," Evyan says, drumming her heels on the cupboard.

I care. I'm fascinated to hear what everyone planned on doing when they grew up. If there hadn't been a war on, if I hadn't been channeled into ASTA via The Game, what would I have wanted to do with my life? I can't think of a single thing. I realize how few careers I truly know about, and I'm struck again by how much we've missed out on.

"Beth?" Quinn prompts, interrupting a burgeoning squabble between Bruce and Evyan.

"The point is, kids learned what they liked and didn't like

doing by being out in the world, trying different things, being exposed to a wide range of work," Beth says.

Neil gets up, and while he fills the kettle and rummages through the cupboards, his sister continues her explanation.

"Adolescence is a time of exploring and forming one's identity, including work identity. What would usually happen is you'd find several fields you were interested in or had an aptitude for. You'd go off to college, take some courses, maybe drop a few as you discovered that wasn't your thing, and sign up for something else. You had freedom to explore and choose, to try and fail, to become anything you wanted." Beth says. "But the plague changed all that. Suddenly kids were trapped inside their houses. When you weren't doing schoolwork, you were playing that wretched game. You were insulated from the world, and your range of choices shrank radically."

Neil, who is sniffing at a box of herb tea, says, "The Game helped distract you from the reality that you were essentially trapped. You were lost in other, fantasy worlds inside your heads and machines. But it wasn't reality."

Insulated. Trapped. Lost. The words capture the essence of my life.

"With virtual reality, it was almost as good as real life," Sofia says. "And probably more fun."

She sounds a little wistful. She was in the games room, too, this morning, looking over the shoulder of a girl lost in The Game, pointing out clues on the screen.

"And *that's* where the real danger lies," Beth says, startling me when she slaps a hand on the table to emphasize her point. "At its deepest levels, the human brain doesn't know the difference between what's real and what's sufficiently vividly imagined."

"Come again?" Quinn is fully alert now. I can almost hear the wheels of his brain turning.

"When you watch a movie, and the killer yanks back the shower curtain and stabs the heroine, don't you get a fright? Jump in your seat and gasp?"

"Or scream?" Evyan suggests, almost smiling.

"Always suspected you'd be a screamer, E." Bruce laughs.

Evyan kicks him hard in the leg, and he hops on the spot, rubbing his thigh and grumbling about how nobody has a sense of humor anymore.

Speaking louder, Beth says, "You react that way because you're so absorbed, that it's *as if* it's real at some level, and you're involved. Consciously, of course, you know it's not happening to you, that it's not even really happening at all — the blood is fake, the knife is plastic, the killer's an actor. But it *feels* real. Now multiply that effect when you're in a virtual reality environment, and you *are* the person running, searching, coding, shooting. As far as your brain is concerned, it's real."

"And the big problem with that is …?" Robin asks.

Pouring boiling water into a chipped mug, Neil says, "Neurological molding."

Beside me, Quinn gasps. He's understood something I haven't yet.

Chapter 32

Come out fighting

"The brain is made up of cells called neurons, millions of them," Beth says, "and what determines your intelligence, your talent and skill in certain areas — music or verbal ability or coding, for example —"

"Or the fine-motor control required for accurate sharpshooting?" Quinn says.

"Yes, or that." Beth nods and smiles at him. She can tell he's got it. "It depends on the number and strength of connections between neurons. And *that's* a product of both nature and nurture. The genetics you're born with, and the stimulation you're exposed to — what you learn, do, and practice in your formative years. And how intensively."

"And just think about what The Game exposes you to," Neil adds, dunking a tea bag in his mug.

"So we learn and practice certain skills in the virtual reality programs. And we get better at them, and ASTA selects the best and trains them to be even better?" Robin says. "But we always knew that. That's nothing new."

"What you didn't know is that the Game tests you the first few times you play, guiding you through different roles, all the while assessing your inherent aptitude for different functions," Neil replies.

I have only the vaguest recollection of playing as anything other than a sniper, but I do remember that Robin tried a bunch of different roles.

"And then it channels you into the one you're best at, and increasingly you play, and learn, only that role. Nothing else."

True. Once I started sniping, I never tried anything else.

"Didn't you ever wonder why you never got bored playing only one role? Why you never even thought of playing The Game as a different specialist?" Beth asks.

Now that she mentions it, no, I never did.

"Weird," says Cameron, frowning.

"Right?" adds Bruce.

"Bitter," says Neil, puckering his face at the taste of his tea and stirring in a heaped spoon of sugar.

"You teens, who are so quickly and easily bored with everything else, get sucked right in and don't stop, don't change course. And, of course, you're too busy playing to take a good hard look at what's happening to your rights, to question the laws the government is passing." Beth gets up and pours herself a glass of water at the sink, turns to face us again. "And parents don't complain, because the kids are occupied, safe at home, not even tempted to go outside, and not whining about how bored they are. It's a win-win."

"And the biggest winners are A Play Test and their government allies, because — and this is the crux of what I found out — all the while, your brains are being hardwired by the smart program," Neil says.

"The program which subliminally gets you to grow increasingly addicted to it, don't forget," Beth adds.

"And you're funneled through a carefully plotted succession of neurocognitive enhancement exercises aimed at developing synaptic webs and neural pathways, which in turn mitigate your behavior and deterministically select your future paths," says Neil.

"Huh?" Bruce grunts, looking at Beth for a translation.

She bites her lip, clearly thinking of a way to explain this simply. "Back at the house, I saw you guys exercising in the yard."

"Yeah, and?"

"Imagine if you only worked the muscles of one leg. Or even of only one calf," Beth suggests. "Imagine how big that muscle would grow, how powerful it would become."

Bruce smiles and nods slowly, slitting his eyes and casting a sideways glance at Evyan. I'll bet he's thinking how far he could kick her with such a leg.

"And the rest of your muscles, that you never used, would shrink and weaken to the point where you wouldn't be able to lift something heavy with your arm, or do a sit-up, even if you wanted to?"

"And so?" says Bruce.

"Well, The Game is like neuro-gym. That's what was happening to your brains," Beth says, waving a finger around the room at all of us. "What is happening to the brains of hundreds of thousands of kids who happened to show an aptitude for one of only a handful of valuable skills."

"The rest they didn't seem to care about — except, of course, as easily programmed consumers and voters," Neil says, sipping on his tea.

The kitchen door bursts open, and a tall girl with lime-green dreadlocks asks us if we're going to be much longer. "We're getting hungry," she complains.

"We won't be much longer, Chesiree," Beth says, and the girl retreats.

"So some kids get good at some skills and get offered jobs via ASTA. While others just buy Style Tapa fashions. What's the big deal?" Evyan asks.

"I think I get it, or some of it," Quinn says. "You, Jinxy,

were just twelve when you started playing. Other kids were even younger. Bruce said his six-year-old cousin plays the cartoon version. Now imagine if you lived in a country where almost all kids from a very young age are removed from their schools and families, tested, and if they show any potential for one of a few desirable skills, then they're channeled into the kind of training that results in only those skills being developed in their brains. Imagine you're one of those kids," Quinn says, looking around at all of us, "and you get specialized training for several hours every single day — three, or eight, or fifteen hours at a stretch. You practice it over and over and over again, honing your ability, until you become a genius at it, until it's automatic, until it's who you are."

"While other areas and potential abilities are entirely neglected," Beth interjects. "And you lose those permanently, because the rule of the brain is: use it or lose it."

"So you're steered in one direction that will prove useful and very profitable for the government, but without consciously deciding to do it, without having a real choice," Quinn says. "The Game takes away your freedom of choice. It *programs* you."

"Maybe you had great hand-eye coordination and excellent fine motor control," Beth says. "That could've set you up later in life to be a violinist or an artist, a basketball player or a brain surgeon. But, instead, you'll be *programmed* to be a sniper — the best sniper that ever was because your brain is being hardwired to do that, and only that. You've been so addicted to The Game, so tightly manipulated through its various programs and neuro-developmental exercises, that you couldn't become an artist, even if you wanted to."

"And you wouldn't want to, not with the way the subliminal messages influence you," Neil says.

I get it now. I didn't choose to be a sniper — I was

chosen. Chosen by someone who didn't care whether it would make me happy or fulfilled, didn't care if that's what I actually wanted to do, didn't care whether the work matched my morals and values. It mattered only that shooting was what I *could* do, and what they could forge me into doing even better. They chose my future for me, they set me on my life course. I was an automaton, hard-wired for killing. No wonder I'm so useless at everything else.

"The training extends even beyond cognitive enhancement," Neil says. "In the sniper units of The Game, for example, they use biofeedback to condition the activation and suppression of sympathetic and parasympathetic nervous system functioning."

"What's that mean?" I ask Beth.

"Aren't you snipers exceptionally good at lowering your heart rate, slowing your breathing, narrowing your focus?"

"Yeah," I say.

"Damn straight," Bruce agrees.

Cameron merely nods.

"Well, that's because your brains and bodies have been developed by The Game to be that way. It would make you able to stay calm and keep your hands steady when you have to shoot, I guess."

It would make you able to be an ice-maiden.

"Wait, some freak scientists decided what they wanted me to do and trained me up so that's all I *could* do?" Bruce demands, his face red with outrage. He stands up, knocking over his chair, and walks over to the window, staring out. But I imagine his focus is inwards. On who we are, and aren't. And why. "They've turned us into lab rats, man! Rats in a freaking maze."

"That's what they were testing and measuring at Stapla," I say. "They were checking how our brains had changed, how we performed on our specialist tests compared to others who'd trained in different areas."

No wonder they were flummoxed by my lack of ability in intel skills. All that neural programming for so many years, and no real ability? It would have made zero sense.

"Super-soldiers," Cameron says.

"Precisely!" Neil beams at Cameron. "The Game is merely a very sophisticated mass-testing instrument to select and neuro-program talented individuals, who are then selected for cadet training programs in real-world conditions. ASTA both harvests and continues to program already specialized brains."

"In some of the email exchanges I hacked into, I found out that ASTA recommends cadets to the Department of Defense and gets a hefty bounty for every one that's accepted," Robin says.

"Soldiers, ready-trained and ready for action. Often at the tender age of sixteen," Quinn says, his eyes resting on me. "And that age will be falling every year as younger and younger kids play."

I think about a child-army of eight- and nine-year-olds, carrying rifles, going about their lethal business on the streets of our nation before they even have any real understanding of the consequences of what they're doing. Perhaps The Game is even designed to suppress moral development. Certainly I was the only cadet in my squad who seemed to have any qualms at all about killing infected people. And maybe I only had that glitch because of what happened to my dad.

"We've been soldiers in this war since the day we started playing," Quinn says. "The Game is real."

"I've been programmed to be a coder. I would probably have gone all the way, too, and become one of their robotic slaves if I hadn't got the creeps with the whole setup when I went to visit Jinx on family days," Robin says.

"I only questioned what we were doing because Connor

used to sit me down and make me think critically. He was almost twenty by the time the Game came out and said he was too old for computer games, so he never played it," Quinn says. Then he scrubs a hand across his mouth and adds hoarsely, "But Kerry plays all the time. *All* the time."

"We've got to end it. We've got to stop that augmented-reality game rolling out on Halloween," says Robin.

Silence falls as we all look around at each other, thinking about free will and the full horror of what the government has unleashed on its own people. Roth said the war was coming. Hawke, too, in his last announcement. Maybe they know something about the next onslaught from our enemies, maybe they've had information about it for the longest time, and that's why they've been building their army of super-soldiers.

I remember listening to Roth's welcome speech on my first day at ASTA. She'd said The Game helped identify and develop the skills of gifted individuals. She told us then, and again at our graduation ceremony, that it was our duty to serve our country, that we'd be valuable in the war against our enemies. But none of us had a clue how deep the training and the "service" went. When she interrogated me at Stapla, before she turned me over to the torturer, she'd said there was *nothing* she wouldn't do to keep this country safe. But I could never have imagined she meant *this*.

My mind ticks back to the night when we rescued Robin. Roth remarked that they'd failed utterly in their goal to "install a correct mindset" in me. She'd meant that literally, I now realize. And Leya had spoken of finding smart ways to thwart our enemies, of training people up to be ready and able to take the fight directly to the terrorists. She must have known about this grand scheme, too.

I glance at Cameron and Bruce. We're patsies, all three of us. I was shocked and appalled when I discovered what I thought ASTA was really up to — that we'd been selected and trained to kill plague victims. But that wasn't the real agenda either, it was just 'real-world practice.' We'd actually been chosen and trained to become soldiers, master snipers who would be deployed in some future war arena, without ever actually having volunteered.

We're freaks and slaves.

Something clicks into place inside me at that thought, something solid and resolute. When I came back from shooting with Bruce and Cameron, I'd challenged Quinn, "So what if PlayState is selling us gloves and games and politicians?" Maybe adverts don't matter all that much when stacked against the ravages of the plague. But this does. My stomach clenches at the thought of how I've been manipulated, brainwashed, and calibrated like a drone robot, programmed to kill.

"It's a masterful plan," Neil says.

"You think?" I say. "I can see a glaring hole in the middle of it."

"What's that?" Quinn says.

"They've trained us to be geniuses at our skills, right? But they can't control *what* we use our skills for."

Quinn's face splits into a grin, and he gives my thigh a squeeze under the table.

"They may have turned you intel cadets," I say, pointing to Quinn and Sofia, "into super-skilled agents who could spot patterns and make sense of mega-loads of data, but they never expected you to use those talents at figuring out what they're up to. They may have trained you to write code, Robin, but they can't control what code you create, or how you use it. They may have turned us into expert sharpshooters," I say to Cameron and Bruce, "but they can't control what we shoot. Our super-specialized brains can as easily be used against them as for them. Because now that we're no longer playing their freaking game, they're no longer playing us."

Part Four

Chapter 33

Out of excuses

October 31

It's the morning of Halloween.

Today, all around the country, children will be dressing up in scary costumes and staying indoors, safe from the real danger outside, waiting to receive their drone deliveries of gruesome candy — bloodypops, liquirats, veined gummy eyeballs, candy bloodbags, coffin crunchies — ready to trick or treat their own families.

Here in the shelter, Halloween will go ahead as Tallulah requested. I've handed her stash of candy to Beth, who's organizing the in-house Halloween fun together with a few of the older teens. All over the house, kids are creating makeshift costumes from cardboard, toilet paper and PPE suits.

I remember, before the plague, getting dressed up and going out onto the streets of the neighborhood with Robin. Mom used to like dressing us in twin-themed costumes, like Tweedledee and Tweedledum, or the Mario Brothers. Or she'd send us out dressed as some kind of punny pair. Once, when we were eleven, she made me go as a piece of bread smeared with peanut butter, and Robin as one covered in jelly.

"It's PB and J, don't you get it?" she'd told my dad when

he stared at us, wondering, I guess, what the heck we were supposed to be. "Oh, come on, it's funny."

"We're supposed to be *scary*," I complained. "We're not supposed to be a joke."

"Yeah, we're supposed to *do* the tricking. You're not supposed to play a trick on us," Robin had said.

The year after that, we were allowed to choose our own costumes. And the year after that we stayed home. There was no need to go out to encounter fear — horror had come to us. The plague ruled the streets, real monsters were plotting our destruction, Dad was dead, and Mom was in a permanent fog of depression and grief. That night we *ate* PB&J's — our standard self-made supper when Mom was going through a bad patch — and stayed indoors, watching not-so-scary old movies on T.V.

"Jinxy!"

Quinn leaps into the kitchen, startling me out of my reverie when he waves a plastic cutlass in front of my unfocused eyes.

"Why are pirates called pirates, me beauty?" Quinn demands.

I shrug.

"Because they just ARRRRRRR! And what d'ya call a pirate with two arms, two legs and two eyes, wench?"

I think for a moment, venture a guess. "Hearrrrrty?"

"No. You call 'em *beginners*!"

I can't help laughing — partly at the first-grade humor, and partly at his getup. He's in full pirate costume, complete with a stuffed parrot on one shoulder and a black eyepatch over one eye. When we discussed costumes for today, Bruce pushed hard to get Quinn to wear a Leprechaun costume, but I said he'd make a fine pirate. And he does.

Bruce immediately chose to be the Incredible Hulk. This morning, he couldn't wait to slip into the green suit and mask, and he's been storming around the shelter, bursting in on the kids with thundering roars and punches to doors and walls. I've never seen him so happy.

Cameron is decked out in the full black garb of a SWAT team officer. When I asked him why he'd chosen that disguise, he'd replied, "I like irony."

It's a good thing it's a chilly day — everyone's already getting hot, because we're all wearing double outfits. Beneath their Halloween costumes, Quinn, Bruce and Cameron are all wearing dark business suits with white shirts and conservative ties, and they have dark glasses tucked in their jacket pockets. Bruce and Cameron also have loaded pistols in shoulder- and ankle-holsters.

Neil was reluctant to wear a suit and tie, but at least he doesn't need to wear a costume since he'll be driving.

"I'd rather wear a costume," he'd protested. "I thought I could go as Sherlock Holmes. Order a deerstalker hat and a pipe. Can't someone else drive?"

"No, we need our strongest muscles as well as Sticky-Fingers over there" — I indicated Evyan — "at the gate."

Sofia is dressed as a witch in black robes and a pointed hat, and she's wearing a fake, warty nose over her own. But it was only when she covered up the tattoos around her eyes with thick concealing makeup that Robin protested, "I don't like it. It's not you."

In reply, she'd merely cackled and offered him a treat from her basket of Halloween candies.

"*You* should have gone as the witch, Evyan," Bruce says when he claps eyes on Sofia. "Or are you scared of being typecast?"

He tugs on Evyan's tail as he says it and leaps aside to avoid the swipe she takes at him. Evyan is wearing a black, formfitting catsuit, though whether she's supposed to be Catwoman or a cat burglar I don't know and don't dare ask, because she is in the mother of foul moods. Maybe it's how she carries her nerves? Even Bruce has refrained from making any ksk-ksk noises or cracking pussy jokes. It must be killing him.

"Did someone mention casting? I want only the best method actors for my project," says an orange-and-black-striped tiger with one arm in a sling. Robin must be getting into character.

Underneath his innocent-looking Tigger costume, he's wearing all black — jeans, shirt and shoes — and has stuck on a small false beard. I only just dissuaded him from topping it all off with a black beret.

"Overkill, Robin," I'd said when he tried to add the headgear to our online Halloween order.

For once, the order — totally unsuspicious for this time of year and to this place, and ordered with untraceable pre-loaded cash cards — could be delivered directly to us.

We're all in the kitchen of the shelter, playing like teens at a pre-plague Halloween party, laughing and kidding around as we dress, but it's a nervous humor. We're under no illusions. Today's mission is deadly serious and undeniably dangerous. Our goals are to drive a stake in the vampire that is PlayState and defeat the monster that is Hawke's presidency.

It occurs to me that *we're* the real zombies — not the M&M's we've always thought of in that way. They at least have agency and power as they run through the streets, attacking and spreading the plague, terrorizing the population into thoughts of, "That could have been me, it still could." We have been mere sleepwalkers, living half-lives in game-induced trance-states, obediently walking down our predestined paths in the service of the twin ghouls of Power and Profit.

I'm dressed as the Grim Reaper in flowing black robes and a skeleton face mask. I wanted to be Robin Hood but, like

Sofia, I needed an outfit that would cover the pin-striped skirt-and-jacket business suit and sensible heels we two are wearing underneath. Back in the woods with Zonia and Connor's band of rebels, when we spied on Alex Hawke's comings and goings at the remote presidential compound, we saw that his guard of secret service agents all dress like conservative business men and women. That's the look we're aiming for today, under our cloaks, stripes, hats and cat's ears. Because today is the day that PlayState aims to release the new Go!Game to the nation.

Today's the day President Hawke will be the guest of honor at PlayState's headquarters, arriving in time to cut the ribbon, or break the bottle of champagne, or whatever it is a dignitary does to launch a new version of neuro-molding, brainwashing software.

We know from the advance publicity that the release is set for noon and Hawke will be there for a live transmission of the event. We don't know what time he'll be arriving, but we aim to be a couple of hours early just in case.

I've slicked back my short hair with wet-look gel, and now I pin a false blond bun to the back of my head. The effect is severe, but I still look way too young to pass as anyone's guard. A pair of clear-lensed, horn-rimmed spectacles helps a bit though, as does an application of Sofia's dark-brown lipstick. It'll have to do.

I fit the new suppressor onto my sniper's rifle and hang it over my shoulder, under the heavy black robe. Then I grab my plastic skeleton facemask, pull up my hood and pick up the scythe that a couple of the teens helped me make from a broomstick handle and a cardboard blade wrapped in aluminum foil.

Robin is still playacting at being a movie director.

"*You!* You shall be my female lead," he says passionately, descending on Sofia and planting a kiss on her witchy nose.

Sofia points a talon-tipped finger at me and says, "I think she's the lead."

All heads swivel to me. Bruce nods, Quinn smiles, Evyan rolls her eyes, and Robin pulls an *I-told-you-so* face.

"What?" I say, startled. "Me? Uh-uh, no way, I'm not the leader."

"Jinxy-love, what are you talking about? You've taken the lead all the way through the planning of today's mission," Quinn says, grinning widely at me.

That's true. Most of our plan was suggested by me, and for the last week I have, now that I think about it, been the one guiding the plan, asking questions, trying to identify potential problems. But …

"That's admin. It's a lot different to being team leader on a life-and-death mission," I say.

"C'mon, Blue. We'll follow you." Bruce thumps one beefy fist into the other, clearly eager for some action.

"No," I say. My heart has started to beat faster.

"Jinxy, we need you to do this," Robin says simply.

"Oh, puleeze. Here we go again," Evyan sneers. "Everyone trying to pressure the biggest coward to take the lead."

"I'm not a coward!"

"She's the bravest person I know," Quinn says fiercely.

"No, she's not. She's chicken-shit. Oh, she's not afraid of facing guns and diseased rats and M&M's, or risking her own life, but those things don't actually scare her. She's a complete coward when it comes to facing up to what does scare her stupid."

"Oh yeah? And what's that supposed to be?" I demand.

"Responsibility. Making decisions and living with the consequences," Evyan says. "Guilt. It paralyzes you."

My heart is hammering, my mouth is dry. I can't think what to say, how to deny this. But she doesn't wait for me to speak anyway. She steps up to me and looks me in the eye.

"You're the most skilled fighter here. You're the best-equipped to lead this team today, but … You're. Too. Scared." She pokes me in the chest on each goading word. "You're afraid to call it in case it goes wrong, and then you'll have to wallow in your self-serving, self-indulgent, miserable guilt again. I call that *cowardly*."

I stand frozen, unmoving, unspeaking as her accusations strike to the core of me. No one else says anything either. The kitchen is so quiet that you could hear a rat's whisker twitch. I look around at the bank of faces turned to me.

Bruce and Cameron don't defend me. I remember our conversation in Neil's backyard, when Bruce told me that my doing nothing was no guarantee that people *wouldn't* get hurt. He'd used the same word as Evyan: chicken-shit. Cameron had said that my refusal to make a decision *was* a decision.

"Jinx, you're not to blame for Dad. Or my arm. Or Sarge," Robin says now, giving me a sad smile.

"It's a kind of narcissism, or megalomania," Neil weighs in. "You think you're responsible for everyone else's decisions and lives. But you're not nearly as powerful as you think you are. We have our own minds and our own wills."

Hot tears are brimming in my eyes. I look up pleadingly at Quinn. He'll defend me. He loves me — surely he'll rescue me from this?

But he loves me, so he doesn't.

"We're not fools. We know the risks. But we have enough faith in you to follow you," Quinn says.

"On condition I don't shoot?"

"No conditions. You do what you need to," he says.

Well, *that* was unexpected.

"The truth is that you *are* a leader. It's time to step up and own it." His voice is soft, his tone infinitely gentle. But his words are implacable.

"Hah!" Evyan snorts derisively. "But she won't. Because she's cowardly *and* selfish."

The words hit me like the one-two blows of a prizefighter.

Because they're true.

I *have* been both cowardly and selfish. I've been too terrified to take action, to make decisions — real ones, ones which put people's lives at risk — and take the lead. Because doing so means I have to take responsibility for how it all pans out. Even if it ends badly. I've always known I don't want to hurt anyone, but ever since Dad died and I felt the pain of losing him, and saw how Mom and Robin suffered, I don't want anyone hurt. In any way, by anyone, and especially not by me. I've thought that by not using my deadly skill and by retreating from the fight, I was protecting the ones I cared about. But that's not true.

There's no way to keep everyone safe. And not taking action, not embracing it, just because I'm afraid of making mistakes and feeling more guilt? That's not wise, it's weak. And it's cowardly.

Less than a month ago, when Quinn came to fetch me from this shelter so we could go rescue Robin, I was clear on who the enemy was, certain about what I had to do, and confident about my ability to do it. But what happened to Robin and Sarge, and what Robin told me about Dad — all that guilt derailed me. I need to get back on track.

I dash a hand across my eyes and straighten my back, blow out a slow breath.

"Okay," I say.

"Okay? You'll lead?" Sofia looks surprised.

I nod.

Quinn and the rest look relieved, but Evyan, I notice, is wearing a sly, self-satisfied grin.

"It's time to go. Everybody got what they need?" I say,

and I'm pleased that my voice sounds clear and strong.

Sofia fetches the handmade signs that she and Quinn designed last night. Evyan grabs the long duffle bag filled with camera equipment, a lighting stand, a reflective photographer's umbrella, the bipod for my sniper's rifle, and extra magazines of ammunition.

Bruce and Cameron pat their concealed weapons. Cameron gives me a nod to indicate that he's ready. Bruce slips an extra item into the slit he's cut into one leg of his padded foam costume, then roars, "*Hulk smash!*" and pounds both fists on a nearby table.

"Yeah, that's going to grow old real fast, moron," Evyan says.

Robin and Neil check their pockets for the umpteenth time. They each have a small thumb drive loaded with the malware that we aim to upload into PlayState*'s* data center servers. In a few hours' time, when the Go!Game goes live and millions of people download the new software, they'll also be downloading a hidden virus intended to paralyze the game and to broadcast an announcement about what has truly been happening in The Game, as well as the truth about the plague — Quinn insisted on that. He'd said, "It'll be a new kind of PSA — one that truly *is* in the interest of serving the public." And it won't end with the SEE-SAY jingle that encourages us to suspect and rat on each other.

Admitting that she had neither "the stomach nor the skills" for this fight, Beth has decided to sit it out at the shelter. She's taking her new role as unofficial house-mother seriously and has grown very attached to the kids living here.

She's serving milk and cookies to a cluster of her charges in the games room when I go to tell her we're leaving. Carlos doesn't lift his eyes from the cookies, but one of the younger girls gives an involuntary yelp when she lays eyes on me.

My choice of soul-harvester costume suddenly seems like

an omen. A chill of premonition ripples through me. Lives may well be claimed today.

Will mine be one of them — or will I be doing the killing?

Chapter 34

Outfits

Go!Game!
Go Prez Hawke!
We ♥ The Game!!

"What do we want? The Go!Game. When do we want it? Now!"

We wave our signs and chant our cry in a bizarre Halloween pack outside the gates of PlayState's headquarters, down the lane from ASTA. Despite the chill breeze, I'm feeling hot and stuffy in my robes and mask. The lenses of my spectacles are fogging up, the hairpins holding my bun in place are digging into my scalp, and the new shoes are starting to pinch. But it can't be long now until Hawke arrives — we've already been going at it for over an hour since Neil dropped us off and then went to hide the van.

My pirate mops his face with a red handkerchief and mutters to me, "You think it's going to work?"

Hell, no. I'm not sure of anything.

"It has to," I say. "It's the only plan we've got."

The perimeter fence is as high as I remember, topped with razor wire and electrified strands. The gate itself is a heavy black palisade barrier that slides on a rail, powered by a gate motor on the inside of the fence. Surveillance cameras mounted on poles inside the compound point in various directions. One is aimed at the gatehouse — where two armed guards control access to the compound — and the spot where the gate opens.

That camera is going to be a problem. I could take it out — it wouldn't be a difficult shot — but if the monitor showing the video feed of the gate suddenly went blank in the security surveillance room, someone would surely come to investigate. And if they see it's been shot, they'll sound the alarm, and our mission will be over before it starts.

I borrow Quinn's pirate spyglass. Inside the fake wood-and-brass housing, the telescope is real enough. I look back down the road. There's still no sign of Hawke. I take another look at the camera aimed at the gate. It's mounted on a screw-tightened, swiveling bracket. If only I had a paintball gun with a white paintball, I could splat it directly on the lens, and it would look like bird poop. There might not even be any immediate urgency to fix it. But today, our weapons and our ammunition are real.

Both guards emerge from their quarters and take up position at the gate.

"Y'all need to clear off, now," says the one, a middle-aged man with a receding hairline and an expanding waistline.

"Yeah, they're on their way," says the other, a rat-faced woman with tightly curled hair.

"OOH-RAH!" Bruce shouts, sounding more like a marine than a comic character.

"Let the games begin," Robin says.

"Go, go, Go-Go-Game! Go, go, Go-Go-Game!" the rest of us chant.

Quinn dances a little jig which makes his fake parrot wobble drunkenly.

I peer down the road through the telescope and see the

approaching convoy.

"Here we go," I say. "Three vehicles. I reckon the president's in the middle one."

"Come on, y'all. Move out of the way there!" The security guard flaps his hands at us, but all our attention is on the convoy.

Two black Chevy Suburbans with tinted windows come to a halt about ten meters away from us. A black van, also unmarked, pulls up behind them.

"What do we want? The Go!Game! When do we want it? Now!"

Bruce roars, Robin bounces, Sofia cackles, and Quinn pats his parrot. Beside me, Evyan flexes her fingers and rolls her shoulders, limbering up for what comes next.

Cursing the narrow eye slits of my death mask, I study the figures who emerge from the front vehicle. Two men and one woman walk toward us, their hands hovering cautiously near their holstered weapons. They're secret service agents, members of the president's own guard.

"Nailed the outfits," Quinn whispers to me.

The agents are indeed wearing suits and shoes very like the ones we sourced from clothing suppliers on the net.

"We need more of them to get out," I say, loud enough for our group of eight to hear. "We need six."

"What's going on here?" one of the agents demands.

"We want the new game!" Sofia says.

"We're demonstrating in support of the Go!Game!" I say, trying to sound girlish and excited. It's not hard because my voice is already high from nerves.

"You need to move off, all of you, so we can get past. This is an illegal gathering in terms of Emergency Regulation 2021.2.35."

We laugh loudly at this and take up our chant again. Even Cameron joins in.

"Go, go, Go-Go-Game! Go, go, Go-Go-Game!"

The agent is visibly annoyed and more than a little perplexed. I don't expect there's a chapter in his how-to-guard-the-prez manual that deals with herding cats and Hulks.

"We want to see the president," Sofia says. "We've got Halloween candy for him."

"Just you stay well back, ma'am!"

The agent stretches out his hands to the side to block her way and, with the help of his colleagues, starts pushing us back and off the road.

I give Robin's hand a squeeze, and he bounds off to the side, flanking the agents. When they spin to try to net him, Quinn runs in the opposite direction, calling, "Land ahoy!" Bruce can't walk fast with his stiff leg, so he circles on the spot, adding to the mayhem by bellowing and beating his chest. Sofia ducks around the agents and runs toward the middle vehicle holding her basket in front of her and screeching, "Trick or treat! Trick or treat! We've got something good to eat!"

Before she's taken more than a few steps, three more agents bail out of the Suburban and storm directly at her. One grabs her by the waist, thumps her to the ground and pats her down, checking for weapons, while another seizes the basket and examines the contents suspiciously.

"Hey!" I yell, lifting my mask up onto the top of my head. "Stop manhandling her, you brute."

"Hulk smash!"

"Shiver me timbers!"

"Ow! What'd you do that for?" Sofia complains when she gets her breath back. "I just wanted to give President Hawke some candy, that's all."

"What's in the basket, Wilson?"

"Just candy," the agent who examined it replies. "Here"

— he shoves it at Sofia — "get back with your friends."

Complaining loudly about police brutality, Sofia gets to her feet and slowly retreats to where Bruce, Cameron, Evyan and I are. We keep moving as the agents close in and try to hustle us off the road. Robin bounds around and around in a way that's got to be hurting his arm, and is pursued by an increasingly annoyed female agent. Cameron pretends to take up a guard position at the gate, yelling, "No game, no entry!" And I stalk about, swooshing my scythe in long arcs until the biggest agent snatches it out of my hand and flings it away. We create as much movement, noise and confusion as possible.

"Abracadabra," Sofia cackles.

"The end is nigh. Death waits for no man!" I drone.

"Avast, me hearties! Stand and deliver!" Quinn shouts, and laughs maniacally, while Bruce, Cameron and Robin chant about tricks, treats and games.

And all the while, a meowing Evyan slips between us and the agents, circling them and pawing their lapels like a cat, moving from one to another in a graceful prowl.

Chapter 35

On the outside looking in

"*Shut up!*" the lead agent eventually bellows above our noisy commotion.

I turn my masked face to Evyan, and when she nods, I start backing up, and the others follow suit.

"We were just having some fun, dude. No need to freak out so majorly," I say.

We allow the agents to propel us to the side of the road.

"Why are you kids out anyway? Don't you know it's not safe?" one of the female agents asks. She looks a little less fierce than her colleagues.

"Not safe!" Bruce roars. He walks stiff-leggedly over to the gate, grabs the bars and gives it a good rattle. Is he testing its weight?

"Hey, now. You stop that," says the rat-faced guard. She unhooks the baton off her belt and tries to whack Bruce's knuckles with it.

"We just wanted to be part of today's big reveal," Quinn says. "You know, the Go!Game launch and all? Today is going to be mind-blowing! Everything's going to change."

"You kids need to head off home," the agent replies and

adds, in a mutter, "Before I shoot you just to shut you up."

"All right, all right," I say. "Someone forgot to take his chill pill this morning."

"Ma'am?" Sofia approaches the least-scary agent. "If you won't let us present our beloved president with these Halloween treats, will *you* at least give them to him?"

"No way," the agent says.

"Don't be ridiculous," her colleague snaps.

It would've been fun if they'd taken the candies, but we never expected them to. Our real targets are not inside the cars.

"Now are you lot going to *back up*, or am I going to arrest you for disturbing the peace, convening an illegal gathering, and jeopardizing the security of a government official?"

Mumbling and grumbling, we shuffle off the road. Each time we pause, the irritated agent gestures for us to retreat further. When he's finally satisfied, all but two of the agents climb back into the Suburbans. The black gate slides open, and the convoy enters. We wave and shout supporting slogans to the middle vehicle as it passes by, but can't see anything through the darkly tinted windows. It would have been great to have one of us slip in after the convoy, but the two remaining agents follow on foot, walking backward, all the while keeping their vigilant gazes on us. The gate clangs shut behind them.

"Did you get them?" I ask Evyan.

"Of course."

I take the small black cloth bag she removes from around her waist, slip it under my robes and tie it around my own.

We groan and sigh in mock disappointment, huddle at the gate and crane our necks as if keen to catch sight of the president. The rat-faced guard walks up and down the gate, rattling her baton along the bars, seeming eager to smash some fingers. Sofia pulls off her witch's hat, removes the false nose, and ruffles her black hair. Then she smiles sweetly at the other guard who — judging by the size of his paunch — is probably fond of candy.

"We were hoping to give these to President Hawke," Sofia says, holding the basket toward him. "But they wouldn't let us. Would you guys like some?"

"Well, now," Big-Belly says, with a sideways glance at Rat-Face. "We're not supposed to take food from outsiders."

"Phhf, it's not *food*. It's just some Halloween candy."

"Whatever it is, it's not permitted," Rat-Face says, and Big-Belly shakes his head sadly at Sofia.

Hulk sidles up to me and mutters, "We're going to have to shoot them, Blue. Want me to do it now?"

"No."

I'm not out of ideas yet. Somehow, we'll get them to take the candy.

"Eh, look, it's the president," Rat-Face says, turning her back on us to watch as the occupants of the cars climb out. This would be a great moment to sneak Big-Belly a few treats unseen, but he goes to stand beside his colleague.

I peer through the bars of the gate using Quinn's spyglass, examining the suited figures one by one.

"Hawke's not there!"

"What?" Quinn says. "He must be."

I check again. It's just the secret service agents, seven in total. Unless Hawke is still inside the car, and I can't see why he would be. Then the occupants of the van hop out.

"Uh-oh," I say.

"What?" Evyan asks.

"Robin," I say, eyeing the three figures lugging cameras and lighting equipment. "They've brought their own filming team."

"Damn," he says.

One of the crew begins mounting a large satellite dish on

the roof of the van. They're obviously going to be doing the live transmission from here, via their own team. I should have anticipated this. Of course Hawke and Roth wouldn't allow public media contingents at the headquarters of their precious games and secret agenda. They'd want to keep control of what gets filmed and released to the public.

"We'll just have to wing it," Robin says, drawing Evyan aside so they can rethink their director-and-camera-operator plan.

At least the presence of the film team must mean that Hawke is still expected. As they set up their tripods, cameras and lighting reflectors at the foot of the stairs to PlayState's main entrance, Sofia has another crack at the guards. They've lost interest in the convoy now that it's clear the president isn't among them and have drifted back to the gate.

"Oh no, they're going to melt," Sofia says, looking down at her basket of soft-centered chocolates and jelly eye-bites. "What a waste. Sure you won't have some?"

Big-Belly edges over. He definitely looks tempted.

"Why don't *you* want it?" Rat-Face asks, narrowing her eyes at Sofia.

"Oh, we've got loads back in the car." Sofia gives her a bright, innocent smile.

"Excuse us for trying to be kind to our folks in uniform," I snap. "I thought we were supposed to support our servicemen and thank our troops and all that."

Big-Belly perks up at this, clearly flattered at being included in the ranks of the armed forces. I can see his reluctance crumbling, and he's actually taken a step toward Sofia when another distraction snags his attention.

Sofia groans softly in frustration and rests her forehead against the bars of the gate, staring down at the dirt. But my eyes are focused on the sky, my ears attuned to the *whup-whup-whup* of an approaching helicopter.

"Helipad," Cameron murmurs beside me.

I follow his pointing finger and see for the first time that there's a helipad located to the left of the PlayState building. The film crew swing their cameras, one toward the sky, one toward the helipad. The two gate guards wander a little way down the drive, the better to catch sight of the president's arrival. Their backs are to us. Everyone's attention is diverted by the impending arrival of the VIP.

The helicopter appears — a glinting flash of blue above the tops of the distant line of trees. I'm guessing that even in the security room inside PlayState, all the officers will be watching the monitors showing the feed from the cameras trained on the helipad.

This is the perfect moment.

Chapter 36

Passed out

The helicopter begins its noisy descent, whipping up swirls of dust beneath it. Hiding behind Quinn, I lift my cloak and extract my rifle, all the while keeping my gaze fixed on the camera pointed at the gate. I'm already gauging distance, calculating angles.

"Gate?" Cameron asks me.

We'd planned to do it later, but it would be better to do it in this moment of distraction.

"Yes! Get ready for the gate, move on my command."

Everyone but me and Robin, who takes the spyglass from Quinn, stations themselves right up against the gate. From the leg of his padded costume, Bruce pulls out a large crowbar, being careful to keep it hidden behind him. The din of the helicopter must now be at its maximum.

"They're landing," Robin says.

He lifts the telescope and trains it on the chopper, while I raise my weapon, rest it on Quinn's shoulder, and train it on the problematic camera.

I take a second to steady my arm and perfect my aim. Then I fire.

I get it right on my first try, just clipping the rear bracket of the camera so that it swivels marginally on its mount. Its view will now be directed just slightly off — to the other side of the gate, not picking up action where it opens, and at the guardhouse. With any luck, those monitoring the surveillance feeds will think that the strong drafts of the landing helicopter buffeted it slightly off its usual range of vision.

"Go now!" I say urgently, slipping my rifle back under my cloak and across my shoulders.

Bruce wedges the crowbar under the bottom rail of the gate, then he and Cameron thrust it down, levering the gate backward off the sliding rail. Everyone grabs a couple of the vertical rails, and on my count, they lift it up and shuffle to the right, leaving a gap just wide enough for Evyan to slip through sideways.

"It's him. It's the president," Robin confirms.

"Now back," I instruct as Evyan disappears around the rear of the guardhouse. "One, two, three, *heave*."

We lift the gate up, move to the left and settle it back into its original position on the sliding rail.

So far, so good. Evyan is nowhere to be seen, and the gate guards are still watching the president, who alights from the chopper and strides toward the building, holding his hair down with one hand. He's accompanied by what I assume is a personal bodyguard, a suited man so big and burly, he makes Bruce look petite.

With a little wave to the waiting agents and camera crew, Hawke bounds up the stairs, and a couple of people cluster around him. I can see the figures but not the details of what's happening.

"What's he doing?" I ask.

"He keeps a comb in his pocket, and he's combing his hair!" Robin says, sounding half-amused and half-disgusted at the president's vanity.

"What is that chick in front of him doing?" Bruce asks.

"Applying makeup," Robin says. "And hairspray, I think."

Bruce snorts in deep disgust.

"What a putz," Evyan says.

Someone comes out of the building and shakes Hawke's hand. I know who it is before Robin confirms, "Roberta Roth."

She disappears back inside then re-emerges to shake his hand again. The performance is repeated twice more, until, presumably, the real director is satisfied they've got the perfect shot.

Quinn glares at Hawke and Roth, who're now posing for photographs. "Look at them, smiling and waving as if they weren't corrupt crooks and killers."

After another few minutes, the camera crew packs up, and the whole entourage enters the building via the multi-person decon unit. The agents go in together first, followed by Roth and Hawke, who go alone together — no doubt seizing the moment of privacy for some last-minute secret conversation. The camera crew are the last to enter.

Now that the excitement is over, the gate guards swivel and walk back to their station.

"Sofia?" I say, giving her basket a significant look.

"Hey guys, we're about to go. Sure you don't want the candy?" Sofia asks the two guards. "It's almost lunchtime. You must be so hungry."

"I really shouldn't," Big-Belly says.

"I'll have some," I say, snatching up a bloodypop, unwrapping it and sucking it with exaggerated relish. Only the soft-centered candies have been injected with fast-acting sleeping medication. We included a few 'safe' pieces in case of just such an eventuality.

"Me, too," says Quinn. He grabs a piece of rat's whisker licorice.

"Save some for us," Bruce says, elbowing his way through as if intending to devour all the treats in one monster gulp.

"Oh, go on then," says the guard. "Just a few won't hurt."

Sofia grabs fists full of the spiked candy and drops them into his cupped hands. After a token hesitation, Rat-Face comes over to claim her share.

"Bye, guys," we call as we peel away from the gate. "Enjoy the candy, and give the president a wave for us when he comes out."

"Sure, sure," Big-Belly says.

"You go straight home, now, you hear?" Rat-Face calls after us.

As soon as we're out of sight of the gatehouse, we signal Neil on the walkie-talkie. By the time he pulls up to the arranged waiting spot, we've tossed the signs into the bushes and stripped off our costumes. We climb inside the van, stuff the Halloween suits under the seats, and then I hand out the ID tags Evyan lifted from the agents to everyone except Robin and Evyan.

"Right, Neil, drive us to the gate," I say, disassembling my rifle and hiding the pieces under all the equipment in Robin's duffel bag.

It's been ten minutes since we handed the guards the candy. If they ate any, they'll already be asleep. If they didn't, we'll have to move to plan B, which I don't want to think about.

But as we pull up at the gate, it slides open. Evyan appears, now wearing the black jeans and long T-shirt she had on under the catsuit, and hops into the van.

"Any problems?" I ask.

"Nah, they were stuffing their faces before they even entered the guardhouse, and asleep five minutes after that. And look, I got a remote control for the gate."

She points it over her shoulder and clicks it, and the gate

slides shut behind us.

We debated, when planning the mission, whether to gag and tie up the guards or tranquilize them, but decided against those ideas, because if someone arrives at the gate, wanting to enter or leave, they would be discovered and the alarm sounded. This way the guards will just be asleep, not unconscious, for a while, depending on the amount of candy they ate before they passed out. And with any luck they, or anyone else, will assume they just dozed off.

Neil takes us down the drive and backs into a far spot in the visitor's lot where the gate guards won't be able to see our van. We climb out, straightening our suits, and gathering our equipment. Robin grabs the duffel bag, and the rest of us each grab a handful of caltrops. These tire-puncturing tacks are designed to always have one spike pointing upwards, and they have hollow cores so that even with self-sealing tires, they'll cause slow leaks and flat tires within minutes. We've learned from our previous disasters. This time, we don't want anyone following us.

As we walk to the steps of the entrance, we surreptitiously toss the tacks just in front and behind the tires of the convoy vehicles, the staff people-carrier, and the only other vehicle in the lot — a sleek Mercedes-Benz sports car in a deep pokeberry purple parked across two spaces right by the entrance. I'd bet good money it's Roberta Roth's ride.

"GAME ON," the custom plates read.

"Game *over*, bitch," I mutter as I drop a few caltrops behind her rear right wheel, nudging them right up against the rubber with a toe.

As part of my disguise, I'm wearing black leather pumps. Even though they're low-heeled, they feel uncomfortable and awkward. I'd feel way better in my sneakers. How are agents supposed to run and jump in these things?

We pause at the top of the stairs and peep through the

glass frontage. This time, the lobby is not deserted.

I take a deep, steadying breath.

"Here we go, people. Good luck," I say.

Sofia crosses herself, Neil whispers, "May the goddess protect us," and Bruce pats the holster at his waist, saying, "In Winchester we trust."

Saying nothing, Quinn presses the button for the decon unit.

Chapter 37

Out and in

All eight of us step inside the decon unit, immediately covering our eyes with our hands. As soon as the UV light bath and decontaminant spray process ends, a beep sounds, and the inner door clicks open.

As planned, we all walk out quickly and pass through the metal detector. It buzzes a protest with each of us — except Sofia — and no wonder. Bruce, Cameron and I are carrying concealed weapons, Quinn is armed with his knife, Neil has an external drive hidden in a pocket, Evyan has her lock-picking kit stashed somewhere on her, and there are more of our weapons and ammunition in the duffel bag Robin holds.

"Whoa, whoa, whoa!" says the security guard inside, holding his hands out to stop us.

I check him out quickly. He's a young man, tall and thin as a rake, with a thick beard and multicolored eyes — he must be wearing rainbow contact lenses. A Taser hangs on his belt, and a communication device is clipped onto the epaulet on his shoulder, but he's not packing any firepower.

"Hey, everybody stop," he says.

The same central core of space, crisscrossed by walkways on the second and third floors, stretches above us. The same board behind the front desk lists the various levels and their offices. Our destination — the data center — is on the fourth floor, along with Roberta Roth's office. This time, though, there's a receptionist with a fuzz of purple hair seated at the desk. She stares up at us, clearly alarmed.

"What seems to be the problem?" Neil asks the guard.

We deputized Neil to handle this interaction because he's the oldest, so we assumed that he would carry more authority. But I'm beginning to wonder if that decision was a mistake. His voice is breathy with nerves, and his forehead gleams with perspiration.

"The problem? I'll tell you the problem," the guard says. "One, I don't know who you people are — I don't have any further visitors listed as due for today. And B, y'all set off my metal detector!"

"We're the president's security officers," Neil says.

I groan internally. That wasn't what he was supposed to say. I shoot a look at Quinn. He's the quick-thinking one here. And aren't all Irish supposed to have a touch of the blarney?

"I don't think so." The guard shakes his head at Neil and hoists the pants hanging loosely around his skinny hips. "They all arrived earlier — we checked each and every one of them against the list."

"All checked off," the receptionist calls from across the lobby, waving a list in the air.

"Officer" — Quinn squints down at the man's nametag — "Murphy, I'm Agent Long." Quinn taps the identification badge pinned to his own chest, and I hurriedly check mine to memorize my supposed name. I'm Agent Morgan.

"That's a coincidence," the receptionist says. "There was an Agent Long in the earlier team, too."

I surreptitiously turn my ID badge around, not wanting her to notice that all our names are duplicates of those on her list.

"What my fellow agent meant to say," Quinn continues easily, gesturing at Neil, "was that we're the presidential security team here to escort the film crew." He gestures to Robin and Evyan, who holds a high-tech video camera in the palm of her hand.

"Everyone who was on the list of expected guests has already arrived," the guard repeats, tugging at his sagging pants again. "And that includes the camera team."

"That camera team is *media*," Robin says, as though stating a deep insult. "We're *art!*"

"Looks like Bert forgot again, like he always does," Quinn complains loudly, treading on my toe. On cue, I groan.

"When I get a hold of Bert's scrawny neck ..." Bruce makes a brutal twisting motion with his hands.

"Who's Bert?" the guard asks.

"I don't have a Bert on my list," the receptionist calls out to us.

"I don't expect you would, ma'am. Bert is the admin assistant at HQ who was supposed to send you notification of our arrival, with all the details of our team," Quinn says smoothly. "Obviously he screwed up. He tends to do that a lot. Couple of sandwiches short of a picnic if you ask me, but he's the boss's nephew, so what you gonna do?"

"Why do they need another camera crew?" the guard asks suspiciously.

"The first crew's going to film the launch ceremony to televise live and distribute to the media." Robin smooths his false beard. "But *this*," he says in an awed voice, gently tapping Evyan's device, "this is an augmented-reality camera. We're going to film President Hawke and use the footage to have him pop up in the Go!Game."

"It was a last-minute decision," Quinn says.

"The president himself asked for it!" Robin's eyes are wide with feigned delight.

"And Bert must've forgotten to send through the details."

"I don't know what the problem is here. They already cleared us at the gate," I say, trying to make my voice deep, and using a cold, unfriendly tone. "*They* had all the relevant documentation. Are you certain *you* checked all your incoming authorizations?"

"And what about the metal detector?" the guard says.

I sigh in annoyance, as if at his stupidity. "Officer Murphy, we're the presidential security team. We are, by definition, licensed to carry concealed firearms."

"We need to hurry!" Robin says, clapping his hands together dramatically. "If we delay here much longer, we'll miss the president's performance."

"You'll be in trouble if that happens," Bruce says in a rough voice, and the guard's Adam's apple bobs up and down. Bruce might not be wearing his Hulk costume, but he's still pretty intimidating.

"Umm," says the guard, clearly unsure what to do.

"I'll call upstairs to check, shall I?" the receptionist volunteers.

I can't let her do that.

I take a step toward her desk, weighing my options even as she reaches out a gloved hand to press a button on the phone system in front of her. But, unexpectedly, Neil is there before me.

"Is it because I'm black? Is that it?" he demands, frowning down at the young woman.

"Because … wh-what?" the receptionist stammers back, confused.

"You don't trust us, because one of us is black, and another is Hispanic, right?"

"N-no!" she gasps.

"Now hold on a moment," the guard protests, yanking his pants up to his ribs.

"I guess people of color can't be presidential guards, right? Because they've naturally got to be felons," Neil continues. Then he adds threateningly, "The president will hear of this."

"No, no. No need. I didn't mean to imply —" Blushing now, the receptionist lifts her hands off the buttons in front of her and rolls her chair back from the desk. "Claude?" she says, raising her eyebrows at the guard. Clearly she wants nothing more to do with this business.

In a masterstroke of inspiration, Quinn says to the guard, "Look, Officer Murphy, if *you* haven't got the authority to let us through, perhaps we should call the guards at the gate."

"Of course I've got the authority. I don't report to *them*," the guard snaps. And with one last, feeble attempt at defending his dignity, he blusters, "I'll have to inspect that bag, though."

"Sure," Quinn says.

"Just be quick," Evyan adds.

The guard hoists the bag onto his inspection table, unzips it and, with a white dowel stick, pokes through the contents, frowning deeply.

"What's this?" he says, pointing at something with the stick.

Robin peers inside. "That's a tripod for the camera. Like a stand?"

"And this?"

"Extra battery packs — please don't open the tins, they often leak," is what Robin says.

Please don't open the tins, they're filled with extra ammunition, is what he means.

"Could you hurry it along?" Quinn says.

We do need to hurry. We'd planned to smooth-talk our way through quickly, but this delay has the potential to disrupt everything. No doubt the security officers monitoring the feed from the closed-circuit camera on the wall near the elevators will have noticed this altercation, even though their primary focus would have been on tracking the president's progress. If one or more of them isn't already on their way to come check what's going on, they soon will be.

"Agents," I say to Bruce and Cameron, "would you please go to the security operations room, which is where?" I look expectantly at the receptionist.

"Down that hallway and on the left," she says, pointing and smiling, eager to be of assistance now.

"Down that hallway and on the left," I repeat. "And check whether the in-house security and video surveillance staff require any … assistance."

I know the boys must understand what I mean, but they hesitate.

"Are you certain *you* won't require our help?" Bruce asks.

Neither he nor Cameron will like the idea of me being the only armed person on the next part of the mission. They'd like to stay with me, to protect me. The irony is, it isn't easy for me to order *them* away, because I'd like to stick by their side, by everyone's side, to protect my team, too. Plus, I'm not sure I trust them to use violence only as a last resort.

"Once you're sure that all is safe and *secure*," I say, pinning them with a warning look that Cameron, at least, will understand to mean that they can subdue, gag and bind whoever they need to, but they should avoid shooting anyone unless their lives depend on it, "then you can follow on and catch up with me. Will the president be going to the operations room first?" I ask the receptionist.

"No. First the data center on the top floor — everyone wants to see that, it's awesome! Then he's scheduled to go down to operations on level three to launch the Go!Game, before finishing up in the gaming arena out back."

"And what's the quickest route to the arena?" I ask.

"The quickest way is via Ms. Roth's stairway — she likes to have her own direct access — but if she's not in her office, you'll have to come back down, and go out and around the side of the building, past the helipad."

"There you go," I tell Bruce and Cameron. "Now hurry!"

Still clearly reluctant, they spin on their heels and stride down the indicated hallway. Immediately, I feel both better and worse — more confident that we'll get this mission back on track, but also more anxious about their safety.

"Look — the president must be moving down to the operations room right now," the receptionist says, pointing at the row of lights above the elevators. The down arrow is flashing, and a moment later the indicator for the third floor lights up. "There's usually no access to the third and fourth floors for outsiders — you have to be on the biometric system and scan your eye for the elevator doors to open on those levels. But they've overridden the elevator system for today, else the president himself and all his entourage wouldn't have been able to get in," she says helpfully. Then, clearly worried that we might be questioning the stringency of the security measures, she adds hurriedly, "Of course, all systems will be reinstated the very minute President Hawke concludes his visit."

"And what the H-E-double-hockey-sticks is this?" The guard lifts a long wooden object out of the bag. It looks exactly like what it is — the stock of my sniper's rifle.

"That's the handle for the steadycam rig," Robin improvises wildly. "It screws into the camera here, see, so you can hold it low for running, low-angle shots like so." Robin takes the stock and scampers about the lobby, miming filming.

"Right, that's enough of this nonsense," Quinn says in his firmest voice. "If we take any longer, we won't be in time to do what we came to do."

I check my wristwatch. It's 11h43. The prez is due to hit the go-button on the game's launch at noon, and Robin and Neil still need to upload the malware before then.

"Pack up there, Rob, we need to get this show on the road. We're running out of time," I say.

Robin grabs the bag. He, Quinn, Sofia and I march over to the elevators, and I punch the button. Neil lingers a moment, takes some candy out of his jacket pocket and insists that the two PlayState employees each have a piece — just to show there's no hard feelings, and because he knows deep down they're not racists.

Whether they really want the treats or are just terrified of causing further offense, they each take a piece, immediately unwrap it and start eating.

The elevator doors open, and we enter. There's a biometric scanner above the control panel, but it's lit with a dull yellow light. I hit the button for the fourth floor while Quinn holds the doors open for the last member of our team.

"You have a nice day, now, folks," the receptionist says, smiling ingratiatingly at Neil as he takes his leave to join us in the elevator.

"I'm sure it will prove to be extraordinary," Neil replies.

The doors close, and with a soft ping, we move up to the fifth floor.

Chapter 38

Out of time

"It's 11h44. We have exactly sixteen minutes before they release the new version," I say as the elevator rises.

When the discreet ping sounds our arrival at the fourth floor, nothing happens. I stare at the retinal scanner. Has it already been reactivated? If so, we're screwed.

"And now?" Sofia asks in a tight voice.

"Let's try the obvious," Robin says.

He presses the open-doors button, and my shoulders relax a good inch when the doors part.

Wait, I signal to the others. I peer out and check both directions. We're at one end of a long, empty hallway. I can see only two doors. One is about twenty yards down, and the other is located at the far end of the hall. There's a scanner on the wall beside the elevator — I guess that's how you get the elevator doors to open on this level — but I don't spot any cameras.

I step out, signaling to the others to follow me. On the section of wall beyond the elevator, there's an illuminated map of PlayState's national network of distributed data centers. Tiny lights mark the location of nodes situated in Arizona, South Carolina, Wisconsin, Washington state and at least half a dozen other places in between. Blue lines between the lights show the connecting fiber-optic web, and all the lines ultimately trace back to here. The data center in this building is the nerve center, the very engine of The Game, and it's where Neil and Robin plan to access the system and upload their malware.

Neil reckons the data center will have strong security, but that fewer people are likely to be present there than in the operations room, particularly on a day when new game software is being released.

"The ops room is where all the action will be for the release," he'd explained. "They'll only have a skeleton staff overseeing the hardware in the server and network rooms."

The door at the far end of the hall must be to Roth's office, because the first door has a sign on the wall to the left of it stating: *DATA CENTER — NO UNAUTHORIZED PERSONS ALLOWED.* On the wall to the right is an intercom system, and above that, an ID verification unit, complete with retinal scanner. Unlike the units for the elevator, this scanner is activated. The indicator glows red, and the display reads: *NO ACCESS.*

The door itself is reinforced with metal plating and is inset with a head-sized circle of thick glass, undoubtedly bulletproof. The door has no handle, and no lock for Evyan to pick. An electronic display screen mounted on the door alternates flashing messages (*Days since last server error: 16; No food or drink beyond this point*) with a Go!Game countdown widget.

0 hours 10 minutes 15 seconds to launch! it reads.

I risk a peek through the glass porthole. Sitting with her back to us at a computer console inside is an operator with a long braid of black hair.

"Robin, Evyan — you're up," I say.

I bang a fist against the door and slip out of sight beside

it. A moment later an aggrieved woman's voice sounds through the intercom.

"You startled me — I spilled coffee all over myself."

"Sorry," Robin says into the intercom. "Can you let us in, please?"

"Who are you? What are you doing up here?" the woman asks.

"We're the camera crew, here to get footage of the data center, for the game launch."

Evyan lifts the camera to shoulder-height and steps up beside Robin, pretending to film the door and the woman behind the glass.

"You're too late. The president has been and gone. He and Roth have gone to the ops room."

0 hours 09 minutes 49 seconds to launch! the display on the door flashes.

"We know that, we just need to get footage of the data center. Like, background stuff," Robin says.

"Your other team already did that."

Robin gives his little explanation about the special camera for the augmented reality, but the operator shakes her head firmly.

"I'm under strict instructions not to let anyone in."

"Fine," Robin snaps, and the annoyance in his voice is real. "But if there are complaints, I'm directing them all your way."

"You do that," the voice says dryly.

Robin and Evyan make a show of leaving in a huff, but they stop a little way down the hall.

"What's the plan now?" Robin mouths.

0 hours 08 minutes 31 seconds to launch!

We're running out of time. I run my fingers through my hair, trying to think of some scheme to con our way into that room that won't involve tripping a bunch of alarms.

Quinn takes a step toward the door, but I hold up a hand, signaling him to wait. I've had an idea, and since I look the least threatening of all of us, I figure I should be the one to try it.

I buzz on the intercom. The woman appears at the porthole after a moment, scowling.

"And what do you want?" she says.

I smile brightly, flash my badge at the glass and say into the intercom, "Hi there, sorry to bother you. I'm one of the president's guards. He sent me back up because he lost his comb in your data center."

The operator looks around at the room beyond the door.

"I don't see it," she says.

"He thinks he set it down in the server room after fixing his hair for the camera."

"Tell me where, and I'll go fetch it," she says.

"Um, he said it's between two of those big things with the flashing lights and the wires, near the back," I say vaguely. "Sorry, it's hard to describe, but if you let me in I can find it in two ticks."

I sneak a quick glance at the display panel.

0 hours 07 minutes 28 seconds to launch!

She still looks unconvinced.

"Please, the president sent me to get it, and he won't go on camera without making sure his hair is perfect. And if he doesn't go on camera, the whole launch will be delayed. He'll hand me my ass if I return empty-handed," I plead with her. "He's very particular about his hair."

"Let him use someone else's comb," she says.

I gasp loudly in mock horror. "Never! He never does that." I lower my voice to a confidential whisper. "This one time, he borrowed a brush from a makeup artist and got an awful case of lice. Please don't ever tell anyone."

The intercom erupts with giggles.

"Come on, give a sister a break," I say. "I've just been promoted to his security detail, and I do *not* want to go back to presidential pooch duty. That poodle has chronic diarrhea."

"Fine," she says, still laughing.

Finally! We literally have mere minutes in which to complete the task we came here for. Six minutes and forty-five seconds, to be precise. I signal the others to approach with one hand, while extracting my Ruger 9mm with the other. Should I take the safety off?

No. Betting that she's more nerd than ninja, I leave it on.

The door hisses as the seal is broken. Neil told us that there would be serious air-conditioning and cooling systems inside. The electronic display flashes a warning as the door begins to swing open: *NO TAILGATING! This door must be closed behind each person. NO TAILGATING!*

But that's exactly what we do.

Quinn grabs the door and yanks it wide open. I bring my Ruger up and point it at the operator's face.

"Inside. Now!"

Her eyes widen with fright. She backs up, and the others slip in behind me.

There are several computer consoles in the network room, but she's the only person on site. It's surprisingly noisy with the hum of machines and the air-conditioning. Behind the bank of computers there's a huge glass wall inset with another door labeled: *SERVER FLOOR.*

"Wh-what's going on here?" the operator asks, her frightened gaze fixed on my firearm.

"Where's the server software access point?" Robin asks.

She points a shaking hand, and Robin immediately sets off in the indicated direction, followed by Sofia, who will be helping him with any typing that's required.

"Who else is here?" I demand.

"Just P-Pete. The rest wanted to be in the ops room for

the launch."

"Call him and tell him to come here. And" — I check her ID badge — "Ananya? Don't do or say anything silly now."

She presses a button on a communication device hanging from a lanyard around her neck.

"Pete? Come in, Pete?" she says in a quavering voice.

"Hey, Ananya," a male voice replies.

"Can you come to the network room for a moment?"

"What's up?"

"I j-just need your help with something," she says.

Is she sending him a signal? I narrow my eyes at her and position the barrel of my Ruger under her chin. Tears well in her eyes.

"Sure, on my way," Pete replies.

"You better not have been trying to warn him, Ananya," I say, putting as much menace as I can muster into my voice.

"I w-wasn't! I swear!"

"Put your hands behind your back," I say, moving around behind her and taking a step back so that Quinn can bind her hands with zip ties.

To my horror, I see that the seat of her pants is wet. Oh God, I meant to scare her into cooperating, but I don't like the idea that I've caused such terror. I want to tell her I'm sorry, that I have no intention of harming her, but that would be counterproductive. I need her compliant.

I check the ties, tighten them a notch. Then I stand just behind her, with my weapon pressed into her back, both of us facing the glass wall, waiting for Pete.

Chapter 39

The only way out is in

Quinn crouches down beside the door, and Evyan hides behind the desk.

There's a deep sigh from beside me. A quick glance confirms that Neil is standing there, staring transfixed at the massive server floor visible through the glass.

"Isn't it beautiful?" he says in an awed whisper.

Beautiful isn't a word I'd use to describe it. But it is impressive. When we were planning this mission, Neil tried to describe what it would probably look like, but I wasn't prepared for the sheer massive scale of the thing. The room is enormous, and filled with row upon row of vertically stacked servers stretching off away from us as far as I can see. There must be thousands of them, each with pulsing multicolored lights. The hard drives are plugged into the stainless steel vertical racks, and each rack is connected to the others and to the power supply, I presume, by great bundles of yellow, orange and gray cables running along the ceiling overhead.

"Can you imagine the processing power? The storage capacity?" Neil says, pushing up his glasses, the better to see the setup.

He sounds like a man in love. Or like he's finally come

home — like if he died now, he'd die happy.

"Neil," I snap. "Shouldn't you be helping Robin?"

"Yes, of course. Yes."

With a last longing look, Neil moves off, and I check my watch.

"Five minutes," I call.

"Almost there," Robin replies.

There's a movement in one of the passages between the high racks on the other side of the glass wall. A man comes gliding toward us on a push-scooter. When he gets closer, I see he's wearing a baseball cap topped with a propeller.

"Is that Pete?" I ask.

Ananya nods.

Quinn tenses. As soon as the door opens, he springs up and seizes Pete. A half-minute later, Pete is also restrained, and Evyan is tying gags around his and Ananya's mouths.

"Three minutes, five seconds," I call, wiping a sleeve across my forehead.

Come on, Robin. Come on.

"Two minutes … One minute forty-five seconds," I yell. "We're out of time!"

The machines hum, Ananya sobs, Quinn drums impatient fingers on the desk, and on my watch, the seconds tick down the ever-shortening time like a burn traveling down a fuse to a bomb.

"Sixty seconds!"

We're not going to make it.

"It's in! It's uploaded," Robin calls triumphantly.

He and Neil slap high fives, and I sag against the desk in relief. But there's no time to relax.

"And now?" I ask.

"Now we wait and hope like hell it works," my brother says, scratching his fake beard vigorously.

If Robin and Neil's code succeeds, the malware will

piggyback on the released software. It'll shoot between the nodes on that map in the hallway at the speed of light, and will start downloading everywhere in seconds.

"We can't wait here," Neil warns. "We need to get out before they detect their system's been breached."

"How long before they find out?" I ask.

"After the first player out there finishes the download and starts playing, things are going to happen quickly. Fifteen minutes into his first game, the hack will activate the announcement. Then, I imagine, phones will start ringing in the support center pretty quick."

"How long will it take to download the software?" I ask.

"Five minutes," Robin replies with a shrug. "Maybe a bit longer — there's going to be masses of traffic on the servers."

Five minutes to download. Fifteen minutes of game time. That means we've got twenty minutes to get out of here. It's more than enough time.

But then Neil says, "Of course, they could always pick up the breach sooner from the ops side. Probably will."

"Thanks for the heads up," I say, but my sarcasm is wasted on Neil. He merely nods.

We push the two operators under the desk, where Quinn positions them with their faces to the wall and then secures each of them to a cross-bar of the desk with more zip ties.

I open the door and check the hallway first. It's still empty.

"Everyone, out — quick!" I say. "Robin, don't forget the bag."

Neil is the last to exit the data center — he probably wishes he could stay. As soon as the door clicks shut behind him, I send a round into the retinal scanner, ducking away from the plastic shrapnel which flies out. I send another round into the intercom system, and it dies with a wheezing moan. Quinn gives the door an experimental push. It's locked. No one will be getting in there to thwart the malware upload and distribution anytime soon.

"To the elevators, run!"

But we're only halfway down the short corridor, just passing the network map which is now lit up with pulsing lights like a Christmas tree, when the elevator pings its arrival on this floor. I skid to a halt, turning my ankle in the stupid shoes.

"Take cover," I yell, dropping awkwardly to one knee in the tight skirt and aiming my Ruger at the opening doors. This time the safety is off.

"Don't shoot the white hats, Blue," Bruce says as he and Cameron step out of the elevator.

I lower my weapon to the accompaniment of sighs and exclamations of relief from behind me.

"How'd it go?" I ask the boys, rubbing my sore ankle.

"Mission accomplished," Cameron says.

"We overpowered the guards in the security room, disabled the video feeds, and destroyed their communication devices." Bruce mimes stomping his foot down on something and crushing it.

"Did you hurt anyone?" I ask.

"Meh, not much," says Bruce. "How did you guys do?"

"Mission accomplished," Robin says, grinning widely.

"And no injuries," I add. "But we need to get out of here now."

At that very moment, a series of beeps sound from the biometric scanner beside the elevator.

"Nooo!" I groan as I run to it.

It's been activated. The light is red, and the display reads: *NO ACCESS.* I thumb the button to summon the elevator. Looking up, I see the light for the fourth floor is illuminated — it's already on this floor. But without the right eyeball, there's no way to get the doors to open.

I look back over my shoulder at the destroyed access system hanging in pieces off the wall beside the data center door. Pete, Ananya and their retinas are locked inside. Stupid. I am so freaking stupid. Why didn't I foresee that this could happen?

"It's active?" Quinn asks.

I nod.

"How are we going to get out?" Sofia asks, sounding panicky.

"We could try forcing the elevator doors open," Bruce suggests, "using Blue's rifle as a lever."

Quinn shakes his head. "Even if we could — and I doubt it would work— it would set off alarms, and there'd be a welcome party waiting for us when the doors opened."

"How did it get switched on if you 'secured' the security room?" Evyan asks Bruce.

"Dunno," he says. "Maybe it was on a preset timer."

"Or maybe the guards have been discovered, or the system breach. They may know we're in here," Quinn says.

We hurry back to the data center on the remote chance there's some way back inside.

"No way, man," Bruce says, after examining the door. "Even if I had explosives I wouldn't know where to stick them. This door is probably reinforced with spokes projecting into the wall. Blue, why didn't you take one of them hostage?"

It didn't even occur to me, that's why.

"What about the fire escape?" Evyan asks.

Quinn and I glance to the end of the hallway, beyond the elevator. That's where the fire escape stairwell was positioned when we used it to access the second floor last time we were here. But on this floor, there's just a blank wall.

"The stairwell doesn't come all the way up to this floor. That'll be part of their security," Quinn says. "They must count the stairs from Roth's office the receptionist mentioned as their fire-escape route.”

"Yeah, that’s the only way out now," I say. "But it means we’re probably going to have to fight our way past Hawke and his security detail to do so."

Bruce immediately cheers up at the prospect, but I’m not pleased. I had hoped for us to get in and out without anyone getting hurt. Now, that’s looking increasingly unlikely.

Chapter 40

Outlook

The door at the end of the hall looks to be plain wood, and the only sign on it is a brass nameplate: *ROBERTA ROTH, CEO.*

There's no answer when we knock, and a quick test confirms it's locked, but Evyan has us inside in under a minute. As soon as we enter, I see that the whole back wall of her office, except for a door marked *FIRE EXIT,* is a slanted glass overhang that overlooks the gaming arena where six months ago, Bruce and I shot our way into the ASTA Academy in a sniper simulation exercise.

Was Roth watching that day? Already selecting her future killers and super-soldiers, comparing our real-life performance in the simulation to our scores in the virtual game? How long had she been keeping tabs on us by means of The Game, through the tinted window of her office and the cameras at ASTA, and via her many eyes and ears — the unit commanders, and the snitches like Leya? Bruce nailed it when he said we were like rats in a lab. Roth has been the experimental scientist, selecting samples, changing protocols, measuring results. Playing with us all the way.

"Evyan, can you lock the door to the hall? And can you guys try to barricade it in some way so no one can come through?"

While Quinn, Bruce and Cameron shove desks and filing credenzas in front of the door, I get the telescopic attachment of my rifle from the duffel bag and peer through the scope down at the arena floor, far below us.

The presidential entourage is already in the arena. The camera crew is arranging lights, someone is touching up Roth's makeup, and Hawke is combing his hair again. They're setting up in front of the statue of a cavalryman astride a rearing horse. That's where I shot Sarge in the neck with a blue paintball, and he praised me for my coolness in a crisis.

Sarge probably ensured every simulation ended at this spot in the arena so Roth could have a bird's eye view of the final players from her crow's nest.

A slim figure with short, spiky black hair stands on one side of Roth. Before I've even trailed my scope up to her face, before I've seen the Chinese character on the outer corner of her left eye, I know who it is.

"Leya," I breathe.

I glance back at my old ASTA cadets.

Cameron's head snaps up, Quinn grimaces, and Bruce's face settles into hard lines. "I want a word with her," he says.

"Those stairs," I say, indicating the fire exit door, "will take us all the way down to street level in the arena. I reckon we'll come out close to where they're filming. Hawke has three of his secret service agents with him, plus that big personal bodyguard. The others must be stationed at the exit, which is over at the far end, that way." I point across the fake inner-city neighborhood of streets, alleys, buildings and abandoned cars.

"Four guards," Quinn says.

"It's not ideal, but it's probably as good odds as we're going to get," I say.

"Only four? We can take them, no problem," Bruce says. "Hell, we could probably take them out from up here — easy as shooting fish in a barrel."

"The glass will be bulletproof. Besides, we are not going to take anyone out unless we absolutely have to. Unless it's self-defense."

"We've got to wait until they try to kill us before we shoot? C'mon, man, that's not what snipers do. We pick the time, the place, the shot. And I've got dibs on Leya."

"No!"

"Blue, not everyone is going to get out of here in one piece. You've got to know that."

I do. And I can't see any way around it.

"Can't we just wait until they finish and everyone leaves, and then we can go down?" Sofia asks.

"No," Quinn says, surprising me. Waiting it out is exactly the sort of approach he would prefer to take. "If our intrusion hasn't already been discovered, it soon will be, then we'll be well and truly trapped."

"Sitting ducks," Cameron says.

I squat down to empty the duffel bag out onto the floor, cursing the tight skirt that makes it difficult for me to move freely, and the shoes which are pinching my toes painfully. While Bruce and Cameron sort out their weapons and ammunition, I assemble my sniper's rifle, check the internal magazine, and stow extra ammunition in my pockets, all the while shooting envious glances at Evyan's jeans. That's what I need — a pair of pants. But hers would never fit me. She's way skinnier than I am.

"Hey, Robin, give me your jeans." My twin is more or less my size — his should fit me.

"My *what*? Why?"

"This skirt is cramping my style. If I'm going to be fighting down there, I need to be able to move more easily."

"So I'm supposed to go down there in a skirt?" he says, giving me an over-my-dead-body look and rubbing hard at his beard.

"No."

"In my *boxers*?"

"No. You're not going down there at all — not until I give the all-clear. You're going to stay up here with Evyan, Neil and Sofia."

"No way, uh-uh, I'm coming with!" Robin protests.

"To do what, exactly?" I say irritably, shoving my rifle into the duffel bag and slipping the straps of the bag over my shoulders. I tuck my sidearm into the back of my skirt's waistband.

"To help you figure a way out."

"I know that you three" — I indicate Robin, Sofia and Neil — "are geniuses, but —"

"What am I — stupid?" Evyan interrupts.

"Unarmed," Cameron says.

"But," I continue, talking over the mutters, "you can do your thinking from up here."

"Where it's *safer* for us, because we're so in need of being protected," Robin says bitterly, ripping off the fake beard and tossing it onto Roth's carpet, where it crouches like a fuzzy little animal.

"Robin, it'll be safer for me down there if I don't have to worry about protecting you three … civilians."

Robin looks mutinous.

"Hey, you insisted that I be leader," I remind him. "Well, now I'm giving you an order — stay put!"

I glance out of the window. They're filming. Hawke is standing alone in front of the statue, gesturing grandly.

"We need to get moving," I say, walking over to the fire exit door.

"What about Quinn?" Evyan asks. "He's not armed, he's a *civilian*, too."

How to explain that Quinn wouldn't leave my side now

even if I ordered him? That I wouldn't want him to. We've vowed to stick together, and it's a promise we're both going to keep. I know that without asking.

"I am armed," Quinn says, holding up his knife.

Robin makes a sound indicating that he thinks this is one of the most ridiculous things he's ever heard and tells me, "Well, you're not getting my pants."

"Here." Quinn kneels beside me and slits the side seams of my skirt from the hem up to my thighs. "Better?"

I flex my knees and kick out sideways. "Much!" I say, flinging off the stupid shoes and removing the fake bun for good measure.

"Why don't you guys try to log onto the Go!Game?" Quinn suggests. "And see whether the hack is working."

Robin and Neil perk up at the thought of that, but Evyan asks, "So we're just supposed to sit up here, unarmed and unprotected?"

I hadn't thought of that.

"If you want, I can stay and defend them," Cameron says softly.

"Oh, Cameron, thank you!" I give him a quick, tight hug and kiss him on the cheek.

I know he must want in on this fight, must be desperate protect me and Bruce, and he's sacrificing that to keep my brother, and the others, safe.

"Aw, man, you're going to miss out on all the fun," Bruce complains, joining me at the door of the fire escape.

"Be careful. Hawke's a snake," Cameron says.

I want to tell them all goodbye, good luck, that I love them. But I superstitiously think that making my peace with them will somehow bring about their, or my, death. So I just give them a tight smile and tell Bruce and Quinn, "Let's go."

"Ooh-rah," Bruce murmurs. Then he opens the door, steps aside and says, "But ladies first, so … after you, O'Riley."

Chapter 41

Truth will out

"Hide your weapons, Bruce," I tell him as we run down the stairs.

It's much easier moving quickly now that I'm barefoot and can take bigger strides in the split skirt. The duffel bag containing my rifle bounces against my back, and I hold a steadying hand against the Ruger 9mm tucked into the back of my waistband.

The stairs end inside one of the buildings resembling an apartment block on the street with the traffic circle and the statue.

Bruce pushes the door open a crack, and I check. The president's guards are standing just ten yards away — within arm's length of the president, who is now chatting to Roth. Leya is standing just behind her. The camera crew is packing up — folding tripods, stowing cameras and lights in storage trunks with wheels.

"What's the plan?" Bruce whispers.

They keep asking me this, like I know. But I'm making it up as I go.

"We wait for the camera crew to leave, then we move."

"When you say, 'move' — do you mean shoot?" Bruce

asks.

"*No!* First, we try talking."

Beside me, Quinn nods his support for this strategy. "Yeah, let's see if we can convince them that the game's up. That they need to surrender."

"Yeah, right. That's likely," Bruce mutters.

"We have to try," I say, even though I fully expect Hawke and Roth to laugh at our attempts at a negotiated solution.

As soon as the film team has cleared out, I push open the door, step outside and, flanked by Quinn and Bruce, walk purposefully toward the group of people clustered at the statue. The presidential guards turn as one to face us. We stop a few meters away and wait. The personal bodyguard, who has already drawn his weapon, alerts Hawke, who turns to face us. Roth follows his gaze, and the sycophantic smile fades rapidly from her face.

"You!" she says, glaring at me, taking in my new hair.

"Hello again, Ms. Roth."

"Jinx? Bruce?" Leya looks stunned.

I spare her a glance, but only to check for weapons. As far as I can see, she's not armed. No way would the presidential guard have allowed it, I guess. Besides, Leya's real gift was never in shooting. Her talents lay in surveillance, camouflage, double-dealing.

"You and I have some unfinished business, Leya," Bruce says, his voice flat and hard.

Leya's eyes widen, and a vein pulses at her temple under the small tattoo, but she says nothing.

"Who are these people?" Hawke asks.

"Cadets, from the Academy," is all Roth says.

Obviously, she has no desire to explain how at least three top cadets have abandoned the program, gone AWOL, and are now working with the rebels.

"Welcome," says Hawke, smiling in his smarmy way.

How could I ever have thought of him as a kindly father-figure? He's a total creep. Without the subliminally-induced favorable attitude toward him, I can see that he's a slimy crook. "I wasn't expecting any cadets to visit today, but you are all welcome!"

He actually leans forward to shake our hands. If we were babies, he'd probably kiss us. As one, the three of us take a step back. Hawke looks offended. Roth looks worried. Leya's eyes move from side to side, scanning the arena. Looking for a hidey-hole?

I realize that Hawke doesn't know who we really are, that he has no clue that Bruce and I are Game-raised, government-trained killers. I guess he has more important things to do than memorize the faces on the most-wanted lists.

"Mr. Hawke," Quinn says, "you should know that the true purpose of our visit to PlayState today was to upload some additional software into the Go!Game."

"Extra special effects? Excellent, excellent!" Hawke says, smoothing his hair. The man truly is a moron.

Roth is nobody's fool, however. She narrows her eyes at Quinn.

"What additional software?" she demands.

"The sort that will tell the nation about the true purpose of the Game."

Hawke's smile snaps off with the suddenness of a light being switched off. Sarge's smile used to do the same.

"We know everything," Quinn says. "We know about the subliminal messages in support of —"

"Stop!" Hawke says, holding up a hand. He turns to his three secret service agents and says firmly, "Go secure the exit, all of you — now!"

When they hesitate, looking confused, Hawke says, "I have reason to believe that the perimeter has been compromised. Go and wait at the exit. On the *other* side of the decon unit. And tell the camera crew they can depart."

Clearly, he does not want them to hear, or record, any secrets about The Game. Maybe the personal bodyguard is privy to everything though, because the big guy stays put, as immobile as a small mountain.

"We know," Quinn begins again, "about the subliminal messages — the ones to boost fear of the plague to irrational heights, the ones to bolster support for you and your party, the ones to get kids addicted to playing The Game."

Hawke shoots a panicked glance at Roth, but before she can formulate a response, Quinn continues, "And we know all about the neuro-molding of children's brains, the creation of super-soldiers and the kickbacks ASTA receives for sending the talent your way. In fact, I think we may know more about The Game than you do. Did you know that there is a whole other set of subliminal messages? Advertising for —"

"Stop right there!" Roth cries furiously.

"Let him speak," Hawke says. "I'm very curious to hear what he has to say."

Roth glowers at us. Leya takes a few steps backward.

"Fact is, the Game is riddled with subliminal ads for ASTA, A Play Test and all their subsidiaries. Anyone who plays is going to be spending their money on those products. Did you know? Or has Ms. Roth here been fooling you into believing you were the only beneficiary of her super-secret technology? You both benefit from your deal, but one of you is making wayyy more money."

"Who are the wolves now, Leya?" I can't resist asking my former friend. "Who are the monsters who prey on this nation, brainwashing children, terrorizing citizens with lies, propaganda, detentions, torture and deceit? Will you stop them, too? Where's your fight now?"

Leya doesn't answer. What could she say?

Hawke looks outraged. His face is purple, and his eyes are

bulging. "That fact that you have not identified, isolated and eliminated this threat is staggering and deplorable, Roberta," he says. "You may correct your failings now."

Bruce's hand slips behind his waist, as does mine.

"Wait," Leya begins. "Let's just —"

"Shut up," Roth snaps.

"The problem is, it's not just us who know," Quinn says quickly. "At this very moment, across the country, the Go!Game will be broadcasting an animated depiction of President Hawke, telling the nation the truth."

As if on a prearranged cue, both Roth and Hawke's phones start ringing.

"There you go," Quinn says. "It's begun. And once *that* public service announcement concludes, the Game will self-destruct."

Hawke answers his cell with a curt, "Yes?"

Roth ignores the strident ringing of her phone. She knows what we're capable of — she's supervised our training since we were kids. She knows we're not bluffing.

Hawke cuts the call and, when it starts ringing again immediately, hands the phone to his bodyguard.

"Give up now, both of you," Quinn urges.

"Roberta, explain yourself!" Hawke spits.

"We had to make a profit somehow. What the government pays us is merely enough to keep us afloat, let alone fund our new research and development. We're a business, Alex, not a charity. We have to satisfy our shareholders and investors."

"You were double-dealing all this time, screwing me? Swindling and conning the nation. The nation's *children*?" he yells above the ringing phones.

"Oh, please don't pretend you care about *them*," Roth says, setting her jaw and spinning to face Hawke. The underside of her hair flashes purple as it swings. "Besides, I think you'll find we were operating within the parameters of the law. Don't think you can pin this on me. I have those contracts, Alex, those presidential exceptions and pardons — all the evidence. And I'll use it. You'll be the one in disgrace, not me. I'll tell the world you ordered it and I was just loyally following orders."

"No, Roberta," Hawke says. His lips are thin, his eyes hooded. "You won't tell the world anything."

He gives his personal bodyguard a nod and then turns his back on Roth. In one smooth movement, the big guy lifts his weapon and shoots her square in the chest.

She falls to the ground — a crumpled heap of black and white and spreading red. Her hair fans out in a halo of poisonous pokeberry purple. And in a pocket of her jacket, her phone rings and rings.

Chapter 42

Out of the blue

Leya bolts, spinning on her heel and dashing back down the street in a zigzag pattern. Hawke nods again, and his bodyguard takes off after her, but I doubt he'll find her. Leya probably knows every nook and cranny of this arena, and there are just too many bolt-holes where she could hide.

Bruce, Quinn and I scramble backward a good twenty yards. Bruce ducks behind a dumpster on one side of the road, and I drag Quinn behind the cover of a rusty, old-model Ford on the other.

"Young fellow, you with the accent? I'd like to talk to you. You're an intelligent young man, I can tell. You know your computers — your bits and your bytes, your programs," Hawke says pleasantly. He still thinks we're geeks and hackers. "But do you know the state of your nation?"

"I know you're corrupt to your core!" Quinn yells back, ignoring my efforts to shush him. "I know you and your allies are profiting off the fear of a nation!"

"If that's what you think, then you know nothing," Hawke says flatly. "War is coming. True war — a hot war. This plague is just a taster — a first blow to soften us up before they launch the real attack on our decimated nation. A nation that was weak — *weak!* — even before they attacked. Divided, partisan, with personal rights at an all-time high. The individual was being prioritized over the collective. You couldn't shoot an armed criminal without being crucified in the media and charged in court. We were easy prey for our enemies."

"So you just started growing a future army from underage civilians?" Quinn yells. "Changing the brains of children?"

"We needed soldiers."

"You should have asked!"

"We did ask!" Hawke yells back. "But serving your country was no longer the fashionable thing to do! Voluntary enlistment in the armed services was at an all-time low after those botched desert conflicts. Those wars weren't winnable, or maybe even worth fighting. If we'd tried to bring back the draft — we would have had a fight on our hands. Even the plague attacks didn't change that, because you can't fight a plague with soldiers and tanks."

"Please can I just take him out? I can't stand this prattling anymore," Bruce says from across the street, just loud enough for Quinn and me to hear.

"Was fighting the plague ever even your priority?" Quinn demands.

Hawke ignores the question. "We've had the intelligence for years that our enemies are planning a full-scale war. And how do you fight a war for the very survival of the nation when you don't have enough soldiers to withstand serious losses? When both sides have the same weapons, the same lethality, and are prepared to use them?"

"What are you saying?"

"Careful, Quinn," I whisper, pushing him down so his head doesn't protrude above the car's protection.

"We needed an edge, don't you see? If either of us went nuclear, the war would be over. But so would the world,"

Hawke continues. He sounds closer. "That left us with the usual weapons, including biological attacks, which, as you've seen, can be difficult to control. Our only advantage would be in our fighters, quality over quantity. Perfect soldiers bred from childhood to succeed better than anyone on the planet in what they were best suited to do. Super-soldiers who'll hit the ground running, trained up, neuro-adapted, and motivated in the extreme. That's our edge. That's how we'll win."

"You can't win a righteous war by sacrificing your own people," I yell.

"Don't be so naïve," Hawke says. He sounds even closer. "That's what war is. One side pitting its finest, its strongest and best-trained youth, against the other. When we deploy our super-enhanced soldiers on foreign soil, the enemy won't know what hit them. It's going to change the global game."

"It's not a game!" I yell, incensed.

"You're talking like this crazy scheme is still going to happen. But it's over, don't you understand?" Quinn says. "All across the USA, The Game is self-destructing. And when players know what you've been up to, when they aren't being influenced by your subliminal programming any more, they'll be able to hear the truth, to figure things out for themselves, to demand change. It's all over for you, Hawke. Everyone in this country knows about you, or soon will. Give yourself up now."

"Not likely," Hawke says contemptuously. "For the man with a little foresight and a lot of money, this isn't the only country there is, boy. It's not even the best. There are a dozen places who would offer me sanctuary."

We hear the sound of running feet and a mumbled conversation. I sneak a peek under the chassis of the Ford. The bodyguard is back. Either he found Leya and eliminated her, or he didn't. Either way, he's our problem again.

Moving as quietly and carefully as I can, I extract my rifle from the duffel bag, then I take up position behind a tire, lying on my belly, aiming my weapon at Hawke's bodyguard. The big guy has his pistol out in a double-handed grip and is moving it in an arc from side to side as he moves slowly down the street. He's completely exposed. As far as they know, we're three unarmed computer geeks.

"Don't move," I say softly to Quinn, remembering Cameron's warning. Hawke *is* a snake. He'll want to leave no witnesses.

The bodyguard comes another two steps closer to where we're hiding. I try to adjust my line of fire, but the position is awkward. The rifle is better for long-distance shots, less easily maneuverable at close quarters, so I lay it down beside me, pull the Ruger from my waistband, and keep it trained on the guard.

"My compatriot, Mr. Smith here, would like you three to surrender yourselves so we can all get together and have a nice cup of coffee and a chat to straighten out these misunderstandings," Hawke calls to us.

"Surrender this, asshole!" Bruce yells, flipping him the bird from where he hides, safely protected in amongst piles of rubble behind the dumpster.

The bodyguard swivels his gaze to the spot on his right where Bruce's voice came from, then glances up and to the left — into a traffic mirror mounted on a pole, reflecting Bruce's position. The bodyguard hurls himself into a forward roll and fires.

So do I.

Bruce grunts.

And my rounds hit the bodyguard in the chest even as Bruce slumps sideways and topples to the ground.

Chapter 43

Out of reach

"Bruce! Bruce!" I scream, leaping up and dashing across the street to him.

Blood spreads in a vicious red blossom across Bruce's abdomen. His eyes are rolling, unfocused behind drooping eyelids.

My heart is hammering, my head buzzing.

I yank off my jacket with trembling hands, sending bullets scattering across the ground, and bundle it up tightly to press it hard against the wound. Bruce groans and goes limp. Please let him not be dead. *Please.*

"Is he …? How is he?" Quinn asks, standing up from behind the car and taking a step toward us.

His head snaps to the right. He lunges sideways, out of my sight, and I hear a thud, a "No!" and then Hawke calls, "I've got a gun up against your friend's head, young lady."

Shit. Hawke must have gone for the bodyguard's weapon, gotten there before Quinn.

"If you try anything, I'll shoot your friend."

I *can't* try anything. Both my weapons are lying uselessly behind the Ford across the street — my rifle where I placed it on the ground, and my handgun where I dropped it when I leapt up to come to Bruce.

My heart is galloping, and I can't catch my breath. My chest feels tight, and a cold sweat breaks out under my arms. I look up into the traffic mirror across the way in time to see a flash of movement, then nothing. I risk peeking out around the edge of the dumpster. Hawke has Quinn in front of him like a shield and is backing up the street in the direction of the exit with the weapon pressed against Quinn's temple. I pull back quickly, but I've been seen.

"I'll kill him! I will," Hawke warns.

"Stay where you are, Jinxy!" Quinn yells.

"You listen to your friend here," Hawke calls, sounding farther away, "and I'll let him go, let you both go safely."

It's when he says that, that I know he intends to kill Quinn. Me too, if he can. He doesn't know there's a gallery of witnesses watching everything from Roth's eyrie. He thinks that Quinn and I — and Leya if she's still alive — are the only ones who know Roth and Bruce were shot on his orders. He plans to use Quinn as a hostage all the way to the exit, then bait me out somehow and kill us both.

I don't know what to do.

The trembling in my hands is starting to spread through my body. Full-blown buck-fever threatens. I close my eyes in panic for an instant. The image of Quinn, with death poised at his temple, is seared into my vision.

At that moment, something inside me shuts down. The trembling stops instantly, as though I've pulled a kill-switch. I hold a hand out in front of me, and it's steady as a rock. My chest expands easily as I take a deep breath. I blow it out slowly, feeling my heart rate ease. My mind is suddenly clear. Ice flows in my veins.

For the first time, I see clearly, as though in a photograph, that I stand at the border of life, like the angel of death. My weapon may be a rifle, not a flaming sword, but it has two sides — save and kill, defend and destroy, good and bad. This is true freedom — the free will of choice, with the weight of responsibility. I cannot have one without the other. Every action has its price.

And there's no running away or hiding any more. This has to stop. I can stop it. And I will.

I close my eyes again, but this time to picture the layout of the arena in my mind's eye. If Hawke continues backing up the street, he'll only have another block before he needs to turn to his right to take the street that leads toward the exit. That's when I'll make my move.

I scan around the immediate area where Bruce is lying, unmoving. With steady hands, I lift a small chunk of concrete cinder block and gently lay it on top of my wadded jacket over his wound, hoping that the pressure will help slow the bleeding. I wipe my bloody hands on my skirt. Crouching behind the very edge of the dumpster, I allow myself another quick glance. Hawke and Quinn are almost at the end of the street.

I count to five. And then in one fluid movement, I dive across the pavement, snatch up my rifle and race down the street after them.

When I get to the corner of the road they must have taken, I stop and chamber a round in my rifle. One up, safety off. I lift it to my shoulder and step out into the center of the street, facing them.

"Jinxy, no! Get back!" Quinn calls as Hawke, bug-eyed from surprise, ducks directly behind him and pulls him close.

"I'll kill him. I can't miss!" Hawke yells.

"If you do that, I'll kill you. And I won't miss either."

"But he'll be dead!"

"So will you. I think this is what they call a zero-sum game." My voice is steady, low, calm.

It unnerves him.

"Don't come any closer!" he yells, his voice high and tight.

"I don't need to. All those games you had me play? They shaped my brain. All that training you made sure I had, it honed my skills. And when the crosshairs are locked on you, Hawke, your dream super-sniper becomes your nightmare executioner. From this range, I could put a round in the center of your eyeball, easy as breathing."

I could, if I could *see* his eyeball. But Quinn is taller, his shoulders broader, and Hawke is tucked in neatly behind him. He must have a hold of Quinn's jacket and be tugging him backward as they take one step after another to the exit.

Quinn is watching me steadily now. He knows what I'm capable of, but he must also know that there's no easy shot here.

The irony is almost amusing. Finally, I'm ready and willing to kill. I know it's wrong. But I also know it's not the worst of evils in this situation either. If it comes to a choice between sparing Hawke or Quinn, there's no contest.

Finally, my head and heart are aligned, but now there's no shot to take. Quinn, my beloved Quinn, stands between me and my target. All of Hawke is hidden behind him. All but the hand holding that pistol, its wrist and the bent arm that sticks out to the side.

I study that arm, that hand, that weapon. If I shot the pistol, it might accidentally discharge its lethal contents into Quinn's brain. If I shot the hand or, say, the arm — I move my scope fractionally so that the crosshairs are centered on the bend of the elbow — would it knock the arm backward, away from Quinn? Or might the finger on the trigger reflexively convulse, and ...?

I stalk my prey, step by barefoot step, as he backs up, his human shield in front of him, past the doors that lead to the shooting range and the changing rooms. They're almost at the exit. Beyond that final door lies the decon unit and escape. Hawke will go in alone, and he'll dispense with Quinn as he does so. I can feel it in my bones.

I half expect Quinn to ask me not to shoot, to try another attempt at talking Hawke into surrendering. But he doesn't. He just stays calm and still. Trusting me?

Options, angles, ideas stream through my mind in a cool, logical sequence. Ideas are born, weighed, discarded. I sift through all the shots I've ever taken, all the shots I've ever seen, in microsecond analysis — Sarge's neck, the rats, the woman with the red shoe, the little boy at the pond, Nicky, the aching M&M man, Tae-Hyun's high-angled shots, my snake-eyes, Robin's wrist and shoulder, Sarge's forehead, Bruce's gut.

Robin's wrist and shoulder. Beth explaining about severed ligaments and sheared tendons.

"Last chance to let him go, Hawke," I say.

The stock is cool and hard against my cheek, the rifle cradled in my steady hands, which make minute adjustments to keep my target centered. I breathe in. Hold it. My eye is at the scope. Breathe out. My forefinger is curled, the pad of the fingertip on the trigger. Gently now.

I take in a breath.

"No!" Hawke yells.

Hold it.

"I'll splatter his brains acr—"

And squeeze.

The round tears through Hawke's wrist, shattering bone, instantly severing tendons, muscles, ligaments. The report cracks loudly at my ear and echoes through the warehouse. The pistol drops from Hawke's limp fingers. His arm falls as Quinn flings himself aside.

I breathe out. Look up over my sights. Move forward.

In the second I turn my head to check Quinn, to ask, "Are you okay?" Hawke is through the exit door and into the decon unit, screaming, "Help me! Get me out of here! Seal this exit, nobody comes out, y'hear?"

My hand is on the door, ready to pull it open and follow my prey, when Quinn tugs me back. "No, Jinxy! You'll be walking into a death trap."

"You're right," I say. I still feel cold with icy logic, fully alert in this strangely detached state. "But I need to stop him."

"The stairs — to the roof. Go!" Quinn yells, thrusting me forward, back in the direction of Roth's end of the arena. "I'll take care of Bruce."

If he can still be taken care of.

I hurtle back down the street, passing Cameron and Evyan, who are bent over Bruce, yelling at him to hold on. I bound over the traffic circle with the cavalryman, yank open the door to the fire escape, and scramble up the stairs, shoving past Sofia, who flattens herself against the stairwell wall as I approach.

"Where's Robin?"

"He's fine. On the phone," she says as I bound upwards without pausing.

His phone? Can he be logged onto the Game, seeing whether the hack is working?

No time to think of that now. Hawke will be racing around the side and the length of the warehouse arena, headed toward the helipad. Maybe he'll stop for a few minutes while his bodyguards fashion a tourniquet around his arm to stem his bleeding. Maybe he'll tell them he needs to be med-evacuated urgently, and even now they're carrying him to the chopper.

It's a race against time. He'll want to be away from here as soon as humanly possible.

I hurtle around the balustrade on the level of Roth's office and keep going, vaulting the stairs two and three at a time as I climb upward. The door at the top is sealed with a padlock. I move to the side, aim and shoot it off, sending a shard of shrapnel deep into the calf of my left leg. A cry leaves my lips, but I have no thought of stopping while I can still walk.

I thrust the push-lever down and slam my body against the weight of the door, driving it open, and step onto the roof outside.

Chapter 44

Out for blood

Chest heaving, I stand still for a moment, taking in my environment, getting my bearings, catching my breath.

My back, at six o'clock, is to the warehouse arena. At the far end of that is the exit where Hawke escaped. Directly ahead of me, at twelve o'clock, beyond the far end of the office building, is the parking lot and beyond that, the gated entrance. The helipad must be at three o'clock, slightly ahead of me and to the right.

The roof of the PlayState building is flat and filled with what I guess is the cooling system equipment for the data center below. Scores of wide, horizontal fans spin lazily in the afternoon sun, pushing out invisible columns of hot air. Giant, tubular water tanks form a perimeter along the outer edge of the square rooftop. They look like submarines, with railed ladders mounted on their sides, for access to the openings located on their tops.

The high-pitched whine of a helicopter engine starting up is like a starter's pistol to me. I spin to my right and run in an uneven limp to the middle of the five water tanks, leap up the metal-runged ladder, climb onto the top of the tank, and peer over the building's edge.

On the ground four floors below me, the helicopter is warming up. A tight cluster of figures approaches the helipad. I lift my rifle and scrutinize the scene through the powerful magnification of my scope. Four of the president's guard have each other's hands grasped in an interlocking formation and are carrying Hawke in a sort of netted seat to the chopper.

I sit on my butt on top of the water tank, my right leg bent up and crossed over my left, which is tucked beneath me, still bleeding and throbbing with a hot pain which I try to push from my awareness. It's not a great position — my balance is precarious on the curved surface of the tank, and I'm backlit by the sun, making me a literal sitting target for anybody who may look up. I brace my rifle on my knee and tilt it down, trying to find my shot.

Target acquisition is impossible. The president bounces up and down as he is carried by the surrounding tight knot of guards. Every time I think I've found my shot, someone moves, and there's a head or a chest blocking my line of fire. I know that my round would probably pierce them and keep going, slamming into my ultimate target, but I can't — I won't — turn human beings into expendable collateral. That's the way of my enemies, both those who spread the plague and those who cultivate child soldiers to fight them.

It's hard to keep my focus on Hawke and still retain an overall awareness of what's happening below. The one requires me to look through my telescopic sight. The other requires me to lift my head and peer over the top or to the side. What I really need now is a spotter. Cameron would be perfect, or Bruce.

Bruce …

I clench my teeth and try to line up a shot. The bodyguards are lifting Hawke into the back of the chopper now. Hawke has his right hand bound against his chest in a makeshift sling. His other hand is holding his hair down. The man is utterly ridic—

The loud crack and the simultaneous blow of ice and fire that punches into my right thigh is the first I know that anyone is shooting. The force of the shot knocks me backward, and I roll over and fall off the water tank, toppling face-first onto the rough cement surface of the roof.

The searing pain in my thigh is bewildering in its intensity. It knocks me clean out of my calm, icy state and into a hot awareness of agony. I am fully present, all here, all now.

It's nothing! I tell myself. This is nothing compared to that room, that chair, those machines, that endless blinding torment of pain.

I make myself say it out loud. "It's nothing! Ignore it."

I press a hand to my thigh, to the nucleus of the radiating pain, and feel a squelchy mess beneath my palm. I taste the salty iron of blood in my mouth.

This leg belongs to someone else. It is somewhere else. I will not think of it now. Will not acknowledge the existence of the shredded flesh and scorching pain in that thigh that is not mine.

A new sound, rising up from below, blends with the pounding of blood in my ears — the rhythmic whirring of rotor blades beginning to turn, slowly at first, then faster and faster.

I crawl on my belly and elbows to the spot where my rifle lies at the bottom of the metal ladder on the side of the water tank. I grab and lift it, rolling onto my back and pointing my sights at the sky where I imagine the chopper will appear above the top of the water tank. But it's no good. The shot will be from an extreme low angle, almost vertically up and directly into the blinding sunlight. I'll be able to hit the underside of the chopper, but there'll be no guarantee I'd get Hawke.

I could aim for the tail rotor, in the hope of bringing

down the whole chopper, but I'm not sure how many other people might be in the craft — the pilot, perhaps another agent? — or on the ground directly underneath it.

I roll back onto my stomach, sling the rifle over my shoulders and grab hold of the second-lowest rung on the ladder. I drag myself toward the tank.

My leg screams a protest.

Ignore it. It doesn't belong to me, I think savagely.

I lift first one hand, then the other to the next rung and pull, grunting with the effort.

Ignore, ignore, ignore.

The sound of the helicopter changes. The engine whines louder. The beat of the blades chopping the air gets louder and faster, until it's a whirring din. It must be ready to take off.

I grasp another rung, pull up, and another.

My legs are dead to me now. My arms are what ache. The muscles twitch and jump with the effort as I haul myself upwards, rung by rung.

It's nothing. Just monkey bars.

A new sound joins the deafening purr — an echoing growl.

I can do this. Pain is good.

My head crests the tank. With a final heave I pull myself to the top, wedge my left elbow between two rungs so I can't slip backward, and reach back with my right hand to slide my rifle forward. Gusts of wind buffet me, whipping my hair around my face and drying my eyes.

I am so tired, so sore, so done.

Blood fills my mouth, tinny and sickening. A welcoming blackness beckons temptingly at the edges of my consciousness, offering relief from pain, an absence of feeling, a respite from having to make decisions. Promising a release from awareness and responsibility.

Failure is not an option. I will not quit.

I'm just this side of consciousness, lying on my belly, eye up to the scope, finger on the trigger, when the helicopter, glinting electric blue in the sunlight, hovers into my line of sight.

The shot, if I take it, will be easy.

Hawke is in the seat against the window closest to me, the golden triangle of his chest and throat is clear and open. My focus is on his torso, not his face, but I wonder — does he sense me there, a bleeding, sixteen-year-old angel of death lining up my crosshairs over where his heart should be? Does he look my way, his eyes surprised at this last turn of fate when he thought he was safely on his way to a beach, or perhaps a snow-frosted mountain range, near a bank where he's squirreled away his obscene profits? Does he curse the choices he made to mold, select and train the expert that would be his downfall?

Does he understand, finally, that the human mind, the individual spirit which powers each of us, cannot ultimately be controlled and determined? That we are humans, not machines. Survivors, not victims. As feisty and adaptable and unpredictable as rats.

I close my finger on the trigger, breathe out, and in that fractional stillness at the center of all the noise and motion, I take the shot.

Chapter 45

Over and out

Done.

Utterly done in, I topple backward.

And land heavily in the soft, strong arms of — "Quinn?"

"Jinxy!" he yells above the noise.

Above us, the chopper banks and pulls away into the sky.

"He shot you! That bastard shot you, and he got away!"

"He didn't get away," I say. My voice is hoarse, rough with emotion. I spit out a mouthful of blood and swallow. It's hard — I'm so thirsty.

"You got him?" Quinn says, lowering me gently to the roof, wedging something soft beneath my head.

"Uh-huh," I sigh, then suck in a breath and squeeze my eyes shut when I feel painful pressure on my thigh.

"You are such a wonder wench. When we get home, when we're safe and together and in a bed somewhere, I'm going to buy you a superhero costume," he says, anointing my cheeks and my forehead with tender kisses, sure as love, light as a blessing.

"You want me to wear a superhero costume to bed?" I sigh, opening my eyes to stare up into the frantic gray depths of his. "Kinky."

He laughs. But he's crying, too. Tears land on my face. Or is it raining?

"Hold on, my Jinxy. Please hold on."

I sigh and close my eyes. I want to go into that dark bliss that's closing in on me. It'll be warm there. Safe. I'll be able to rest.

"Jinxy!" Quinn gives my shoulder a little shake. "Please hang in there, Jinx — for me."

I can hold on for Quinn. I can do anything for him.

"Hold on," he says. "Help is on the way. Can you hear the sirens?"

Help is on the way?

"Who?" I breathe. "How?"

"Robin did the obvious. He called 911. The cops and ambulance are on their way, just hold on, *mo chuisle*."

There's a loud bang, and a man's voice yells, "Hands in the air where I can see them, both of you!"

The lids of my eyes are so heavy. They drag down, but I force them open. Quinn's hands are not in the air — they are still pressing down on my leg. I don't mind. It doesn't hurt anymore. None of me does. But he should do what the man says.

"Freeze! And put your hands in the air."

I want to tell him, *do what they say, Quinn — be clever, be safe.* Because he is being neither. He is angling his body around mine, bending over me, blocking me from the man.

Drops splash on my face.

"I can't put my hands in the air, officer," that Irish voice says, thick with emotion. "She's been shot, and she's bleeding heavily. I'm applying pressure to the wound."

"What the hell happened here?"

"I'll explain later. Right now she needs urgent medical attention. Please, just lower your weapon and call for help. Neither of us is armed."

In my mind's eye, I wag a finger at Quinn. Not true, Pirate. You've got a knife, and I've got a pistol digging into my back. But I couldn't reach either weapon, not for all the will in the world.

I open my eyes for a final look at my pirate, taking in his gray eyes — the color of frozen steel, as they always are when he's angry or afraid. His olive skin and chestnut hair. The circle of silver through his brow.

Circles never end.

"I'm coming closer, no sudden movements," the man's voice says.

"I'm with her. I'm not going anywhere."

Quinn lifts a hand and cups my cheek. I'm sinking into the soft, velvety darkness.

"*Mo chuisle*," he says. "*Mo stóirín*, I love you."

"Love you too. Got in last," I say, with the last of my breath and strength.

And then I'm gone.

Epilogue

Chapter 46

Out of the gates

When I wake up, I brush my teeth and, still in my shorty-pajamas, sneak downstairs. Quinn is fast asleep on our sofa where he spent the night, as he regularly does. I lift the sheet and lie down next to him, cuddling up close.

"I love you — I got in first," I murmur softly, running a hand down the stubble of his jaw and kissing the tiny dent in his chin.

"No fair. I'm not even awake yet," he mumbles, pulling me close against the length of him.

I yawn widely, stretch and wince, grabbing my right thigh.

"Sore?" Quinn asks, opening his eyes.

"Yeah, it's going to rain today or tomorrow."

Six months after the bullet tore through my leg, it only aches when I've been exercising hard or when rain is on the way.

"Shall I kiss it better?" Quinn asks with a sexy grin and a raised eyebrow.

"Uh-huh."

He disappears under the sheet and trails a circle of kisses around the old wound. It tickles, and I giggle as I rub a hand over the spot, feeling the dented hollow in the flesh of my thigh. Quinn lifts his head and smiles wickedly at me.

"Any other booboos you want me to kiss better while I'm on the job?"

"Here," I touch the scar on my left calf where the shrapnel left a jagged scar, now faded to a pale silver line.

He pushes me onto my back and moves back down to kiss the old wound.

"Next?" he asks.

"My arms, please."

He moves under the sheet, trailing a line of kisses over my hip and side, up to the top of my left arm, where the old, round blotch still marks the spot where an electrode burned me in my torture session. Quinn kisses first one arm, then the other.

The scars have healed nicely. I don't pick at my sores anymore, not the ones on my skin, and not the ones inside. What is, is. And what is, right now, is a lot better because of what happened, back then.

"Any others?"

I tap my mouth. The cut where my teeth smashed through my lip, when I toppled off the water tank and face-planted on PlayState's hard roof, has left me with a distinctive bottom lip — it's more rounded, a little uneven, undeniably unusual.

A bit like me.

"When I get there, I think I should kiss your tooth," Quinn says. "It was injured, too."

True. The outer corner of my right front tooth was chipped off in the fall. For a while, I toyed with the idea of getting the edge repaired in gold, teasing Quinn that I'd join him in piracy. But in the end I decided to leave it. I like running my tongue across the missing bit. It reminds me that I'm a survivor. Damaged, edgy, but *here.*

Quinn moves his mouth over my shoulder, brushes it

along my collarbone, and sucks gently on my neck. The air around us shifts, tightens, intensifies. His lids go heavy. The pit of my belly contracts. I knot my fingers in his hair and pull his mouth up to my own while he slips the straps off my shoulders and moves his hands lower.

"Quinn," I gasp.

"Jinxy!"

The voice calling my name is not Quinn's. It's Robin's, and he's standing in the doorway of the living room, frowning at us. "Canoodling *again*? Don't you two ever stop?"

"Don't you understand the meaning of privacy?" I say, scowling at him.

"Are you blushing, Quinn?" Robin teases.

"Ignore him, Quinn. He's just jealous because he's not getting any action."

Robin expertly dodges the pillow I throw at him and shrugs. He and Sofia didn't work out, but neither of them were heartbroken about it.

"Mom says that it's time to get up and get going." Robin holds up a thumb. "That you don't want to be late for the opening ceremony." He extends his forefinger and points it and his thumb at me like a gun. "And that the traffic across town is likely to be heavy, so we need to leave in good time."

Three fingers are in the air now. They're the fingers of his left hand. His right arm is still thinner than the left, and the fingers don't work properly. He can use a specially adapted mouse with his right hand, but for almost everything else, he's now a lefty.

"What's that red mark on your neck?" says Robin, arching an eyebrow at me. "Is there a new plague I should be worried about?"

The old plague is still more than enough to be worried about, but the Center for Disease Control announced just last week that "the tide is turning", and I think I might actually believe them. Deaths are down, and the mutant rat population is being brought under control by a combination of new poisons and elimination units. The sniper squad is still operational, though none of the old team except Tae-Hyun and Mitch are still on it, and these days, only rats and infected animals are shot. There's still no cure for rat fever, but there is a new vaccination in final trials, and results so far are promising.

"Robin, go away — or I'll give you something to worry about."

"Fine, fine, blame the messenger."

Robin steps into the hall, and I hear my mother calling from the kitchen, "Are they awake, Robin? It's breakfast time."

"Oh yeah," he says, with a last cocky smirk at Quinn and me, "they're all ready for action."

Mom was right, the traffic *is* hectic. Not as bad as before — the people who still remember say — because so many people switched their business to working virtually. But it's astonishing for someone like me who remembers deserted roads with cracked pavement and weed-overgrown sidewalks. These full lanes of bumper-to-bumper cars, trucks and buses are still a novelty to me. I love staring out of the window of our vehicle, peering into other cars alongside us, catching glimpses of other lives.

A kid with red hair and rosy cheeks in the car adjacent to us waves at me and then sticks out his tongue just before we take the turnoff to ASTA.

I've got to stop calling it that. It's been renamed and is now called the New Horizons School of Achievement. Quinn says they should have named it after me, but he's biased. ASTA and its various subsidiaries and holding companies have been put out of business and charged with hundreds of crimes. The list of offenses grows by the day as more of their underhanded dealings emerge in the official inquiries and hearings currently underway. Of course, they've got insiders giving them information, too. Leya was one of the first to do a deal in exchange for becoming a state witness.

"Like the proverbial rat jumping the sinking ship," according to Quinn.

I'm off the hook for the deaths of Hawke and his bodyguard — the grand jury declined to return indictments, so I never even went to trial. But while *I've* been given awards, the entire government of the Southern Sector was forced to resign, and an early election has been called. There's also talk of disbanding the three super sectors and returning to the federal system we had before. Things are changing faster than I would have thought possible.

As we drive down the access road, I note how different it looks. There's still a fence around the campus, but the guard huts and electrified tops have been removed. The gate is now a fancy wrought-iron affair with the school's crest — a phoenix against a sun rising above the horizon — and it stands open in welcome.

Muttering about how we were very nearly late, Mom finds one of the last spaces in the lot and backs into it. It takes her a good few tries to get it right — Mom has never been great at parking — and while she's maneuvering, an advertisement comes on the radio, extolling the virtues of the new rat-flu vaccine which is due for release next month.

"Such good news!" Mom says, wrestling the wheel to one side and reversing in jerky bursts.

"Better health for a better future," the voice on the radio says sunnily, "brought to you by *Type Atlas*."

Robin, Quinn and I exchange glances.

"That name, though?" Quinn says.

"Yeah, I caught it." Robin frowns. "Do you think —?"

"I don't want to know." I hold up a silencing hand.

"Wouldn't surprise me," Robin mutters as we get out of Mom's car. "Money always finds a way to survive."

"A luta continua," Quinn says. Or that's what it sounds like.

"Look, there's Cameron!" I wave and run to the steps at the entrance, where my big friend stands, smiling.

It's a warm May day, and I'm wearing a light-blue sundress. Much to Mom's chagrin, I'm wearing it with sneakers. As a concession, they're covered in lacy detail, so they don't look too strange with the sundress, but I won't wear heels. For one thing, they make the muscles in my right thigh ache and twitch, and for another, I'm not so over the past that I'm comfortable with being hamstrung by heels. I want to be able to run if I need to.

"Hey, Cameron! How're you doing?"

I give him a tight hug, pull back to check his face. He's smiling.

"Good. You?"

"Great!"

Quinn and Robin catch up with us and shake hands with Cameron, while Mom hustles us up the stairs. They've retained the decon unit for folks like my mother who still want it — old fears and habits die hard, I guess — but the boys and I simply walk through the open door into the marble-floored lobby of the old ASTA building.

I'm struck by a moment of déjà vu. This is where I stood that first day as a nervous, green recruit, eagerly listening to Roth and Hawke spew their deceit-filled speeches, excited to be out of the house, and already interested in the tall, handsome boy standing beside me. It was just over a year ago, and although I'm only seventeen, I feel years older than that girl.

There are a lot of familiar faces, and some that are noticeably absent, but Mom hurries us into the auditorium, saying, "You can catch up afterwards, Jinx, and we'll meet up with your family then, too, Quinn. The ceremony is about to begin."

There's some music from a string quartet and a few speeches about how the school will serve gifted children from across the state by exposing them to a wide variety of academic, cultural, artistic and sporting subjects in hope of "fostering well-rounded, broadly educated future leaders". I have to stifle a giggle when I think what Sarge would say if he knew that the old shooting range is now the site of a new school theatre. Because one thing they will certainly no longer be teaching at this school is sniping.

We get a mention in the speechifying, the names of our little team — "the liberators" as the press called us — who brought down The Game and revealed the truth about the government and ASTA, are read out one by one, and we stand briefly to acknowledge the applause.

"A medal would have been nice, or a reward," Robin says, not bothering to keep his voice down.

Mom shushes him so we can hear the end of the new principal's address. He holds up a large brass plaque with our names engraved on it — "Yours had better be at the top," Quinn tells me — and informs the audience it will be mounted in the entrance hall of New Horizons "as a reminder, because those who forget the past are doomed to repeat it."

Afterwards, we shuffle out of the auditorium and are guided through the school to admire the new music center, the converted classrooms and the fully equipped art room. When we pass the high-tech computer lab, I have to hook a finger through a loop on Robin's trousers to prevent him sneaking inside. They've laid on a champagne breakfast in the gardens at the back of the school, and there's a moment of awkwardness when Robin and Sofia bump into each other in the crowd thronging out through the doors.

"How are you doing?" Sofia asks.

"Good, you know, okay. I'm starting college in the fall."

"Me too, at Emory. Pre-law."

Robin nods like that fits what he knows of her.

"I'll be doing biomedical engineering at Georgia Tech. They've got a research program underway using virtual reality to help people regain use of paralyzed limbs by reactivating the nerve connections."

"Cool. It would be great if that game technology could be put to better use," Sofia says. "Good luck, Robin."

"Yeah, see you."

I walk around inspecting the revamped gardens. The bench that I liked to sit on at sunset is still there, but the cameras are gone. There are new flowerbeds filled with blue hydrangea bushes and white anemones, same as Mom has planted at home.

"It's an improvement, I'd say," Quinn says, handing me a tall flute of orange juice when we get to the long tables laden with a variety of drinks and platters of snacks.

"You bet." I take a sip. "Is this spiked?"

He winks.

"How's the leg?" Cameron asks, noticing me rubbing it.

"It's okay."

A dent, a scar and a limp aren't too much to live with. Others weren't so lucky. Like Bruce.

"Hey, you," someone says next to me, and I turn to find Evyan there.

She's almost unrecognizable. She's let the shaven side of her hair grow out and has cut the long side, so that now she's sporting the kind of cute pixie cut I was aiming for when I hacked off my long hair last year. She's wearing only six studs in her ear and none in her nose, and although she's still dressed entirely in black, she's eased up on the eyeliner and looks — there's no other word for it — pretty.

"You look …" If I say, "pretty," she'll probably deck me. I'm still thinking of a good word when a familiar voice supplies the right word.

"Hot! She looks hawt!"

Bruce has arrived, and he's holding a flute of champagne in each hand.

He gets a long hug from me and a bro-hug from Cameron, and then he shakes hands with Robin ("How's it hanging, Thing Two?"), and Quinn ("Wassup, Leprechaun?"). Evyan gives him a cool lift of the chin.

"I'd offer you a glass, but I think you might prefer water, Evyan," Bruce says, nodding toward the rows of bottled water with their pink and blue labels.

Evyan catches my eye, and we both smile, remembering the days when I called her by the brand names of bottled water.

"You clean up nicely, Goth-Girl," Bruce says.

Evyan ignores him and tells me, "You did okay, Jinx."

Wow. Coming from her, that's high praise.

"Yeah, we did okay," I say.

"I don't guess I can call you Goth-Girl anymore, huh?" Bruce says, taking a large gulp from first one glass and then the other.

"What are you up to these days?" I ask Evyan.

"Traveling, mostly. Tomorrow I'm off to Thailand, I've got a three-month gig teaching English there."

"Teaching!" Bruce says.

"And you guys?" Evyan asks.

"I've still got to complete my high school diploma, but I'll be finished by July."

I've spent the last six months recuperating, learning how to drive, and fulfilling the requirements to finish high school. Even though schools are reopening, I decided to finish high school the way I'd started it — online.

"Are you sure?" Quinn had asked when I told him my decision. "Don't you want some of the real thing? You know, friends and teachers and prom?"

I knew I'd be missing out on some stuff. I would have liked to play guitar in orchestra. And it might have been fun to try cheerleading.

Quinn had grinned when I'd mentioned that. And when he saw I wasn't being sarcastic, he'd laughed so hard, he actually fell off the bed.

"I'm sorry, I'm sorry," he'd said when he reappeared, wiping his eyes. "It's just the thought of you as a cheerleader — would you shoot the opposition?"

"In September, Quinn and I are going to Duke together," I tell the crowd now.

"Architecture," Quinn says when Evyan wants to know what he'll be studying.

"You?" Cameron asks me.

"I don't know yet."

I'm considering half a dozen subjects — European history, game theory, anthropology, classical guitar, biology — none of which seems to fit with the others, and none of which I'm certain I'll be able to hack. Plus I keep changing my mind about what to do. It's part terrifying, part exhilarating — this freedom to choose, this not knowing.

"Do whatever interests you now. You've got the rest of your life to change your mind," is Mom's view. Unlike her guidance on shoes, I think I'll follow this advice.

Mom has loosened up a lot over the last few months, and she seems to have a new zest for life. She's even taking ballroom-dancing lessons and has extracted promises from Robin and me to attend her studio's show in July.

"Can I call you Teach?" Bruce asks Evyan now. "Will you give me extra lessons? Spank me if I'm a naughty boy?"

I've got to laugh. Same old Bruce — on the outside, at

least.

"Should you be drinking with only one kidney and no spleen?" I ask him.

"Blue, Blue, Blue," he tuts, shaking his head at me. "You don't drink with your kidney or your spleen. You're hooked up with an Irishman — I would have thought he'd have taught you how to drink by now."

I laugh, but I give him another hug, too. "I'm glad you're here, Bruce," I say.

I don't just mean at the function, and he knows it. The slug ripped through his back and abdomen, and between the blood loss and the massive infection which set in afterwards, it was touch and go for weeks.

"Likewise, princess," he whispers at my ear and then sets me free, complaining about the wet patches I've left on the shoulders of his snazzy silk shirt.

"Control your woman, Paddy, there are some babes around here I still want to impress."

Bruce is now a shooting instructor at a military academy in Texas. "Spoiled little punks from rich families mostly, but I'll turn those little piggies into soldiers, yet!"

Cameron and I exchange glances and smile into our drinks. I'm sure he's imagining, like I am, Bruce channeling the spirit of Sarge — making his charges do push-ups in the rain when they miss their targets and yelling at them, "Pain is …? What is pain, my little piggies? Pain is good!"

Cameron tells us he's going to spend the summer on a ranch out in Wyoming, herding cattle and training horses.

"I need some time away. To be quiet, figure things out," he says.

"You're going to be a cowboy," I say, giving him a punch on the arm. "That suits you."

"Hey, look who it is! Come say hi," Quinn calls over my head, waving someone over.

It's Neil, looking pretty much exactly the same as when last I saw him. He tells us he's working on new software to detect and protect against surveillance intrusions, and another program to analyze computer games.

"The government may look all different," he says, in a low, suspicious tone, "but I don't trust them. Or big business. That technology is out there, man. It would be a fool who doesn't think some crowd or another's going to try using it again."

"How's Beth?" I ask him.

"Happier than I ever remember her being," he says, looking surprised at this turn of events. "She says you're never too old to be a mother."

"Still managing the shelter?"

"Yeah, she lives there now. Volunteers at the local clinic twice a week, too. She sends her love and told me to tell you that they've officially renamed the shelter Tallulah's."

We're all quiet for a moment, feeling our sadness, remembering the kind, loving woman who was our soft place to fall. We drove all the way to Tuscaloosa, Quinn and I, after I got out of the hospital. We spent an afternoon visiting Miss Edna, handing over the envelope of memories, and sharing stories of the grand woman. I told her about Carlos, who wants to be a chef when he grows up, and the teens staying off the streets, and about how Tallulah's legacy was continuing with Beth giving them love and a shot at a future.

"To leave the world a better place," Miss Edna had said, dabbing her eyes with a small handkerchief. "That's all any of us can ask for."

My mother and the O'Rileys come up to join our group. Mr. O'Riley gives me a huge smile and a friendly greeting. He's a fan for life, crediting me with saving his sons, toppling the government and saving the world, too, I think. Mrs. O'Riley is a little more reserved, but Quinn always said she was the tougher nut to crack.

"She's coming around, though," he'd said after my last visit to their house. "She's not blind, she can see you love me and that you make me happy. And that's what she wants most for her children — to be loved and happy."

Connor, standing beside his mother, greets me politely, but not warmly. He still doesn't look very happy — not to see me, and not with things in general. According to Quinn, he's finding it difficult to adjust to life after the rebellion and isn't sure what to do with his future.

"He's at a loose end," Quinn said when we last spoke about his brother.

Kerry had other words for it. "Dad says he wanders about the house like a lost fart in a perfume factory."

"He just needs to find a new cause to fight for, or against," Quinn said. "And he may have found it. Last week Mom suggested he might like to join the campaign to bring down the wall between us and Mexico, and his eyes lit up with the old fire."

Kerry is now nine years old and has both her front teeth. Her eyes, gray like Quinn's, sparkle when she marches up to Robin and demands, "Don't you have something for me? You said you were bringing me a present."

"I did not forget," he says. "It's in the trunk of the car."

"We should probably be on our way," my mother says.

The O'Rileys agree, and the whole crowd of us walk around the side of the building to the parking lot out front. Robin disappears and then reappears a minute later carrying a large parcel untidily wrapped in red paper and tied with a jaunty purple bow.

"Wrapped this yourself, did you?" Kerry asks.

"It's what's inside that counts, young lady," Robin says in a dignified tone.

Kerry rips off the paper and pulls out a skateboard. It's

Robin's, the one that hung above his bed ever since the plague started.

Kerry gives a loud squeal of delight, puts the board on the ground, climbs unsteadily onto it, and smiles at Robin.

"Teach me!" she commands.

"Faith, she's got him wrapped around her little finger," Quinn says, watching Kerry skate down to the gate and back while Robin runs behind, shouting instructions.

"The O'Rileys are charmers, all right."

My mom and Quinn's parents have moved off and are chatting down by the cars. The rest of us stand on the stairs of the entrance, watching Robin and Kerry getting in the way of the departing visitors. We'll all be going our separate ways, soon. Thailand and Texas and Wyoming.

"Hey, guys?" I say. "Let's not ever get so far apart that we can't get back together."

Cameron nods.

"Why don't we set a date for a reunion?" Quinn says.

"Yeah! Get the old crowd back together, shoot the breeze and down some brewskies," Bruce says enthusiastically.

"Labor Day? Or Thanksgiving?" Neil suggests.

"No," I say. "Halloween. I want a proper Halloween this year, I want to dress up and, okay, maybe not go trick-or-treating, we're a bit old for that. But have a street party or something. I want to be outside and watch the kids go by, see everybody out having fun."

I'll go as Robin Hood. Or maybe not. Maybe I'll go as a vampire, or a fairy, or a wizard. I could go as anything.

It's heady stuff, this freedom.

Evyan checks the calendar on her phone. "Cool," she says. "I'll be back stateside by then."

"I'm in," says Cameron.

"Me too, and I'm sure Beth will want to come."

"Yeah, man, let's do it!" says Bruce.

We exchange hugs and numbers and promises to stay in touch. And then one by one, the gang drifts off and leaves.

Quinn and I stand on the steps, holding hands, watching them go. The sun is warm on our faces, and a light breeze stirs my hair. The gate, still wide open, beckons to the world beyond.

"You know," Quinn says with a frown at Bruce, who blows a kiss at me out the window of his sports car as he drives off, "Bruce wasn't the only one who lost a part of himself last year."

"Oh yeah?"

"He may have lost a kidney —"

"And his spleen, and a bit of stomach, too, I think."

"Yeah, alright, very heroic, I'm sure. But I, *mo chuisle*, I lost my heart."

"You did?" I say, laughing up into his gray eyes, dark today with just a hint of blue, like a cloud before the rain. "You shouldn't go about losing your organs. What if you never find them again?"

"Oh, I know where it is. It lives outside my body. You carry it, here." He places the warm palm of one hand softly over my heart.

We kiss then. And it's a meeting of more than mouths, a merging of more than bodies, a sharing and a blending beyond words.

It feels like Quinn and I are alone in the world. Especially when Mom and Robin drive off with a jaunty honk of the horn, and the O'Rileys leave in their pickup, Kerry waving goodbye from a window.

"But," I say, watching them disappear out the gate, "how are we going to get home?"

"I never told you what my family got me for my nineteenth. Sure and it only arrived day before yesterday," Quinn says, grinning mischievously and tugging me down the stairs. "They brought it today on the pickup."

At the end of the parking lot is a sleek silver motorbike with a helmet hanging off each handlebar.

"Yours?" I ask, grinning in delight.

"Mine!"

He climbs on the bike and hands me one of the helmets, looks surprised when I put it on without any objections.

"You know me — I always like to play it safe," I say, fiddling with the straps under my chin, until he brushes my fingers aside and secures the fastening.

"Here, you wear this." He grabs a black leather jacket from a storage compartment on the side of the bike, and I slip it on. It smells of my pirate.

I zip it up and climb up behind him, glad again that I'm wearing sneakers.

"Hold on tight!" he says over his shoulder as he kicks off the stand and starts the motor.

"Always!" I call back.

I wrap my arms around his waist and snuggle up against him, my face curved against the back of his neck. He revs the engine a couple of times, and then we're off — through the lot, out of the gates and onto the open road.

And though I'm flying, moving faster than breath and thought, I'm also still. There's a calm, quiet spot in the center of me, a place of peace and contentment that I feel at my core.

I used to think that freedom was a place, and maybe it is. But it's a place inside of me. A place where I choose, where I decide, where I hold the ones I love.

It's the spot where the heart of me is now. And I think it's where Quinn's heart must also be, beating gently inside of me.

~ the end ~

Dear Reader,

Thank you for staying with Jinxy and Quinn to the end!

If you loved this book, I'd be very grateful if you'd leave a review on your favorite online site — even if it's just a sentence or two. Every review makes a difference and helps other readers discover the trilogy.

You might like to join my Readers' Group to receive my monthly newsletter, with advance notice of my latest releases, competitions, giveaways and offers for free review copies, as well as a behind-the-scenes peek at my writing process. I won't clutter your inbox or spam you, and I will never share your email address with anyone. Pinkie promise! You can join up at my website: www.joannemacgregor.com

I'd love to hear from you! Come say hi on Facebook (@JoanneMacg), or Twitter (@JoanneMacg), or reach out to me via my website (www.joannemacgregor.com) and I'll do my best to get back to you.

- **Joanne Macgregor**

ACKNOWLEDGEMENTS

I would like to thank my magnificent beta-readers, Nicola Long, Emily Macgregor and Edyth Bulbring, and my editor Chase Night, for their invaluable help and feedback, and to express my gratitude to James Bristow of Magnum Shooting Academy for his patient advice on weapons and shooting — any inaccuracies are on me!